BLOOD REEF

JEFF WALKER

Wasteland Press

www.wastelandpress.net
Shelbyville, KY USA

Blood Reef
by Jeff Walker

First Printing – May 2021
ISBN: 978-1-68111-407-1
Library of Congress Control Number: 2021907360

Printed in the U.S.A.

0   1   2   3

Dedicated to Marshall Law
A Real Ball Coach

ACKNOWLEDGEMENT

Thanks to Thump Phillips for sharing the greatest football coach name, ever.

CHAPTER ONE

Jack Rache's lower back spasms harmonized with the drone of the Tahoe's tires. To his right, the sunset appeared as if the wedding planner had prearranged an amber-stained horizon. Ahead, in the southbound lanes, recreational vehicles intermingled with pastel Jeeps crammed with meagerly clad teens and fat blue coolers headed toward their mutual summer destination, St. Pete Beach, Florida.

It had been a long drive from Nashville where he had lectured before the American Football Coaches Association. A brief stop in Atlanta to visit an old Marine buddy, and he was back on the road to Florida for the wedding of his daughter, Gretchen.

May had turned out to be a stellar month for the gray-haired coach. Two weeks prior to the Nashville conference, the Ohio Sports Hall of Fame had honored him for his years of service and accomplishments as a four-time state champion.

After a quick check-in at the resort, Jack opened his suite to find a plush, queen mattress beckoning. He dropped his keys on the nightstand where he spotted a booklet featuring a sandwich coupon for his favorite fast-food joint, Subway.

No expensive hotel food for me, tonight. I'll have my fill of that stuff at the wedding.

He remembered that he'd passed a Subway which occupied part of a gas station. His aching back, the shop's nearness to the hotel, and the well-lighted, upscale stone facade convinced Coach Jack to overlook his resolve to never eat food from a gas station.

Ten minutes later, a slim blonde with brown eyes and sun-bleached eyebrows took his order.

Surfer, he thought.

She reminded him of a girl he once knew as a young Marine stationed at Pendleton back in 1969. Jack watched her assemble a 12-inch cold cut combo with his usual toppings; spinach, tomatoes, banana peppers, and extra mayo. He dropped two bucks into the tip jar and climbed back into his vehicle.

Two blocks from the resort, he waited for the light to change. The girl's face had triggered some memories. Good memories.

Witnesses at the corner convenience store saw a dark green Accord with blacked-out windows stop next to Coach Jack's Tahoe. The Honda's passenger doors popped open, and two males brandishing chrome-plated handguns vaulted out.

Bits of tinted safety-glass cascaded downward into the door's mechanical workings as multiple gun shots silenced the intersection. Jack recoiled from the blasts, then slumped over the console.

Nearby vehicles scattered. From behind the counter, store clerk Jamaal at first thought the stricken Tahoe to be involved with a collision, a common occurrence. Then he saw the shooters walking alongside the vehicle, emptying their clips.

Pilotless, Coach Jack's Tahoe edged forward until it crashed into the corner of the nearby pawn shop. When the Tahoe came to a stop against the brick wall, the first assailant opened the Tahoe's driver side door and leaned in as the second assailant menaced onlookers.

Jamaal told sheriff's deputies that both shooters appeared to be young males. One assailant wore a black hoodie, jeans, and a Miami Dolphins baseball cap with its bill turned to the back. The second gunman, the one from the rear seat, wore a wife-beater and jeans. His straight black hair flowed back into a braided ponytail.

A second witness recalled hearing the getaway driver rev the Accord's engine during the attack. Familiar with street racing, he recognized the sound of a customized engine.

Other than shell casings, Pinellas County Sheriff Department investigators found no physical evidence from the gunmen. The shooting appeared gang-related, but one strand of circumstantial evidence dangled ominously out of sync with the nature of the crime.

Jack Rache, the targeted victim, had lived a pristine life. Nothing in his background connected him to the usual motives behind an orchestrated, gangland hit.

In the second week of the investigation, an informant confirmed that a crew of the West Pen Warriors claimed the hit, but law enforcement failed to find hard evidence.

The Warriors had annexed that intersection into their territory soon after their group's mass immigration to Florida. Since the 1980s, Gulfway Drive had been patched – gangland turf. The Sheriff's Department knew they wouldn't find any cooperative witnesses. A patched street betrays no one.

For law enforcement, the street execution of a bride's father, a lifelong educator and high school coach, defied explanation. Travel websites long-touted trendy St. Pete Beach as the safest vacation spot in Florida, and the gang's reputation as a complaisant middleman of the local high-end drug trade didn't jibe with a violent street encounter. Trafficking cocaine to the jet setters and college kids was the West Pen Warriors' game, not murder.

Months passed as rumors swelled, then ebbed. Two years of investigation yielded no new clues, and a Pinellas County deputy shelved the Rache file. A third year passed, then a fourth. Justice anticipated aged into justice denied. In Urbana, Ohio, Coach Jack's legendary presence faded from the rites of autumn.

Five seasons would pass before a frigid December night in Texas resurrected the case and revealed the truth behind the murder of Coach Jack Rache.

CHAPTER TWO

The faded white line snaked under Thump Sutton's pickup. Another new job, another blind venture down a gray county road, it wasn't like he hadn't been here before. His devoted companion, Jenny—an Irish Setter-Black Lab mix—lay along the threadbare bench seat, head resting on his thigh. In the pickup bed rode his grandmother's rocking chair and a dozen waxed chicken boxes packed with the evidence of a transient coach's life: a deflated football, his daddy's Bible, bundles of playbooks, hundreds of comic books, a trove of *Texas Coach* magazines, three pairs of running shoes splattered with field paint, and Jenny's toys.

Only the most experienced coaches knew the roadside chicken joint's dumpster diving secret. The waxed cardboard shipping boxes previously filled with chicken parts included a waterproof coating. A quick spray from a hose washed away the lingering raw chicken remnants and blood. Then, after a few hours in the Texas sun muted the ingrained odor of chicken guts, that cardboard box was the poor man's Louis Vuitton. Within an hour, the transient coach had a nice-sized waterproof moving box. For transporting papers, clothes, and memorabilia in the back of a pickup, nothing beat waxed chicken-box luggage.

Thomas Udall ("Thump") Sutton estimated it had been over three hundred trips in which he and his old Ford truck connected the dots on the worn Texas state road map he kept in his glove box. His guess may have hit low; he wasn't sure. After his second divorce, the actual number of interviews and schools blurred into speculation. Whatever the number, the tired pickup with its homemade rear bumper, and the white grill with the inward-facing twin rockets outline, had carried him to every coaching job he ever landed.

Time after time, he had packed the old truck with chicken boxes and filled its tank with Premium. As the interminable rows of cotton plants cascaded past his half-open window, he wondered if this trip would be the last one.

A decrepit remnant of a greater era in America's auto world, the 1966 Ford F100 was the only truck his daddy ever purchased new. The pipefitter named his first, and last, brand-new pickup Blue. While not as smart as the fiery red Galaxie his mama wanted, Blue had an optional black padded dash and a cigarette lighter. More importantly, the glistening Caribbean turquoise pickup with three-on-the-tree sported a long bed, perfect for hauling a cacophony of foxhounds or a load of hay.

The Coastal Bermuda hay stacking record was ninety-eight bales, set by his brother, Brian, just two days before he left for Vietnam. To Thump, then an imaginative country boy from the Big Thicket of East Texas, the towering hay formation in the truck's bed looked like the Great Pyramid of Giza.

Now, after five decades of navigating unpaved back roads, the old truck's springs would be lucky to handle a dozen bales. In the back, a corroded spring-release handle that bit like an angry possum operated Blue's battered tailgate, and when viewed from the rear, the truck appeared to shimmy down the road in two directions at once.

Seen as an expired member of the coaching profession, Thump Sutton often assumed the role of the "staff old guy," more a source of ridicule than knowledge. Like his truck, he was from another era, a deteriorating anachronism in the modern world of the tech-savvy twenty-something educator.

To further cloud his vision quest of earning a head coaching position, phrases such as "must be enthusiastic" and "must show high energy" pockmarked the Texas High School Coaches Association's job postings. Everyone knew those phrases were code for "no one over 50 need apply."

While today's coaching world grew rife with gel-haired millennials who had obtained the bulk of their knowledge from online videos, Thump had learned to coach the hard way, coming up through the junior-high feeder system. Most of Thump's coaching buddies had died or slipped into the abyss of retirement, but he couldn't surrender his whistle, not before getting his chance. Now, in the twilight of his career and past the usual retirement age for high-school assistant coaches, Thump Sutton finally had landed his first head-coaching job.

A quirky old Stealers Wheel tune filtered through the static from Blue's original AM Philco. Wind whipped from behind the side mirror as Thump substituted his own improvised verses. Mrs. Marcantel's third-grade criticism of his "Froggy Went A-Courtin'" solo may have broken his heart, but his spirit remained unhurt. Half a century later, his own sun-leathered ears continued to confirm Mrs. Marcantel's tone deafness. He knew he possessed a beautiful singing voice. Ever since his playing days at Texas Christian University (TCU), he exhibited an unusual knack for composing new lyrics out of any oldie ever heard on the radio. One-hit wonders from the 1970s were his specialty. Though the other coaches—the visor-wearing types—never appreciated his talent, the kids loved it when he redubbed the old songs during practice. The team might be in the thick of a big drill when Thump would burst into an improvised song with the kids' names inserted into the lyrics.

They loved him, the players. To him, they weren't just players; they were his kids. Thump was a kids' coach.

The only thing Thump loved more than kids was Jenny. Thanks to her mother's preference for a neighboring Labrador retriever, a flowing midnight black coat highlighted Jenny's Irish Setter profile.

Middle-aged but still a great athlete, she could swim 400 yards, operate a pushbutton water fountain, and walk the track unassisted while remaining in lane six. In the daily chauvinistic banter of the football office, Thump once got a riotous laugh when he told the young coaches Jenny was the only female ever known to "stay in her lane."

Ten hours on the road had passed when Blue eased past the yield sign where Texas 114 and U.S. 93 intersected. Blue's tired twin I-beam suspension strained to remain steady through the extended curve toward the coast. As they crested an overpass, Thump saw a settlement where an abandoned school had lost its battle against the vines scaling its walls. Across from the school stood Dime Less, the staple grocery store of over a thousand rural communities scattered throughout Texas. Just down from the store, a faded billboard shaded a tangle of weeds.

"Welcome to Godsend, Texas," the sign said.

Shoot, if this place is the godsend, I sure don't want to see the curse, Thump thought.

He had only a second to enjoy his own joke before she scolded him.

You need to check yourself. This time, we make it work. It's our last time. It's your last chance!

The voice belonged to Rose. Born of his isolated childhood, she was his life partner, a monitor of conscience who played the role of either a morality compass or a morality stalker; he wasn't always sure which. She was ever present and awake, even in his dreams. Sometimes, she moderated his teetering edginess or calmed his quick-to-rage temperament. Other times, she mediated his failures. He christened the voice "Rose" because the name invoked the warm memory of his mother's striking presence as she tended her flowers out by the cattle guard in front of their house. And, like his mother's sharp reproofs, Rose's thorny reprimands and honest observations could prick his ego. His savior from two bad marriages and his latest mistake whom she nicknamed Ten-Months-in-San Antonio, Rose had nursed him through his recovery from all the regrettable terminations and relationships he had suffered.

7

Ten-Months-in-San Antonio had familiarized Thump with Jamaican Green. Jam-G-Roast, as the hipster crowd knew it, was the only coffee Thump touched. Once introduced to the bean, he ordered it online from a San Antonio coffee shop. It was the only drink that could compete with what Thump called the sweet nectar of Texas, the original formula Dr. Pepper infused with pure Imperial sugar.

As a coach, Thump enjoyed the support of less than a handful of confidants. A civilian, somebody who had never coached Texas high school football, might think it strange to have such an anemic body of friends, but that was the nature of the calling. During his decades of teaching and coaching high school ball in a culture where the mandate was to win football games or get packing, Coach Thump Sutton had learned something vital. Though his fellow coaches might seem to be his family—he spent more time with them than anyone—the fluidity and random movement in the profession dissolved the bonds of the closest coaching staffs. But he didn't mind much; he had grown accustomed to the life.

CHAPTER THREE

Because the Port Verona job broke late, rumors on the internet coaching forums circulated that fewer than nine candidates had applied for the job. One homegrown assistant on staff had an inside track, but support for his appointment teetered at the precipice. Three tattooed millennials from the suburbs of Houston applied, each from large, elite 6A schools, but Port Verona was way too far from a Starbucks for those boys. Only one other prospect posed a threat, a West Point graduate who had retired from the Army after a decade of service and three tours in Afghanistan. His bio alone could sway a rural school board's patriotism, but the rest of the story was even worse. Not only was the retired soldier a combat veteran who had been a four-year starter at the academy, the assistant superintendent was his aunt. Still, as Rose had been quick to point out, the military man may have held the pole position in familial advantages, but he had no Texas high school coaching experience. For the first time, fate had stacked the deck in Thump's favor. Rose assured him his résumé would beat the weakest hand he had ever faced from an applicant pool.

As usual, Rose was right. The offer came less than an hour after the interview. And by awarding Thump the position via teleconference in late July, just two weeks before two-a-days, the superintendent and the board of trustees would test the range of his abilities. He had no time to waste. In 13 miles, he would sign a contract to be the new head football coach of the Port Verona Barracudas. There he would meet his newest best friends who carried in their pockets a contractual clause, one that stated if you want to remain their friend, you'd better win a lot of football games.

No one doubted the Port Verona football program needed a change. By the time the old ball coach hit town, the 'Cudas had suffered a streak of thirty-two losing seasons. The town had not seen a district championship since LBJ signed the Civil Rights Act. No current Port Verona Independent School District student had seen a Barracuda homecoming win.

Still, Thump believed. His long service record as an assistant provided the knowledge that he needed to jury-rig a competent staff and resurrect what had long been dead. While ecstatic over his new job, he wasn't blind to the challenges ahead. Port Verona was a hurricane-afflicted football hellhole if the cards fell wrong. And for Thump, the cards often fell enormously wrong.

A Texas high school football coach might never know when he would walk into his first period class and find a "see me" note. During the daily wash of the practice gear and cleanup of the locker room, Thump would entertain the old dogs and pups around the fieldhouse with his numerous termination yarns. Most infamous was the story of the December dismissal carried out by one particularly pompous necktie-wearer named Grover Godling. After a playoff game in which Thump's secondary allowed three miles of passing yardage in a 54–52 loss, Grover left a "see God" note on Blue's windshield. God fired Thump the following Monday.

In Texas, high school coaches are nothing more than a hired gun with 10 bullets. Should less than six hit the mark, the coach could have a problem. In some situations, one errant bullet will finish him. For example, if he plays the wrong quarterback, he's gone. If he turns to the wrong page of his playbook during a big game, he's gone. If he forgets to turn in his class lesson plans after a few losses, he's gone. If he dents the bus bumper when he hits a deer on a midnight return trip to school, he's gone, especially if he is 0-and-5. If it's rumored that he cheated on his wife, he's gone. If his wife cheated on him, he's still gone, but she can stay. In Texas, a coach's life isn't fair.

CHAPTER FOUR

Blue rattled past the Aileen Nugent Wetlands Sanctuary at the northern edge of town. The old Ford's musty cab had reached its customary afternoon sweltering point. Thump's old pickup had no air conditioning. The July coastal prairie heat and humidity stirred Jenny from the seat. Thump leaned over and opened the passenger window vent. Jenny pushed her long muzzle into the rushing air and Thump stroked her back.

"Rest easy, girl. Let's stop and get you a cold treat here in just a minute."

Jenny's tail patted the seat in response to her dad's reassurance.

At 10:13 a.m., the Port Verona Police Department received a call. A citizen reported a strange truck parked outside Nguyen's Bait Shop and Store. The caller said a tall, muscular, silver-haired man and a large black dog had abandoned the truck.

Just prior to the call, Thump had ducked into the bait shop for a Dr. Pepper, a bottle of cold water, and a box of frozen waffles. The Dr. Pepper was for Thump; the water was for Jenny; the waffles were for both. It was their favorite hot weather snack. When they passed the checkout counter on their way to the coolers in the back, an older Asian woman behind the counter fussed in stilted English.

"No dogs! Dogs not allowed here! Leave dog outside now!"

Thump raised his palms.

"Yes, ma'am. I apologize. It's just that she's my service dog. I have a medical condition."

Thump retrieved the waffles and approached her at the register.

The woman pointed to the door. "No, I don't know you! Dog must stay outside!"

Thump peeled open the waffle box, pushed open the door for Jenny, and tossed a waffle just outside by the ice storage unit. Jenny grasped it between her paws and gnawed at the frozen treat.

Thump returned his attention to the woman.

"Sorry, I'm new here. I didn't mean to upset you. She's my medical service dog, and we are used to doing everything together. You know, doctor's orders, medical needs, and so forth. I'm the new head football coach up at the high school. Coach Sutton is my name."

"Coach who? Port Verona High School?" She was unaware of the connection, and her brows furrowed as she studied Thump's features. "Wait, something about you look familiar."

"Coach Sutton, ma'am." Thump pointed to a stack of newspapers, "Look, that's me right there on the front page."

The woman's etched face turned from indifference to interest. "New football coach? Port Verona? My grandson, he play football. He play linebacker. You make team better this year, yes?"

Thump handed her his bank card. "Oh, yes ma'am. I will get them better. You can count on that. Do you mind adding that bandana to the total, the red and black one on the wall behind you?"

Swiping the card, the woman beamed. "No problem. You come back anytime. We have good hot food for a big coach. Next time, leave dog outside."

Thump flashed his easy smile. "Yes ma'am. Leave the dog outside. Got it."

Outside, Jenny had just finished her waffle and was sitting pretty for the next one.

"Jenny, load up. I'm sure the Americans with Disabilities and Dogs Act doesn't carry much weight in this town, but we got our waffles," Thump said.

In the truck, Thump pulled out a waffle for each of them and popped the top of his soda.

"Jenny, we have a few minutes before the reception. Let's drive over to the By the Bay Cottages and see what the booster club arranged for us."

A Port Verona police cruiser passed as Blue eased out onto Gulfway Drive, the main artery into town. The officer, her elbow bent and her arm flat on the door, lifted her left index finger in a form of a traditional Texas rancher-style greeting. Thump returned the finger nod and added a big smile as Jenny continued to chew on her waffle.

"Jenny, the vetting process has begun."

The booster club had rented unit 5 at By the Bay Cottages for its new head coach. Six one-bedroom cottages, draped in pastel shades, formed a horseshoe. In the center of the horseshoe, a circle of eight towering palm trees surrounded several picnic tables. Each studio, with its own small back patio, welcomed its newest tenants in the style typical of a sparsely furnished Gulf Coast bungalow. Thump's rental was one of two bungalows nearest the water.

A smiley face clock hung on the door of the manager's hut, and a note on the clock said the manager would return in one hour. They would have to catch up with the manager later.

Thump remembered that the booster club secretary had hidden the apartment key under a potted red geranium near the front door. They had a brief window of time to scout the property then hurry over to the Port Verona Independent School District's central office for the community meet and greet. Like everything in a small Texas town, the central office stood just a minute or two away.

Thump stopped short of the administration building and parked. With two wheels on the pavement and two in the grassy ditch, Old Blue tipped precariously toward the passenger side. Jenny whined, but Thump reassured her that Old Blue would be okay.

Rule number one: Coaches must never take the quality parking spots.

Despite the quick turnaround of the job offer, Thump had done his homework on Port Verona. Everyone across the state realized the depth of the rooted frustrations within the Barracuda football program, but Thump's talent was finding that rare flower which thrived in the desert. He believed coaches who coached the upside could win anywhere. To find the upside was to find the key to winning.

Whatever the downside, Port Verona's upside was its locality and diverse history. During the prehistoric era, coastal Texas nomadic natives known as the Karankawa subsisted in the humid, mosquito-infested wetlands of Tiburon County and the area that would become Port Verona. Five hundred years later, a melting pot of Texans replaced the Karankawa.

The locals, the hundreds of birdwatchers, and coastal cyclists perceived Port Verona as an idyllic coastal enclave publicized as the shrimping capital of Texas. A great place to fish for any kind of deep-sea catch, a self-sufficient community emerged between two bays, De LaSalle Bay and Port Verona Bay. In Port Verona, a retired couple could own a beach house with stunning sunsets and around-the-clock access to fresh air and marine life for the same price of a home in a Houston suburb. Colorful beach houses embraced the bank in a conga line of structures that extended far past the city limits and wrapped around the neck of De LaSalle Bay.

Rule number two: Always scout your opponents.

Thump tied the bandana around Jenny's neck and gave her new Barracuda red leash a tug. Now that he was the head man, his first order of business would be to claim the standard, fire-engine red used in the school color scheme as Barracuda red. From this point forward, Port Verona's athletic teams would sport Barracuda red jerseys. Plain red was what other people wore.

As the two newcomers approached the front door, a freckled teenager in a pristine white cheerleader outfit trimmed in Barracuda red opened the door. A gust of icy air rushed from the administration office.

Upon seeing Thump and Jenny, the freckled cheerleader cried out, "Welcome to the Cove! What a cute doggie!" Script embroidery just below her uniform's left shoulder identified the cheerleader as Ashlyn.

"Why, hello, Ashlyn. Jenny meet Ashlyn. Jenny is my service dog." Jenny's tail wagged. "She always recognizes a good person when she meets them. I'm Coach Sutton."

Ashlyn blushed.

"Coach Sutton! Oh my gosh! And I am the first one to meet you!"

Thump had arrived 20 minutes early. To the side of the lobby, he noticed the boisterous boardroom stuffed with Barracuda boosters.

After another cheerleader named Maya volunteered to babysit Jenny, a woman who identified herself as the receptionist clamped onto Thump's arm and led him past the mass of bodies to where he would meet the superintendent for the first time.

The spacious but sparsely decorated office reminded Thump of a library. Diane Tran stood in front of a large portrait of a shrimp boat crowded with people. Thump recognized Tran from the video conference interview.

"Dr. Tran, glad to meet you," Thump said.

Dr. Tran displayed her characteristic broad, toothy smile. She offered her hand as she spoke in a boisterous, lyrical fashion.

"Coach Sutton, call me Diane!"

Thump's hand swept his gray hair back from his forehead. The tic was a nervous habit. His palm turned upward as he accessorized his handshake with a touch of her elbow. Dr. Tran reciprocated the greeting and grasped Thump's arm. He glanced at her left hand and noted the absence of a wedding band.

Dr. Tran's office was typically academia centric, walled with hundreds of hardbound books and the framed evidence of her education; a bachelor's degree from Baylor, a master's from Virginia, and a doctorate from Georgetown. In one corner, two fabric wingback chairs faced each other. A small. three-legged, round table separated them. Coffee gurgled from a coffee machine, with seven black ceramic mugs nearby on a side bookshelf. At the back of the room, three hardwood chairs fronted Tran's oversized desk. Their style reminded Thump of an old photo he had seen of Louisiana's electric chair.

Thump smirked as Rose whispered in his ear. *Careful. Loose lips.*

Photos of Dr. Tran's family lined the shelf just behind her burgundy leather desk chair. On the left wall hung a large portrait of a sizable group of individuals aboard a wooden shrimp trawler, the *Nho Lai*. Beneath the portrait was a gold plate with the engraving, "We Are One."

"Well, let's go meet our fans!" Tran said.

Because the careers of several coaches had sunk in Port Verona Bay, Thump's aim was to land ashore with dry feet. Not a problem. Few educators could charm a room as Thump could. Within minutes of his introduction, the capacity crowd of Barracuda boosters were cheering several of Thump's remarks.

From the back of the room, Tran glowed. Though she had interviewed him online, she had also researched his career. The perennial dark-horse candidate for head-coaching jobs, Thump's hiring appeared arranged by the stars. Red flags littered his career path. His only consistent success lay in the realm of jousting with administrators. Still, he had served under a half-dozen legends of the game, and he carried a reputation for refusing to compromise in his drive for excellence. His immodest machismo fit Tran's expectation of a high-school football coach.

Uninterested in the extracurricular activities of the district, Tran was often absent from athletic contests. Given her antipathy toward high-school sports, it seemed strange that she would bother to strong-arm Thump's appointment over a popular, inside applicant. But Tran needed a man like Thump.

While Thump may have won the board's approval with a tepid one-vote margin, by the conclusion of the meet-and-greet, he had cemented unanimous support. Everyone who was anyone in town appeared to love the new Great Barracuda.

CHAPTER FIVE

Cabin 5's wooden screen door slapped shut. Thump and Jenny turned downtown on their run. From the southeast, tangerine rays tinted the bobbing shrimp boats moored to their slips. It was time for their father-daughter daily ritual, an old habit that kept them looking and feeling younger than their peers.

Passing through downtown at a brisk pace, Thump grasped Jenny's lead with one hand so he could maintain his free hand in a position of wave-readiness. In a town like Port Verona, a coach must wave at every passerby. Whether he gets a return wave is irrelevant. Should he fail to wave upon eye contact, he has not only lost the chance to win a friend; he has seeded an enemy—a weed. In a small Texas town, it took only the seeding of a single weed to fill the field with enemies.

Rule number three: Wave at everyone, particularly the weeds.

At the outskirt of town, Thump and Jenny stopped to rest across from a field of switchgrass, the tall, indigenous perennial that grows in clumps and flourishes throughout the remains of the abandoned World War II military installation known as Camp Dayson. Jenny lifted her nose toward the morning's cool bay breeze. From where they stood, he could see Blood Reef.

It was the season of Port Verona's 1964 state championship when sportswriter Hershel Maine stirred the embers of history. Shortly after the establishment of the first Spanish settlement, the Karankawa slaughtered the Spanish *colonizadores*. A supply ship's landing crew discovered the silent, smoldering village littered with body parts and blood-soaked pelts; tranquility disrupted. Only a pack of native Karankawa dogs stirred as they argued over the disarticulated skeletal remains. Exaggerated legends of Karankawa atrocities and suspicions of cannibalism soon immortalized the place between the bays, the place the Spaniards called *Arrecife De Sangre* (Blood Reef). Hershel Maine invoked the legend and tagged the nameless venue with an aura that stuck despite the long decline of Barracuda football that followed the stadium's christening.

Blood Reef—Thump loved the name. However, since 1964, most of the blood spilled in that stadium had belonged to the home team. In just over a century of high-school football, the tally was 99 losing seasons and counting. Thump expected to bring that name back to life by resurrecting the spirit of the 1964 Barracudas. He would remind the boys that they descended from a Texas state champion; he would make them believe they are the Gulf of Mexico predator that their nickname implies.

Rule number four: Reestablish the glory.

Kids embrace change. Cynical adults pose a tougher challenge. Thump had less than a week to reprogram coaches who had suffered through years of endless blowouts. Despite the situation, Thump would have to be patient with the staff. He couldn't clean house. Still, the bottom line held firm: Coaches who wouldn't get onboard the resurrection cruise would suffer reassignment or termination.

A colony of gulls circled near the port. Jenny's tongue drooped while Thump attempted to overcome the grinding pain in his bad knee. The only sounds he heard were Jenny's panting and the nails of her paws clicking on the warming pavement.

Cloistered within the morning's calm, the coach and his four-legged daughter were approaching the town proper when a whooping sound blasted behind them. Jenny yanked the leash as the Port

Verona PD Charger roared past them like a lion claiming its kill. Outside the driver's window a hand raised, its index finger pointed to the sky.

CHAPTER SIX

Tuesday morning, on entering the fieldhouse for the first time, Thump and Jenny encountered a mound of damp workout gear, overflowing trash cans, and desks cluttered with chaotic piles of dog-eared forms and handouts. Loose weights and power bars littered the weight-room floor. Both the coaches' and the players' restrooms reeked. From the clogged toilets, eruptions of raw sewage had mushroomed across the bathroom tile. Paper towels and wads of tissue cluttered the floor. In a clear act of degradation, someone had used a "Barracuda Athletics" red T-shirt to clog the head coaches' toilet. Jenny recoiled from the overflow of water and human waste pooled throughout the locker room and assistant coaches' office. An oppressive stench permeated the entire building. The fieldhouse appeared vandalized.

Enraged over the chaotic mess, Thump calmed himself after Rose convinced him to see the situation as an opportunity to put his walk before his talk and use his time, money, and energy to show his coaches he was more than just the latest snake-oil salesman with a bag full of catchy slogans.

Thump spent $300 of his own money on cleaning supplies, and a full day on the fieldhouse makeover. Jenny wasn't much help with the labor. Thump was on his own, but by the time Ole Blue sputtered out of the lot that Tuesday night, the Port Verona Chernobyl resembled a Silicon Valley clean room.

He just couldn't get it out of his head. *Why had the condition of the fieldhouse descended to such a state? Where were the assistant coaches all summer?*

Supervision of the facilities in both the women's and men's realms fell under Thump's auspice. Still, facility upkeep was just a peripheral part of the job. As every athletic director/head football coach from 6-man to 6A knew, it was football, not facility upkeep, that got them fired.

Despite his Athletic Director title, Thump had no time to spread among the other sports. Barracuda volleyball shared the calendar with football, but the spikers would be on their own. A polite email inviting the women's staff to a breakfast or a cup of hot chocolate would suffice. Women's sports weren't the problem at Port Verona. Barracuda women's basketball owned the region, and the coaches in the women's program lived on the right side of the fence. Good guys.

Athletic directors delineated the good guys from the bad. If the system tagged a coach as a bad guy, that coached lived with the mark for the rest of his or her career. Years ago, rumors tagged Thump as one of the bad guys. That designation was one reason it had taken more than 30 years for him to land his first head-coaching job. But Thump was okay with the indistinction. He recognized that for myriad reasons, the necktie-wearers mislabeled coaches. Switching jobs too often, getting divorced, and offending a district superintendent were the top three reasons. Thump had hit the trifecta decades ago.

After a quick shower and a glance through the summer edition of *Texas Coach*, Thump settled in for the night. He wrapped himself in the thin sheet.

A momentary foul vibe passed through the room, but Thump fell back to sleep unaware. Rose felt it on Monday and had since carried the baggage of that awareness in silence. She just could not reel in the cause for her concern. Whatever it was, Thump's emotional gatekeeper decided this was not the time for chasing rabbits. She would let him be for the night.

The following morning, Thump cut their run short, but he thought it a shame to quit early. He stopped to gaze upward. Even the Little Painter Fellow hadn't painted a canvas as starry as the predawn Gulf sky. Overhead in the great black-box theater, Rita Hayworth and Bob Hope were back entertaining the ghosts of Camp Dayson, but Thump couldn't take time to enjoy the show. He had work to do.

All eyes were on him. Even though the coaches' meeting wasn't until 8:00 a.m., Thump and Jenny reported before 7:00 a.m. He knew that an early-bird assistant or two would love to tell their buddies about having to wait for the new head man.

A pot of gourmet coffee brewed in the assistant coaches' office. To promote the spirit of collegiality, he stacked a variety of kolaches near the coffee.

Most of the staff arrived early. They wanted to impress the new head man. Laughter and humorous barbs soon flew about the room. At the stroke of 8:00 a.m., Thump called their first coaches' meeting to order and introduced himself.

From the look of it, he had a nice mix of coaches and personalities. Seven assistant football coaches, counting the junior high coordinator—an understaffed allotment by Texas standards—it allowed the Barracudas just four on the home sideline on game night.

Not knowing much about the men, he would live with during the next five months, Thump asked them to introduce each other rather than introduce themselves. While the coaches revealed each other's supposed talents and listed their personal superlatives, Thump focused on their body language and eye discipline. He felt it would be their demeanor, not their words, that would reveal their social inventory.

Senior to the rest of the staff, Harrison Dye had been the Barracudas' outside linebacker coach and supervisor of the high school's in-school suspension module since before the reign of the Karankawa. Built like a fire hydrant, the silver-haired, slow-talking Killeen, Texas native spoke with the ratcheted voice of a film noir gangster. In his off time, he loved to break bricks and punch the heavy bag which hung in his sunroom. No cut of stone or brick could withstand the force of the egg-sized calcium deposits found on his elbows. Harrison was a Taekwondo Grand Master and the oldest Black Belt in Tiburon County. A coaching dinosaur who, other than the occasional off-color joke, didn't say much, Harrison didn't need to talk. His cold blue eyes could sear a kid's heart.

In charge of the defensive line was Isaac Sewell, a cornerstone of the community. Slow to anger, quick to chuckle, Isaac owned the wisdom of Solomon. Isaac's greatest gift lay in his innate ability to size up a person's character. A team captain during the era of the Black Rain of Death, Isaac led Texas Tech to the Southwest Conference title. The old guard has a saying about coaches like Isaac: "He knows the game."

Coaching Thump's linebackers was Dirk Mason, a special education teacher and a member of Port Verona's Class of 1990. Both his grandfather and father were legendary high school coaches, their names enshrined on the Texas High School Hall of Fame in Waco. Dirk's enthusiasm and talent for leadership had gone unrecognized by the earlier head coaches. He didn't realize it yet, but Thump would elevate him to defensive coordinator.

Prior to Thump's arrival, Dirk's high school classmate, Grant Lee Davis, had been the Barracudas' defensive coordinator. Grant Lee resigned that duty in contempt of the board's decision to name Thump to the athletic director post. At the meet and greet, several concerned boosters leaned in to offer Thump early warning alerts as to Grant Lee's dissatisfaction over not getting the head job. The three original nays for Thump's board approval were Grant Lee voters. Grant Lee appeared smart and charming, but he struggled in his classroom performance as an English teacher, a deficiency that had landed him in the execution chair in front of Dr. Tran's desk more than once. His distaste for the mundane duties of a classroom teacher may have cost him the swing vote he needed for the head job. With the Barracudas understaffed for a large 3A program, Thump kept the mercurial Grant Lee as his secondary coach.

The Herrera twins would coach the quarterback and wide receivers. Identical in appearance and demeanor, the two Port Verona sports legends were the superstars of the last Barracuda team to win more than two games, Miguel at quarterback and Roberto at wide receiver. After college, they traveled overseas to play professional soccer for several years. They are inseparable. When Miguel's career ended with a torn anterior cruciate ligament, Roberto called it quits. They returned home to establish what had become the top soccer program in the region.

Port Verona hired Jason Maldonado in June to be the junior-high coordinator. Thump received scarce information about him other than his wife was Dr. Tran's niece. He had enjoyed a productive career as an offensive lineman at Sam Houston State. Jason would act as head coach for the seventh and eighth grade teams and scout future opponents on Friday night. Despite the growth of instant game video sharing online, Thump was old school and wanted boots on the ground to scout in person. Jason would also float among the individual and group rotations during two-a-day drills. Floating would give him a precise understanding of Thump's blueprint, and his junior-high troops wouldn't report until the first day of school.

After Thump's dissertation of expectations, the staff broke for lunch. Thump noticed that the staff went their separate ways in a hurry. From just outside the fieldhouse, watching the dust cloud created by the simultaneous exit of their vehicles, Thump felt as if he was watching the start of a seven-car demolition derby. Thump stroked Jenny's head.

"We should work on our staff unity, Jenny."

The afternoon session consisted of prep work for the players' arrival on Monday. Throughout the afternoon, Thump met with each coach. They would work late.

It relieved Thump to see Grant Lee onboard with Dirk's appointment to the defensive coordinator spot. Grant Lee was popular with the kids and had skin in all facets of the diverse Port Verona landscape. He even operated his own deep-sea fishing tour company, and *Texas Wildlife Magazine* once named him the top duck hunting guide in South Texas. Besides, this wasn't the first time the bull bucked Grant Lee. Passed over three times before, he never missed a step. Each time he returned stronger. He was a darn good coach if he could keep his ego in check. Thump appreciated the ingredients of Grant Lee's stew. He would need him to contribute in a big way to turn the ship.

With the staff excused just before midnight, Thump and Jenny locked up. Old Blue sat alone under an imposing shelf cloud encroaching the western boundary of town. Thump surveyed the ghostly lot, then secured his lump of keys on a Barracuda red lanyard as his boots crunched on the grit and pebbles. Jenny tiptoed behind him. As much as she disliked a wet floor, she abhorred rough surfaces.

Once back at cottage 5 and wired tight from the stress, Thump needed some outdoor time with his girl. He grabbed his childhood wishing blanket, and Jenny's favorite toy—a red synthetic ball with eight streamers attached. The thing resembled a squid, so Squid became its name.

He spread the blanket on a spot between his hut and the water's edge. Despite the alluring coastal breeze and the gentle lapping of the bay, Thump stayed near to the bungalow. He hadn't heard of gators living in the neighborhood, but perhaps that was because their presence was as routine as the migratory birds that flew south via the coastal airway.

Tiburon County was an international bird-watching mecca, and it was not unusual for the seasonal snowbirds and retirees to glimpse a diving eagle or a hawk plucking its meal from a swatch of prairie grass. And as fast as a hawk could snatch a field rat, so could a stealthy alligator seize a lounging man, not to mention a watersport loving part-Labrador retriever. Thump had heard of saltwater crocodiles living in India, but he wasn't sure if Port Verona Bay was saltwater or freshwater. The old shrimpers told tales of freshwater gators venturing out in the Gulf for a snack, so he figured it was better to stay alert.

Thump lay back and chuckled. He remembered a joke Rose once told him.

Thomas, where does an alligator sleep?
I can't guess, Rose. Where does an alligator sleep?
Wherever it wants, Thomas. It sleeps wherever it wants.

After an hour of tossing Squid and cloud-gazing, Thump and Jenny let the mosquitoes have the rest of the night. Day two would be installation day, the most important day of preseason.

CHAPTER SEVEN

The next day, following their run, Thump and Jenny found a dilapidated establishment that offered his morning fuel, one large *carne guisada* with cheese and green sauce and an ice-cold Dr. Pepper. Through the front door's marred plexiglas, they saw that the locals had packed the joint.

"That's a good sign, Jenny."

Thump left Jenny in the truck and squeezed in line behind an old rancher in coveralls. In the back kitchen, he spied Maya with both her hands flying about as she filled the orders.

Thump ordered 12 breakfast tacos for the staff: four bacon-and-egg, four chorizo-and-egg, and four potato-and-egg with an extra container of red sauce and green sauce.

Years ago, when Thump coached at Lorraine Hansberry High School in Houston, the only place he could find his morning fuel was Elias's Food Truck on Fry Road. Elias's wife Rosalita made the green sauce from fresh peppers in her garden. After loading her homemade tortilla with pot roast, gravy and cheese, she spread a double pump of her green sauce on the gravy-soaked meat, then rolled the overloaded tortilla into a burrito fatty from heaven. A local deputy sheriff, one of Thump's former players and a regular customer, once said that Elias's truck pulled in six figures, selling only breakfast and lunch dishes. Thump had asked Elias and Rosalita to adopt him, but they knew he wanted them for the green sauce.

With Port Verona's best taco joint just a few blocks from the Barracuda fieldhouse, Thump decided to give Old Blue a quick workout. He slid the shifter upward on the steering column, then popped the clutch and floored the gas pedal. Blue's engine revved as she scorched the carbon off her valves. Signaling a left turn into the alleyway that runs behind Blood Reef, Thump glanced at his rearview mirror.

A white sedan topped with a red and blue lightbar changed lanes to pass. This time, the lightbar wasn't lit, nor the siren active. Thump coaxed Blue's rickety suspension into the tight left-hand turn as the Charger sped by. He peered through the passenger window and saw an index finger pointed skyward.

I'm losing the wave war with this gal.

Thump looked down at Jenny's soulful brown eyes. His bacon-scented fingers smoothed her coat. She licked his hand in hope of a taste.

"Jenny, it's a good thing you and I didn't come to rob this town. That lady cop would have already put us under the jail. She's everywhere."

Jenny's tail tapped twice in agreement.

Later at the fieldhouse, with tacos consumed and the staff settled in for the workday, Thump asked the coaches to meet in the conference room to create a depth chart and plan the two-a-day preseason conditioning phase. While Thump versed Dirk as to the specifics on his 3-4 defensive scheme, the rest of the staff would complete preseason practice plans for the four main position groups: defensive backs, inside linebackers, outside linebackers, and defensive linemen. Thump had allotted Jason and the twins three hours to grasp a strategy that had taken over 20 years to develop. Despite the narrow window, he expected to have the youngsters qualified as experts in the formational philosophy and the distinguishing elements of his run and pass game before noon. Both sides of the ball would meet again as a full staff at 6:00 p.m.

Just before the lunch break, he received his first text from the superintendent's private cell number: PLEASE SEE ME.

That didn't take long.

As usual with a "see me" text, he held no clue what it could be. Thump's stomach growled louder than Jenny guarding a T-bone, but he dismissed the staff early and headed over to the Cove.

Dr. Tran's secretary greeted him at the reception desk.

"Coach Sutton, Dr. Tran would like to see you in her office. Come with me, please."

Thump ran his hand through his hair and followed. Her back to the doorway, Dr. Tran typed at her computer. Thump waited as the secretary leaned over her shoulder and whispered. Dr. Tran swiveled to face Thump.

"Coach Sutton! Glad you stopped by. Did you get my text? I hope I didn't interrupt your day. Please take a seat."

"No, ma'am. I'm always happy to talk with you."

His hand pushed aside the hair from his forehead.

"Well, I know you're busy planning and organizing things at the fieldhouse. I just wanted to visit with you about a few matters. We may have an issue with our master schedule. I see we scheduled you for two athletic periods and two conferences." She glanced down at a colorful chart on her desk. "We appointed you to teach two sections of United States history, as well?"

"Yes, ma'am. I believe a coach can do the most good in the building by being in the classroom as much as possible."

"Excellent. That was one thing that stood out about you in your interview. So many football coaches want to focus on the athletic side of their job, but it is through the academics where they can make the greatest impact in a scholar's life."

Putting her hands to her chin as if she were praying, Dr. Tran smiled, awaiting Thump's response.

"I agree."

His throat tightened. He could hear Rose talking, but he couldn't make out the words. It was as if someone was ringing a cowbell in his ears.

Dr. Tran leaned forward.

"I am so glad that you are a man of principle, Coach Sutton. It isn't often we see that anymore. We will require you to pick up a section of English 3 besides your two history classes. My plan trades one of your conference periods for the English. I know that will be hard on you, but you will still collaborate with the social-studies department. And you will work with juniors in both the history and English, so it will be an easy two preps."

"We do what we must do," Thump said. "Our job is to serve kids."

The clanging in his ears intensified.

Dr. Tran rotated the massive leather chair to look at her computer screen. She appeared to read an email, then spun around and leaned forward with her elbows on the desk. Her eyes measured Thump.

"Well, I know you are busy, so let me get right to the second item on our agenda. I received a call from maintenance, and we have a concern regarding the fieldhouse."

"Yes, ma'am. The facility was dirty, but I bought cleaning supplies here in town and scrubbed all night. The place is in great shape now."

Tran's smile faded.

"Is there a problem?" Thump asked.

Dr. Tran leaned back in her chair. Her eyes focused on the expensive droplights above her desk.

"Coach Sutton, here at Port Verona Independent School District, I have put in place a hierarchy which follows a precise direction of accountability. Each department has prescribed duties and a budget administered according to the limits of those duties. When I first arrived here, no policy of accountability was in place how to apply the budget, nor was there an inventory of the man hours budgeted to execute those duties. It was bedlam. Do you understand?"

"Yes, ma'am."

Tran scratched her nose and chuckled.

31

"Well, I am sure you will get the hang of things. Be sure to check with maintenance before taking any action on the facilities. And get with Principal Saltzman as soon as possible regarding the English 3 section."

"Yes, ma'am. Thank you for your time."

"No, thank you, Coach Sutton. I look forward to seeing you and your staff at the Rotary Club breakfast on Wednesday!"

"Yes, ma'am."

"Oh, Coach Sutton."

"Yes, ma'am?"

"Don't forget: Call me Diane!"

How about I call you crazy?

She offered to walk him out, but Thump was in a hurry to get back to Jenny at the fieldhouse. He had just lost 30 minutes of his lunch break, and Jenny would be restless after being locked in his office.

The clanging in his ears subsided as he hustled back to the fieldhouse. He swiped the sweat from his forehead. He couldn't believe he had been on the job only three days before Dr. Tran flexed on him.

Well done, my love. You showed an abundance of poise. I'm proud of you.

Rose's soothing validation brought him back to the joy of the moment; he had passed his first test.

The afternoon saw the coaches scurrying nonstop about the fieldhouse. Around 7:00 p.m., Thump recognized the thousand-yard stare in the faces of his younger coaches. He dismissed the staff early. They deserved time with their families and needed to recharge their batteries for the next day's challenge: demonstration day.

While the coaches gathered their belongings, he would catch up on preseason paperwork and submit the preseason data sheets to the area newspapers and sports journals. The Texas High School Coaches Association questionnaire was late, and the Texas Interscholastic League eligibility report was due by Monday. He was reviewing the athletes' physical forms the staff had completed last May when Coach Sewell appeared at his door.

"Sorry to bother you, Coach. Do you have a minute?"

"Isaac, come on in. Sit down."

Jenny's tail tapped in agreement.

"Well, I'm not sure if you know it or not, but we have this place here in town, right near where you stay at By the Bay. The state Methodist association once owned the property. Been so since 1928. The Methodists used it as a summer camp and what-not. The thing is, the Methodists sold it to the state. Then, the state ended up leasing it to a medical conglomerate, and now it's a residential center for boys from around the state. Some of them have behavioral issues. Some have criminal records for petty crimes and what-have-you. It's a place for kids who had bad family situations and ended up with no place to go."

"I didn't know about that, Isaac."

"Yeah, they call the place Camp Promise. They have 20 to 30 kids who stay there, all boys. Some of them take their classes right there at the facility, but a good many of them attend school right here in Port Verona."

"What are their ages?" Thump asked.

"Oh, they have all ages. Around half are the younger kids who go to East Bay. That's the elementary where Dr. Tran's niece is the assistant principal. It's over by your place. Well, the thing is, my pastor called me two nights ago. He said that Camp Promise had just taken in two new high-school boys."

Thump leaned forward.

"Anyway, Pastor Mike from my church is on the board and works with the intake of the clients. That's what they call the kids, clients. He also runs the recreation department. And he wanted to let me know that these two boys wanted to play football."

"Do you know anything about them? What grade are they in? Have they played before?" Thump asked.

"Well, it was late when he called and the wife was getting on me to take my meds, so I'm not sure as to all what he said; but I remember he said for me to tell you to call him as soon as you got settled. It was something to do with those two boys."

"Sure, no problem, what's Pastor Mike's number?"

"I got it right here for you."

"Thanks, Isaac. Appreciate you."

"Oh, you welcome, Coach," Isaac said as he turned to leave, then hesitated. "You know, Pastor Mike never asked me to reach out on his behalf. He didn't think much of the last few head coaches who came through here. But he swore to me that you're different. He said he had checked up on you, done his homework." Isaac paused. "Yeah, he said you are different."

"Pastor Mike's words honor me. I promise to call him here in a minute, before you and that lime green Dodge Barracuda leave the parking lot."

Isaac smiled.

"Yeah, that's my baby. You like her?"

"Man, I love that car. That's a man's car!" Thump replied.

Isaac pointed at Thump and grinned.

"Okay, Coach, I'll see you in the morning then."

"See you in the morning, Isaac."

Jenny's tail tapped. She liked Isaac.

True to his word, Thump called Pastor Mike before Isaac left the parking lot.

Pastor Mike informed Thump of the details behind his recent intake of the two half-brothers with a football pedigree. The elder had been the quarterback of his freshman squad at Dallas Douglass High, a tough inner-city school known for its stellar basketball teams. The younger brother had been a novice running back at one of the middle schools within the Dallas Douglass feeder pattern. Removed from their grandmother's home when an assistant principal at the feeder school detected the two brothers living without supervision or help, the boys became wards of the state. Before the state took them in, they had fended for themselves, living for four months without electricity or running water. Despite those hardships, the brothers won perfect attendance awards during the second semester. School was the only place where they could get a hot meal.

Pastor Mike told Thump he planned to bring the brothers by the fieldhouse the following day.

Known for low participation at the varsity level, the Barracudas had just gained two in the numbers game. Still, Thump had expected the uptick.

A new head coach results in an initial increase of the numbers, and Port Verona was no different. The Herrera twins had alerted Thump to three soccer players who were reporting on Monday, and Harrison Dye had remarked that "a thick-necked kid who said his family had just moved to Port Verona" approached him at the grocery store. Harrison remembered the kid saying he was a junior and he had played on the offensive line at Corpus Christi High, the class 6A state champion of the preceding season. If his information was correct, the kid was a player.

Coaches call a kid who displays an exceptional skill set a player. Port Verona was a place of few players.

Rule number five: Find the players.

CHAPTER EIGHT

Saturday morning, after scoring the coaches their breakfast tacos, Thump arrived to find a large bald man accompanied by two athletic-looking kids waiting outside the fieldhouse. One tall and thin, the other more muscular. Thump's legendary eye for talent told him he was looking at a quarterback and a running back, but not a typical Port Verona quarterback and running back.

"I hope you three young men are hungry! I got a mess of the best tacos in Tiburon County, so I hear!" Thump said, as he held up the white paper bag.

Pastor Mike greeted Thump with a hug.

"Coach Thump, so good to meet you. You know, I was out of town the day of the meet-and-greet, but I heard a lot about you."

"Well, you just make sure you don't believe 90 percent of that," Thump replied.

The taller kid smiled.

Pastor Mike said, "You know better than that, Coach Sutton. Everybody knows the story of that Le'Montellier boy in Port Arthur, and how you lost your job over taking care of that young man. People don't forget that."

"Yeah. It's just that I'm not sure that was so much of a good thing in a couple places. Why don't y'all come sit in my office and let's visit? I need my morning go juice. Who do I have dining with me this morning at Coach Sutton's Café?"

The taller boy grinned and snickered. He had a big smile.

Easygoing, a good quality for a quarterback to have.

Pointing to the taller kid, Pastor Mike said, "Coach, this here is T'Darian Law. He is an honor student and has a big left arm."

A left-handed quarterback?

Thump had never coached a left-handed quarterback. Neither had he ever coached a six-foot-four quarterback.

Dressed in a white polo and jeans, T'Darian grinned and extended his hand as if he were selling Thump a new truck or maybe a recliner he didn't need.

"Good to meet you," T'Darian said.

His hand swallowed Thump's, and the grip was what a Port Verona fisherman needed to land a Texas-sized swordfish.

Touching the second boy's shoulder, Pastor Mike said, "And this here is Derek Donaldson."

Derek wore a ragged white wife-beater and baggy red gym shorts. "Panthers" written on the left side identified the shorts as equipment issued at Dallas Douglass. The chiseled teen betrayed no emotion.

So, this is the serious one.

Derek was less than enthusiastic in his handshake. His grip cloaked his strength and power.

Jenny wagged her tail and whined.

"Does that dog bite?" T'Darian asked.

Before Thump could answer, Derek looked toward T'Darian and said, "Hey, it got teeth, don't it?"

Thump laughed.

"No, she would never bite you, not unless you were trying to hurt me."

"I don't know about that. I'm with Derek. That dog has fangs, and I never heard of fangs being used for anything but biting," Pastor Mike said.

T'Darian chuckled at Pastor Mike's comment as Derek looked at Jenny and moved behind T'Darian. Just as they entered the building, the lime green Barracuda skidded to a stop in the parking lot.

Thump waved to Isaac.

Once in the office, Thump gathered the waivers and medical forms while the boys enjoyed the tacos with two Dr. Peppers from Thump's office refrigerator. Sitting at Thump's desk, Pastor Mike and Isaac sipped Jamaican Green Roast and exchanged tidbits regarding the upcoming Houston Texans season.

A little after 8:00 that morning, Pastor Mike and the boys stepped in to meet the rest of the staff. Later, as Isaac walked the three to their car, Thump briefed the staff on their history and assigned Grant Lee Davis the critical role of academic contact and compliance officer.

The most popular staff member on campus, if not in the entire school district, Grant Lee was Thump's choice for the academic liaison role. It's a position in which he can influence the counselors in their scheduling of the classes for the players. While his outdoorsman persona designated him the alpha male of the faculty, his good looks, wit, and charm anointed him as the hypnotist of the hens, those old birds who had grown tough and coarse after years of scratching out their subsistence in the schoolyard. Regardless of their gender or their ages, staff members were warm putty in Grant Lee's presence.

Grant Lee's first task as an academic coordinator would be to navigate the enrollment process for T'Darian and Derek. After that, he would oversee their class registration. As the compliance officer, it was his job to review each player's transcript and confirm that the player had completed the minimum credits required to be eligible. He would then move on to the next phase of the compliance spectrum and validate their residency as required by the Texas Interscholastic League. Because of the custodial situation, T'Darian's and Derek's path to attaining varsity eligibility was problematic, but Grant Lee was the man who could get things done no matter what the obstacle.

Thump excused Grant Lee from most of the installation day lectures; he could catch up later. Grant Lee had served as a defensive coordinator for the past 10 years. He excelled at the game.

Harrison Dye remarked, "That ole boy doesn't need meetings. Grant Lee could coach four cats raised in a burlap sack to play Broadway."

Rule number six: Football is a game of adjustments.

Installation had always been Thump's favorite day of the preseason prep sessions. It's the day that each staff member lectures on the techniques, responsibilities, pre-snap keys, and post-snap keys of his position while detailing every nuance of coaching and playing the position. Throughout the chalk talk, the head coach quizzes the presenter. Sometimes, the coaches assemble in a breakout session on the practice field. After the lecture and position coach's demonstration, other coaches may contribute to the discussion. If a disagreement arises, no one leaves until they agree. The typical installation is a three-day event held during a preseason retreat. The Barracuda staff had one day. It was to be a long one.

By 10:00 p.m., that night, burger wrappers and drink cans littered the office. When Grant Lee returned, he was the last of the bleary-eyed staff to present. It took the former defensive coordinator less than an hour to present the stance, alignment, and assignment of each of the nine techniques of secondary play versus the three ball levels a defensive back could face. To enhance his lecture, he embedded game video into a Microsoft Power Point presentation. Thump had seen no presentation done better.

A booster told Thump the former defensive coordinator used a similar slide show during his interview for the head job. Grant Lee was in the process of identifying the coaching points of rotating a zone to adjust the strength versus wide receiver motion when Thump noticed Harrison Dye's chin sinking to his chest. Thump interrupted the session.

"That's impressive stuff, Grant Lee. Let's stop here and call it a day. Dirk, get with Grant Lee on those motion adjustments before the first practice. I'm proud to be associated with you guys. We have the knowledge and coaching ability in this room to change lives. I'm convinced this will be the most memorable season Port Verona has seen in half a century of football. See you dressed in Barracuda red,

Monday at 6:00 a.m., in the morning. The kids will hit the field at 7:00 a.m., right Grant Lee?"

"That's right, Coach."

"Okay, men. Good night. Let's have a restful Sunday and hit the ground running. I love you all."

Because Thump was a man to follow his own orders, he would also rest on Sunday.

Being a Methodist, Jenny slept late while Thump debuted at Second Baptist Church. Thump chose Second Baptist because of its size, not its affiliation.

With a towering steeple that loomed over the bay like a sentinel, its fellowship hall was a two-story stone building featuring a regulation basketball court and an oval arrangement of classrooms upstairs. The classrooms overlooked the court. Harrison Dye told Thump that 500 souls rode out Hurricane Darla on the second floor after 16 feet of water inundated the town. Thump wasn't as much a Baptist as he was a football coach, but he learned from Harrison that Second was home to the largest congregation in Port Verona. It didn't hurt that three of the seven school trustees were members in good standing. To Thump, Second's most inviting feature was Dr. Tran's membership in the Catholic church across town.

On this pristine morning, Reverend Ben Wallace preached from the Gospel of James. Thump understood James to be somewhere in the New Testament, but he wasn't sure where. He thumbed to the middle of his Bible, trying to appear nonchalant as he searched.

Reverend Wallace bellowed what he called the fundamental truth of his sermon.

"James 4:14 says, 'You do not even know what will happen tomorrow! What is your life? You are a mist that appears for a little while and then vanishes.'"

Thump shook his head.

A mist that appears for a little while and then vanishes?

For Thump, a guy who believed in the immortality of his accomplishments, that was a tough line to swallow.

Because Reverend Wallace owned a taste for fried okra, cornbread, catfish, and pro football, he religiously called for the benediction at 11:57 a.m. After the prayer, Thump scurried out to the truck.

Reverend Wallace wasn't the only person who ate on time; Jenny expected her lunch served no later than half past noon. But on this Sunday, Thump's celebrity status derailed Jenny's expectations. Before he could get two steps down the red-carpeted middle aisle, a mass of blue-haired Barracuda fans surrounded Thump.

If only Dirk and Grant Lee can get our defense to swarm like that.

Near the foyer, one of the blue-haired women accosted Thump.

"Coach, how are our boys looking this year? You think we can have a winning season?"

The elderly woman clutched an aluminum walker with two pink tennis balls at the bottom. Arthritis had twisted her near-transparent hands. She grasped Thump's arm as she spoke in a shrill Texas twang.

"My name is Dorothy Jean Butler. I was head cheerleader when we won the state championship, and I still have my pom-poms."

"Yes, ma'am. It's always good to meet an alumnus. I expect this year will be a transition year, but I believe we can win a few games."

"Transition year? Heavenly day, Coach. Please hurry and whip our boys into shape. As you can see, I don't have much time left to wait. No, we can't wait for a transition year. I'm just so tired of our boys losing. Last year, I almost canceled my fall subscription to the *Sentinel.*"

"Yes, ma'am. Praise the Lord and go Barracudas!"

Thump wiggled his way to the main exit where the reverend stood shaking hands with the people filing outside. The assemblage of parishioners surrounding Thump had drifted along with him down the crowded aisle. Out of the corner of his right eye, he noticed a teenager holding her cell camera high above her shoulders and pointing it in his direction.

He was within 15 feet of the foyer when a thick arm collared him from behind. His first impression was that someone had hit him with a pressure treated four-by-four. From behind him, a surly voice boomed.

"Thump Sutton, wait up!"

"Rodney Dwain Venson! We are in the house of the Lord!" a woman nearby said.

Thump turned to see the piece of timber that struck him. It was Rod Venson, his roommate at Tallulah College. They had worked together as graduate assistants on Ed Hattaway's staff.

Rod had been an All-American nose tackle for the Baylor Bears with a future of earning millions when an Aggie chop block at the 50-yard line of Kyle Field ended his career. Baylor won the game, but Rod lost the ability to walk for the next nine months. His playing days over, an emotionally lost and aimless Rod thought he might want to try his hand at coaching. He once occupied the lower bunk under Thump in a residence hall at tiny Tallulah College. Thump hadn't seen his old roomie since the day after the Tallulah Board of Regents dropped the football program.

Rod leaned into Thump and said, "Thump, meet me outside. We need to talk."

The old roommate bulldozed his way through the parishioners and bypassed Reverend Wallace. Thump followed in his wake, squirting through the logjam of congregants like a slippery watermelon seed. He glanced at the reverend, who was busy thanking the attendees for coming. Reverend Wallace, both of his hands entwined with those of two well-weathered little old ladies in pink hats, nodded and smiled in Thump's direction.

Rod stood next to a large four-wheel-drive pickup which had been lifted to ride on oversized tires. His calloused thumb flicked the gold plated lighter he had earned his junior year as the Durham Tobacco Bowl's most valuable defensive player. He attempted to light a short black cigar.

"Thump! Get your tired old butt over here! The Texans kick off in twenty!"

He was still as intense as ever. The chiding woman from the sanctuary had just scaled the passenger side when Rod lit his cigar. One hand on the door handle, Rod repeated his phone number and ordered Thump to put it in his contacts.

Thump was still punching in the number when Rod climbed the footsteps of his Country Cadillac and fired up the engine. Rod was in a hurry.

Thump sprang back as the truck's massive rear mudder nicked the tip of his church boot's silver toe cap.

Over the engine's roar, Rod yelled, "Call me, Thump! I mean it. It's important!"

Thump blinked and the pickup carrying Rod, the woman, and the cigar sped north on Gulfway Drive.

By the time Thump got home, Jenny's head hung low. At the sound of the key sliding into the front door lock, she was at the door giving Thump the business. The penultimate sulk that always ended her pouting fits would follow.

After some prodding and a half-hour of Thump's apologies, she skulked toward her dog dish. Once she saw her Sunday special treat in the bowl, Jenny bounced and wiggled with joy. Thump appreciated the fact that Nature's Best topped off with a squirt of cheese spread always paved an expressway to this woman's heart.

If only that had worked with Ten-Months-in-San Antonio.

South of the cottages, an overcast of dark clouds tamped the Sunday afternoon heat while small whitecaps promenaded like tots in a Texas beauty pageant. It was an inviting canvas of blue for the sailboats and jet skis skimming just offshore.

On the grocery-store hurricane map, Port Verona was dead center in a weather witches' cauldron. Nestled in the crook of the Texas coastline, just north of the sweet spot for the Gulf of Mexico hurricanes, Port Verona often landed on the dirty side, the side of the storm where, according to the National Oceanic and Atmospheric Administration, the wind and the storm's forward velocity combined to level everything in its path.

A high-school football coach has no time for weather watching, so Thump could only hope that a tropical storm had not arrived in the Gulf. Still, having grown up in Southeast Texas, he knew warm south winds accompanying fast-moving clouds were a valid concern. He turned on his weather radio and sat in his grandmother's rocking chair.

Thump's lunch tardiness absolved, Jenny climbed into his lap and laid her head on his shoulder. This was his cue for their Sunday afternoon ritual. He rocked and sang her favorite lullaby, the one his mother used to sing.

Jenny let out a long sigh; her almond eyes closed. A few hours into their rock-a-bye nap, the National Weather Service Alert tone screeched from the radio. A startled Jenny leaped to her feet.

"We have a storm in the Gulf of Mexico, Jenny." Thump rose from the chair to turn off the radio. "We're good. We're miles away from its expected landfall."

He pulled the cord on the blinds. His adventurous side loved the suspense of an approaching hurricane, but it was only a temporary insanity that dissipated once the electricity failed and the oak trees bent like cattails in the wind. Besides, he had a greater thrill awaiting him. In a little over 12 hours, he would see the hand dealt to him.

CHAPTER NINE

The next morning, with a storm in the Gulf, Rita Hayworth and Bob Hope stayed tucked away in a blanket of high-level clouds. Just before dawn, the storm had stalled off the Louisiana coast, then drifted eastward. Its counterclockwise rotation pushed a nice predawn breeze across the emptiness of downtown Port Verona.

Jenny's paws danced along the cool pavement. Two hundred yards away from breaking the tape, the high beams and pulsating light bar of a police car lit up the street. He and Jenny halted on the side of the road. The blinding illumination caused Thump to shade his eyes in the manner of a salute. He made out a thin, athletic figure clad in uniform blue emerging from behind the glare.

"Morning, Coach Sutton."

"Good morning, Officer. Was I speeding?"

"No, you definitely weren't speeding, but it seems you have a defective taillight."

"Sorry about that, Officer. I'll try get it worked on as soon as possible."

"You're a funny guy, Coach. Hey, I know you will be busy this week. Two-a-days start today, right? I just wanted to give you a shout-out from the force. The boys and I think you will turn the program around."

Thump strained to read her name tag. "Thank you, Officer—"

"Mendoza, Sergeant Sara Mendoza," she said, pointing to the stripes on her sleeve.

"Sergeant Mendoza, got it."

"Okay then, Coach. You and your companion are free to go about your business. But I would like to see you get that taillight repaired before too long. Maybe get a vehicular safety expert to look at it for you?" she said with a wink.

"Yes, ma'am. Will do."

Jenny groaned. She was eager to finish the run.

The red and blue lights darkened, the car's engine growled, and the Charger's taillights merged into a single point of red.

"Jenny, I think we have a new friend."

As the players arrived for Monday morning's practice, Thump greeted them at the door, taking note of each handshake's firmness. Because the staff had recorded their foot sizes on the last day of school in May, Dirk had their cleats waiting for them in their lockers. Above their cleats hung the softwear: a pair of black shorts, a pair of white socks and a Barracuda red, form-fitting, drywear t-shirt. On the second hook of the locker compartment hung a laundry bag. A locker number written on the front identified the owner of each item.

At 7:30, Grant Lee locked the front door of the fieldhouse. Any player late for practice would watch from the sideline. The team and the coaches assembled around Thump, and he addressed his team for the first time.

"Eyes up, men. Right knee on the ground. This is how we do things here. We keep our head up, and we look people in the eye. It's called focus. I don't talk much, and neither should you, so let me get right down to it. You are looking at three days of conditioning. Pure conditioning only, for 90 minutes a day, twice a day. Drink all you want whenever you want. We have two student managers and two student trainers on hand to help you. We are a family; we will have faith; we will have a fire in our life. Everybody on your feet. When we break out, you will report to your defensive position coaches. Coaches, call out your positions."

Coach Mason raised his arm and yelled, "Linebackers!"

Coach Davis raised his arm and said, "DB's, defensive backs!"

Coach Sewell raised his arm and said, "Defensive line, that's TNTs, with me."

"I got the outside linebackers," Harrison Dye said.

The team crowded around Thump. Each player raised a fist.

Thump said, "When someone says, 'One Team', you respond, 'One Heart.'"

"One Team!"

They responded, "One Heart!" and broke the huddle with a burst.

Thump watched with reverence. To him, this was everything good about football in one concise moment.

He had arranged the first 60 minutes of conditioning practices in the model of a county fair. Each coach operated an activity around the fairground. Two huddles of team-run versus barrels for 20 minutes followed.

To the Port Verona players, Thump's offense terminology would at first appear to have come from Mars. At least, that's what Harrison Dye had said during installation day.

Instead of the traditional system of numbers to identify the plays, the places or teams and their associated nicknames represented the plays. The snap cadence married each play. For example, runs to the left were on "hut" while runs to the right were on "hut, hut." Other plays were on the first sound the quarterback uttered. Still more plays were on the third "hut." The system had to be second nature for the kids and coaches before the first scrimmage in two weeks.

Pleased by the effort and intensity of the players and coaches, Thump sent the team to the 50-yard line at the completion of the team-run periods. He offered them a deal.

Thump said, "If anyone can beat Jenny across the goal line, practice is over."

"Who's Jenny?" one of them asked.

"Who's Jenny? Who are you?" Thump asked.

"I'm Lucio, Victor Lucio."

"Why, thank you for asking, Victor Lucio. Jenny is our assistant head coach emeritus and doubles as my medical service dog. She will be at every practice. This morning, she's been waiting under the stands for the big race."

Thump yelled for Jenny.

Galloping in a large circle toward Thump, Jenny relished having all eyes on her. Her long, black, tresses flowed as if she were the star of a woman's shampoo commercial. Except for Derek Donaldson, all the boys laughed.

"Okay, here we go," Thump said as Jenny walked to the middle of the line and assumed her spot. "If any one player beats Jenny to the goal line, practice is over."

Thump raised his whistle to his lips. The whistle sounded, and the team launched off the line like dozens of bottle rockets. Jenny pirouetted like a prima ballerina. In a flash, the fastest players owned a 5-yard lead on Jenny. Thump and the coaches laughed and cheered as the seven speediest boys, three of them soccer players, reached the 20-yard line. Crossing the goal line, they pounded their fists into their chest. Two seconds later, the rest of the team rumbled across the goal line like a stampeding herd.

Jenny had disappeared during the race. It took Victor Lucio to figure out what happened.

"Look, she's running around the track! Dumb dog!"

The team howled with laughter.

Coach Mason called the boys to one knee. A few boys continued to giggle at the sight of Jenny galloping around the track in lane six. Grant Lee reminded them to keep their eyes up.

Thump pointed to Jenny and said, "Men, there runs my most loyal companion. She is more than a dog. She is family. She's loyal beyond your imagination because she has an unbreakable bond with her coach. Her love is unconditional. Men, to her, it's simple. She wakes up every morning with a desire to serve and a desire to do what's right. I trained her to stay off the field. Trained to run in lane six, she will stay the course, no matter what. That's what we must have from you guys."

Thump placed his hand on Victor's shoulder. His words dripped with a subtle, sure intensity. He pointed to Jenny. "That athlete will stay in her lane and go and go and go until the final whistle blows. I challenge you to do the same."

Thump blew the final whistle of the practice, and Jenny stopped. She trotted in his direction.

Thump raised his arm. Several boys yelled, "Everybody up!"

Victor Lucio said, "Let's do this! One Team!"

"One Heart!" the boys replied.

Thump had found a leader.

Rule number seven: Let loose your leaders.

The booster club had provided each boy with a quart of iced sports drink. Thump knew that the free drink violated Texas Interscholastic League regulations, but rule compliance was at the bottom of his list of daily musts. People in business clothes make laws while they sit in an air-conditioned office. These boys needed a tasty drink to supplement their water intake. As the boys ambled by the cooler, Thump gathered the staff for a quick conference.

"Coaches, great job out there. I'm pleased with our numbers this morning. How many did we have, Jason?"

"You had 47 present. We have five unaccounted for. I'm getting on the phone right after this meeting to see if I can round them up."

"Great work, Jason. You brought your A-game today."

"Thank you, sir."

"Okay, you guys make sure you lay the love on them. I want each one of them spoken to personally, even if it is just a greeting. Make them feel that we are a family. Make them feel the love."

The coaches nodded and moved through the fieldhouse, speaking to the players. Thump grabbed an icy blue drink and went to his office. He poured a cup of ice water into Jenny's dish.

"Jenny, you're too young to remember when they wouldn't let us drink more than a cup of warm water during practice. If we upset the coach, we wouldn't even get that one cup."

Back in Thump's office, the box fan from Hardee's Hardware sent a stream of cool air toward his face. Thump loved the feel of the rushing air and the droning sound of the blades. Soon, Jenny snored on her new dog pillow. Thump changed into dry socks and put on another pair of shoes. He placed his first pair in front of the fan, but not before pulling the tongue and insole out of each shoe so it would dry.

Time flew. With the sun higher and the kids' gas tanks half-empty, the second practice would be the gut-check practice. The steps on the field would be a little slower, the pep a little lower.

During practice, a few of the boys forced out a primal yell or two, but they were half-hearted. Thump didn't blame them. He didn't feel so great, either. The practice field had turned into an old iron stove griddle.

Looking up, Thump noticed the clouds had disappeared. He wondered why seagulls swooped low over the south endzone. He would soon find out.

As promised, Thump had few words for the team. A player had to find it in himself. Pep talks can't do it for them. Sympathy can't do it for them. It's player versus the pain one-on-one, and by the last ride of the defensive circuit, the softer boys had tapped out.

First two, then three, then four boys fell to their hands and knees. Down on their hands and knees in the endzone, they heaved the remnants of their breakfast mixed with quarts of Gatorade warmed to the elevated temperature of an overheated athlete. The seagulls squawked in joy and settled to the grass like white feathered pterodactyls, slurping the fluid and gobbling the solid portions of the boys' vomit. Thump gagged and squeezed off a shot of ice water into his mouth from one of the water bottles the trainers carried.

"Thank you, trainer."

Unaffected by the bird buffet, she replied, "No problem, sir. I'm excited to be here. We will finally win this year!"

Hands on his knees, attempting not to retch, Thump smiled and threw her a thumbs-up. The segment clock showed it was time for the 10-minute break between the circuits. Grant Lee sounded the horn to start the offensive portion of the county fair.

So far, they had lost eight players to the medical tent, where the water-infused fan circulated a cool spritz over their bodies. Harrison Dye reported that he counted at least four more who were showing the early signs of heat exhaustion. Thump watched while Harrison and the trainers carted the incapacitated boys into the fieldhouse so they could get out of their sweat-soaked softwear and lie in the air conditioning. The failure of Port Verona's summer conditioning program was in full view.

Thump skipped the offensive fair circuit and moved immediately into the team-run section versus the barrels. This was the time to grind. They couldn't become winners on the field unless they learned to beat themselves. He had to show them they could win over weakness and teach them that he would accept nothing less than their full effort.

The horn blew to start the team-run session. This time, Thump would blow the whistle to end a play. Every player had to drive his 55-gallon plastic barrel until the whistle sounded. Depending on their effort, the whistle might blow after 10 yards, or it might blow after 100 yards. Once the whistle blew, the blocker picked up his barrel and ran to set up the defense for the next group. Thump expected the players to move like their hair was on fire. With the kids responding to Thump's pressure, the intensity built among both huddles. Thump shook his head and marveled at their effort.

These Port Verona boys are winners. We just need to light the way.

Following the team period, Grant Lee sounded the final whistle, and the boys sprinted to put away the barrels and return to Thump.

After they assembled around him, Thump said, "I can hardly talk. I'm so darn proud to be your coach. Nobody will believe what will happen at Blood Reef this year. Coach Mason, how do they handle the laundry?"

Coach Mason stepped forward and said, "I need you to place your softwear in your laundry bag. Do not take your gear home. If I catch you wearing that gear home, things will get medieval around here. We will wash and dry the softwear before tomorrow morning. It will hang in your locker when you arrive. Men, look at me. Look at my eyes. You will be here tomorrow morning. You are part of something bigger than yourself now."

Thump nodded to Grant Lee and said, "Coach Davis?"

"One thing, Coach. No one can leave the family. Your second set of brothers need you at practice. Don't get scared of the pain and go home and cry to Mama. You will be sore. You be here. If you aren't here, I will come for you. And, if I come get you, then you and I will make up the lost work. Those of you who know about me, tell those guys who don't."

"Coach Sewell?"

"Nothing here, Coach. We will be ready to roll tomorrow at 7:00."

"Anyone else? Everybody up!" Thump nodded to Victor. "Victor?"

Victor said, "One Team!"

The boys responded, "One Heart!"

Touching every player in the locker room, the coaches congratulated the boys as they switched out of their soggy workout gear. Coach Maldonado stood by the rolling laundry basket to check off each player's name as they dropped in their clothes. Having drawn the first week of laundry duty, he would wash and dry the gear before he left for the day.

A stack of fresh towels lay outside the shower area. High school boys rarely showered after practice anymore, but a few of the older players remained in the shower. Silent, with their necks bowed, they leaned on the shower stems with their eyes closed as the concentrated spray from the shower head assuaged their exhausted muscles.

Once their position group exited the locker room, the coaches retreated to the comfort of the office to cool off and compose their thoughts for the post-practice meeting. Thump sat down on the floor in front of a cheap evaporator Isaac had purchased at Walmart in Reed City the week before.

Thump said, "Well, men. What do you think? I thought it went well. Harrison, what's our injury status?"

"Seven went down with symptoms of heat exhaustion. T'Darian Law came by to get a bag of ice for his back," replied Coach Dye.

Thump swept his damp hair back and said, "Yeah, he's one of those long-waisted kids. I imagine that he has done little over the summer. We need to keep our eye on him. I have a feeling he's our golden ticket."

Grant Lee said, "We need to monitor those kids who went down with exhaustion."

"Exactly," Thump said, "and what's the deal with those seagulls? Have they always hovered around waiting for somebody to vomit?"

"Coach, those birds been doing that ever since I can remember," Harrison Dye replied.

Jason said, "That was nasty, I thought one of them would walk up to that one kid and try to eat the puke right out of his mouth, like it was a baby bird or something."

"That's sick, rookie," Harrison said, as he wiped his face with a wet paper towel.

"Yeah, as head coach, I am going to lay down the law. As of this moment, we shall never again speak of this matter," Thump said.

The coaches laughed.

"That's it. Let's all make sure the locker room is clean and the outside doors are secure. Jason, after you finish the wash, be sure to turn off every light in the building. I heard where a head coach got fired in San Saba for leaving the lights on. The superintendent was one of those environmental nuts from up around Austin or someplace."

"Got it," Jason said.

"See you tomorrow, first thing. We have to grind it out these next two days, then the fun part starts," Thump said.

The coaches filed out, leaving Jason to watch *Sports Center* on his phone and wait for the laundry to finish. Thump coaxed Jenny from her cozy nest in his office corner, and they headed out to the truck. Just before he and Jenny could get in the cab, his phone dinged. It was a message from the local sports editor who wanted to write a season outlook that detailed Thump's thoughts on the team and the upcoming season.

"That will have to wait, Jenny. We need some groceries."

After scarfing a hot sandwich from the Bright Star, he and Jenny passed out under the ceiling fan. It was after 3:00 when Thump awoke. He wiped his face and checked his phone. Thump sighed.

Another message from the sports guy? I guess the Sentinel never sleeps.

Thump punched in the number as Jenny stood and reset her nest with a moan.

"Thank you for calling the *Sentinel* sports desk. This is Rory Brendle."

"Rory, Coach Sutton. How are you doing?"

"Just great, Coach. Thanks for calling me on such a short notice."

"No problem, Rory. What can I do for you?"

"Coach Sutton, I just have a few questions. The *Sentinel* is doing a season outlook report on the area teams. Naturally, we want a thorough feature on the home team at the front of our area outlook section. And we would like to piggyback this interview for our companion news radio station out of Reed City."

"Sure, let's get to it. I know this is an exciting time for Port Verona, new coach and all that," Thump replied.

"Exactly right, Coach. Well, let's just get started. If it is okay with you, I am recording this interview according to the laws and guidelines of the national sports ethics commission. Should you wish to stop this interview, you may do so. Is that clear, Coach Sutton?"

"Yeah, but that all seems a little scary. To clarify, this isn't about that endangered Kemp's ridley sea turtle found under my rear tire last night, is it? Because I don't have a hair of an idea who could have put that turtle's crushed body under my tire."

Rory seemed confused at Thump's failed attempt at humor.

"No, no, Coach. We don't have any reports like that. I just want to ask you a few questions regarding you, your team, and the outlook for this season. We've heard of unusual developments this year regarding the upcoming season and we will use this interview as our radio spot intro to publicize our coverage."

"Well, let's get to it," said Thump.

Rory clicked on the recording device and said, "Great, my first question is, who is Thomas Udall Sutton and why is he here in Port Verona?"

"Rory, Tom Sutton is a ball coach, and Port Verona called him to coach their ball club. That's why I'm here."

"Great, so you've had your first day with the Barracudas. What do you think?"

"I think that the boys are courageous beyond measure. I don't know all their names, but I know their hearts. These boys will win this year."

"Wow. That's a bold statement, Coach. You have been here, what, for just one day? You probably don't know your players yet. I'm sure you know Port Verona has gone some 32 consecutive years without a winning football season, over 50 years without a district championship."

"Rory, these kids in Port Verona today haven't lost for over 30 years. That was somebody else from another time. This moment is their time. Let me tell you something else. We are all but a mist that disappears. Poof. We don't have a lot of time to waste. We have now, and that's all we have. And I want to give these boys and this town the now they deserve."

"Okay, there you have it, Barracuda fans. Optimistic words and deep thoughts from Coach Thomas Sutton, the new athletic director and head football coach at Port Verona Independent School District. Coach, in a few days we will speak with you again as to which players Coach Sutton expects to take the lead in the new direction of Barracuda football."

"I look forward to it," Thump said with a deep sigh.

"That will do it for the Barracuda football *Sentinel* radio preview. Be sure to pick up the upcoming special edition of the area football season outlook in the *Sentinel*. Have a great day, and 'Go, Barracudas."

Rory stopped the recording.

"Thank you, Coach, for taking my call. I really look forward to working with you this season. We can talk more Wednesday at the Rotary Club breakfast, I hope. Also, we will need your schedule, roster, lineups, and some blurbs on your key players, in addition to your assessment of the opposition. If we can get that by Friday, it would be great."

"My schedule is a little tight, but I will get your old friend, Grant Lee, to help both of us on this. He's a great hand to have around," Thump said.

"I agree. Before you arrived, I hoped Grant Lee would get the job. He works so hard, and everybody loves him. Not that you aren't probably going to be great." Rory paused. "I guess that didn't come out right. You understand, right?"

"No problem, Rory. Grant Lee is a special guy, and you can now add one more to his fan club."

"Oh, great. Great. Okay, Coach. See you and Grant Lee on Wednesday morning!"

"Thanks, Rory. It was great talking with you."

CHAPTER TEN

Darkness crept over By the Bay Cottages as Thump scrolled his contact list for Rod's number. Worried the call might take a while, he poured himself a large iced tea. When he opened the back door for Jenny, she decided it was time for a game of fetch. She went to her toy basket to grab Squid. Thump would have to multitask.

Rod answered on the first ring. His blustering prompted Thump to take him off speakerphone.

Motioning Jenny to go deep, Thump launched a spiraling Squid across the courtyard.

"Thump, my man, what were you thinking coming to Port Verona? This place is a ball coach's graveyard."

"Let me tell you, Rod. All that doesn't matter to me because I am here to resurrect this program."

"Yeah, well, you will need more than a bad Jesus pun to turn this place around. You don't understand what you're facing here, Thump."

"I'm sure you're about to tell me."

"Listen, Thump. Been a long time, but I ain't forgot what you did for me back at Tallulah College. You pulled me from the ditch, my friend."

"That was no problem. You know that."

Thump wrestled Squid from Jenny's mouth and launched another bomb.

"Yeah, well, I got your back, Thumper!"

"Only you, brother. Only you."

"Okay, so let's get serious, Thump. This deal here at Port Verona is a trap, my friend. She hired you to fail."

"What do you mean?"

"The superintendent."

"What about the superintendent? She's a bit of a micromanager, but I can handle her."

"She doesn't even want football at Port Verona, Thump. Tran petitioned the board back in April to drop football before the upcoming season. She presented a portfolio of facts and figures from studies from all over the country about how the district must remove football from its extracurricular status because of the publicity about how that head injury stuff manifests at an early age. In executive session, three board members voted for her plan to disband football after this season."

"Executive session? How do you know that? That stuff is confidential, Rod."

"You're not in Kansas anymore, Dorothy! Do you think anything in this town is confidential? Heck, I knew you were coming before you did!"

The silence dripped from Thump's phone. He pried Squid from Jenny's mouth and threw a lame duck end-over-end toss into the weeds near the water. A puzzled Jenny looked back at Thump, as if to say, "Do you expect me to fetch that?"

"Thump! Did you hear me?"

"Yeah, I got you. No secrets in Port Verona."

"Thump, she claims football has no place in education, what with all the concussion talk and so forth. It doesn't help that they haven't had a winning season in 32 years. That's why she pushed the vote in your favor. She realized if Grant Lee got the athletic director position, he could use his support in the community to influence the board to take her to the mat over her push to drop football."

"Well, if that's true, how come Grant Lee didn't get the job? I mean, if he has the power to sway the board?"

"Don't you understand, Thump? This was all supposed to be hush-hush. Known but unknown, get it? Grant Lee couldn't bring it to the table without putting his key supporter in jeopardy. Besides, if he flexed before he got the job, Tran would have chopped him off at the knees. An assistant coach can't win against a superintendent. No school board would back a coup like that; it wouldn't matter what was at stake. She just needed to stop Grant Lee from getting the job and then bring in an outsider, one with a checkered past and a musty old closet she could dig into and find skeletons to use when the time was right."

"So, it wasn't that she hired me as much she didn't hire Grant Lee?"

"Thump, I haven't seen you in over 25 years, but I need you to know that they cut us from the same herd. Since the first time I saw you light up that smart-mouth running back we had at Baylor, I recognized we were brothers from another mother. I loved you even when you wore that puke purple uniform with the frog decal on your helmet."

"Rod, I already told your dumb tail; that's no frog. It's a lizard that spits blood from its eyes."

"Back to my point, Thump. That woman superintendent wants you to fail. She had you researched to where she has copies of your high school detention slips. She set up the late dismissal of the previous coach just to further undermine the new head man by allowing him less than a week to get ready for opening day. And I heard about what you did working up there by yourself to clean up that fieldhouse. Did any of the assistant coaches mention anything about that? Did you ask any of them about why it looked that way? Why didn't they keep it clean? Thump, it was because they didn't even know about it! It was clean all summer, cleaner than the cafeteria!"

"What are you trying to say, Rod?"

"I'm telling you, for a fact. Tran ordered maintenance to trash the place before your arrival. She explained she was 'conducting a study noting the reactions of her mid-managers to an unexpected encounter with a significant stressor,' and they needed to keep it quiet. My poker buddy Virgil is the number two guy over at the bus barn. He told me the whole story, even showed me the memo. She's meaner than a wild hog, Thump. Nobody up at the main building dares to question her. She played you with that messy fieldhouse setup. Her mission was to get you to lose your cookies. She counted on you being the hothead of your younger days. She figured that after you pitched your keys at her, she would play Pontius Pilate and the board would back her plan. Football in Port Verona would be extinct."

"So, it's more than her being a micromanager?"

"Yeah, buddy. She plans to emulate you and your program."

"Emulate?"

"Yeah, emulate. You know, like those monks in Vietnam back in the '70s."

"That's immolate, Rod."

"Okay, Daniel Thump Webster. Whatever. She's going to torch you and your program."

Jenny returned with Squid, but she didn't lay it at Thump's feet. She sat at the back door while a stunned Thump turned to face the gentle push of warm Gulf of Mexico air across the bay.

"Thump, I know it sounds bad, but back in the day, you told me nothing can break a winner. They shattered my leg. They destroyed my future, part of my soul. But you convinced me I was still a winner, and nobody can stop me. Let me tell you something. Thump, I now own a multimillion-dollar shrimp processing business right here in Port Verona."

The line went dead quiet. Thump stared at some boat lights flickering on the bay.

"Thump! You used to say God has a plan for guys like us. Well, you were right. Look, the wife is making faces. I got to go. We'll talk more later. Take care, brother."

The phone screen went to background. Thump felt nauseous. Dumping his tea onto the webbed St. Augustine lawn, he went inside and sat for a spell in Grandma's chair.

Jenny moaned. It was her bedtime alarm. Thump thought that an icy Dr. Pepper in the original "10, 2, and 4" bottle might soothe his anxiety. Rod's revelation had watered his eyes. He sighed and tried the amaretto-tainted buzz of the 40 grams of sugar surfing his palate.

"Jenny, no great expectation goes undeterred. This superintendent wants to detour us from our destination."

At the foot of his grandma's rocker, Jenny sneezed twice and closed her eyes.

CHAPTER ELEVEN

During Tuesday morning's practice, no one got sick in the endzone. The first day had forged the boys' toughness.

The soccer recruits continued to show why Port Verona ruled the area in *futbol*. They had one gear: high. Luis, Jose, and Carlos went one, two, three in every sprint.

On the last sprint of the day when Jose won, he pulled the Barracuda red dryfit shirt over his head and ran around the entire field waving it as he sang, "Jose, Jose-Jose-Jose," in the style of the *olé, olé-olé-olé* soccer chant. Thump wanted to kiss the Herrera twins for getting those guys out. They would cover the opponent's wide receivers better than one of Aunt Polly's homemade quilts.

Historically, in Port Verona, winning football games was the farthest thing from people's minds, and their priorities reflected that mindset. It was a Port Verona tradition to shift the Wednesday morning drills to the evening because of the Rotary Club breakfast, but Thump broke that and kept the morning schedule intact. He wasn't about to put the squad's momentum in jeopardy with a sudden switch to an evening practice schedule.

A lot had changed in football since the days of Stagg and Rockne, but one thing was a constant: If a coach wanted to make boys tough enough to win at this game, rousting them from their beds at the break of dawn in the first week of August was mandatory. Thanks to the leadership of Victor, Luis, Jose, and Carlos, a new energy permeated the workouts. Coach Dye said he had seen nothing like it at Port Verona; neither had Coach Sewell. Thump wanted to keep it that way.

The only exception to the two morning workouts was the surreptitious afternoon passing drills at Camp Promise. Unbeknown to everyone but Isaac, Pastor Mike conducted clandestine afternoon passing workouts at the Camp Promise picnic grounds. After meeting T'Darian and Derek that first Saturday morning, Thump had arranged for an overnight shipment of footballs to that facility's recreation department. To the Camp Promise staff, it looked like a great recreational outlet for the kids. To prying eyes who might alert the Texas Interscholastic League's compliance department, the workout was invisible.

Only Thump and Grant Lee would attend Wednesday's Rotary Club breakfast. Dirk would run practice in Thump's absence. Dirk didn't possess the Grant Lee's charisma, but if he were to be the defensive coordinator Thump needed, he had to show he could command the respect of the other coaches and more importantly, the kids. Besides, Thump could use a morning off.

Tuesday evening, Thump bathed Jenny in the clawfoot tub of his bungalow. Jenny loved bath time, but she hated a wet floor. Thump always laid out a few towels so she wouldn't have to step in the water that splashed over the edge. She loved to do the dog thing, slide and roll around on the towels to dry her coat. He would let Jenny air dry while he made a run to Nguyen's Bait and Store for a new bandana.

Entering the store, he saw the place packed for the early evening dinner crowd.

Who would have thought that a bait shop would have the best Vietnamese food in town?

Rose quickly interrupted Thump's self-aggrandizing thought of doing standup comedy when she admonished him for his tasteless joke.

63

It's getting difficult to think funny things with you always in my head, Rose.

Good thing for you, Thomas, that I'm always alert. One slip of that loose tongue of yours and we are back teaching at an alternative school in El Paso.

Thump approached the counter and took stock of the bandanas.

"Can I help you?" the cashier asked. It was the same woman he'd met when he arrived in town.

"Yeah, I need two of those bandanas, one red and one black," Thump said.

"Oh, you're Big Coach. The big coach with black dog. I know you."

"Yes, ma'am, and as you can see, I left her home this time."

"Very good. You going to win this year, right? My grandson says you are a tough coach."

Thump handed her his card and smiled. "Yes, ma'am. We're going to win."

Thump had noted whom he suspected was her grandson. Dan Ngo was stocky and a little too slow to be a linebacker. Still, if Thump learned anything from 30 years of coaching, it was that a shorts-and-shirts workout is a mediocre assessment tool for identifying the best players.

It took more than size and speed to be a starter, something the gel-haired college recruiters with their pocket tape-measures didn't seem to appreciate. He remembered the day that a middling NCAA Division 1 program passed on one of the best players he had ever seen, solely because the kid measured one-eighth of an inch under five-feet-eleven.

Handing him the bandanas, the woman said, "You come back soon. We have good food and more bandanas for the big coach with black dog."

A loud clang in the kitchen rang out, followed by two women arguing in Vietnamese. The old woman waved Thump toward the door.

"Yes, ma'am. Thanks again."

Back at the cottage, he plopped onto the bed beside Jenny. The ceiling fan chopped the air in a hypnotic groove as Thump's mind drifted. How had his end-over-end car crash of a *coaching career suddenly morphed into success?* Thump's eyelids drooped as the fan's rotating blades blurred into a spinning saucer above him. Still, the normally soothing whir of the blades offered no comfort. Rod's dark phone call had anchored into in his subconscious. He would fail.

Rose stroked his temples and whispered. *Rest, big guy. Free your mind of static. Nothing matters now but tomorrow. They will love you just as I love you, just as Jenny loves you. Sleep.*

Jenny snored while Thump tossed all night, his last moment of sleep—an enemy lance thrust into his heart as he fought alongside a knight in blue armor.

CHAPTER TWELVE

The following morning, Thump and Jenny skipped their morning run because Thump needed to stop by the fieldhouse and check in with Dirk and the boys. Grant Lee waited outside as Thump and Jenny rolled up to the parking lot.

The boys wore their third-day faces. The third day was always the worst. Thump could almost hear their muscles and ligaments crying as the kids filed by. He and Grant Lee remained outside the door, slapping backs and encouraging the kids.

Thump whispered to Grant Lee, "We must win the battle of the mind before their bodies throw the fight."

Thump admired those boys who sacrificed to play the game, those Friday night heroes of Texas. They could do anything they wanted: sleep all summer, play video games, or work at a little part-time job to help their family with the bills. Instead, they sacrificed their bodies and their free time to be part of something that was monumentally hard; all at the risk of being ridiculed by their peers and some of the more obnoxious members of their community. He loved those boys and empathized with their 32-straight losing seasons. But if he allowed himself to obsess on that thought, a distracting resentment of the failed coaching inflicted upon these boys and this town for more than a generation would cloud his vision.

Grant Lee pointed to his watch, a gold-plated Sun Bowl memento. It was time for them to head over to the Pavilion to meet the Rotary Club. Thump had been to a few Rotary shindigs as an assistant; it was always a first-class experience.

The Rotary's mission was to advance the measure of goodwill around the world, community by community. They were the business leaders and the professionals of the county. Behind anything good in Port Verona stood a Rotary Club member.

During a game, the head coach could recognize a Rotarian in the stands just by turning his head and looking up after a turnover. If he saw a fan who wasn't cursing or saying derogatory things about the coach, that fan was probably a Rotary Club member.

Part eating establishment, part tourist mecca, the Pavilion Restaurant was a replica of the Port Verona Pavilion destroyed during Hurricane Darla. It was so popular, 82-year-old Vera Mae Miles and her two best friends from Reed City traveled the 30 miles in her Pontiac Bonneville once a week just for the hush puppies.

The size of the crowd amazed Thump. The parking lot at the Pavilion was bumper-to-bumper pickups with one conspicuous white Charger parked off to the side of the restaurant.

Jenny, in her braided Barracuda red and black bandanas, led the way. She sported her Sunday leash, the black one with the silver rivets. Thump always got a kick out of people's reaction to Jenny. He could almost hear their thoughts as they walked in the door together.

What kind of dog is that?

You think the coach has a disability?

How in Sam Houston is he going to coach with a disability dog on the sideline?

You think it bites?

Thump directed Jenny to nest behind the candy counter by the cash register. Because the breakfast was on the Rotarians' tab, nobody would man the register and step on her tail. Thump nodded and smiled as Grant Lee carved a path to the club's president.

Grant Lee worked the room handily. Thump owned a great speaking voice and had a way with the microphone, but he labored through the small group conversations out on the dance floor. When his second wife, Amy, told him that he was the most selfish person on the face of the planet, Thump thought her statement to be hyperbolic, particularly since Amy hadn't been out of Karnes County more than twice in her life.

Amy had once read an article in *Good Housekeeping* that warned wives about husbands who were too selfish to give back in a relationship. The author of the article said that a woman could determine if her husband is selfish by observing him in social situations. For example, he is selfish if he is inept at remembering names, especially right after the personal introduction of a stranger. After Amy confronted him with her source, Thump accepted her assessment that he's a selfish person because he has trouble remembering names. When he was a kid, he had seen *Good Housekeeping* on his mother's white wicker nightstand. Mama read it. And that was good enough for him.

As he sat down to breakfast with the officers of the Rotary Club and Dr. Tran, Thump felt confident his play calling would compensate for his lack of name-storage neurons. Grant Lee would run interference at the table so Thump could score at the microphone.

Following Reverend Wallace's offering of grace, the conversations harmonized with the clinking forks and teaspoons. Plates piled with yellow mounds of scrambled eggs, bacon strips, and sausage links were topped with buttermilk biscuits and a scoop of grits. Channeling the card-shark linebacker who owned poker night in the TCU athletic dorm, Thump smuggled an extra biscuit into the pocket of his plaid sport coat.

It was approximately 8:30 a.m. when the Tiburon Guaranty and Trust vice president went to the podium to introduce Dr. Tran. In a room full of the community's most influential leaders, Tran looked the part of a CEO who ran the county's largest job-producing entity. Her red power lipstick and stylishly cut silhouette-black hair played supporting roles to her red dress and slender waistline.

Old Diane is not an unattractive woman, Thump thought.

Although she hadn't spoken to him at the table, she prefaced her address with an auspicious glance at Thump.

"Today, I would like to revisit a time in this town when two groups of people from two very different cultures came together in unity and love. As many of you know, when I arrived here as a small child in my grandmother's arms those many years ago, I had nothing. No clothes, little food, and few of my family still alive. Two years earlier in a South Vietnam village savaged by war, neighboring villagers had rescued me lying scared and alone under the body of my mother. The enemy had murdered my family and burned my village. The last living soul in my village there in the Mekong Delta, I lay under the remains of my mother and sister for two days. A mixture of my mother's blood and soot from the fires caked my fragile body. Somehow, the neighboring villagers identified me and took me to the mother of my father.

Now, thanks to the love and encouragement that little girl received from you, I stand before you as the leader of a school system that has produced 116 National Merit Scholars. And just yesterday, I received a letter from the National Endowment for the Arts granting Port Verona High School $1.5 million for an elevated, storm-resistant, combined robotics lab and fine arts facility, the very latest educational breakout concept of the Instructional Overlap Design Model."

Everyone stood in applause. She soaked in the adoration and looked at Thump.

"But enough about me for now," she said with a smile. "We are here today to entertain the hopes and dreams of another person, the person I hired to fix what time has broken for as long as anyone in this town can remember. And today, in the language of a forever Texan, I tell you that if Thomas Sutton can't get it done, then no one can." Pointing to Thump, she said, "I give you Coach Tom Sutton!"

The Rotarians and their guests applauded. Dr. Tran patted Thump's shoulder and smiled as she left the dais. Silent faces met Thump's gaze as he surveyed the floor.

"Like the band that played on as the Titanic slipped beneath the icy waves, Dr. Tran is a tough act to follow."

The Barracuda fans laughed in unison. Back by the door, Sergeant Sara Mendoza applauded.

Thump locked eyes with her. His thoughts drifted back to the traffic stop.

Wake up, silly goose! Rose's admonishment rocketed him back into the here and now.

"Thank you all for inviting my staff here today. You may have noticed that most of us could not attend because of their obligations on the practice field this morning. That's unfortunate for them, but good for me as I can double down on a triple serving of grits.

Because of Dr. Tran's vision, we see a new pathway for Barracuda football, I am here to tell you that this year's team will wash away the past footprints of failure. I am here to tell you that your boys wearing the Barracuda red jersey will set a new course for Port Verona football. I am here to tell you that your boys will receive a standard of coaching that has no rival in the state of Texas. Thank you, Rotarians, for an amazing breakfast. Thank you, Dr. Tran, for the opportunity. Now, Coach Davis and I have to get back to work."

The audience stood and cheered as Thump sprang from behind the lectern and made his way to Jenny. Grant Lee followed close behind. Jenny's lead in hand, Thump turned and waved to the crowd as he left.

Standing just outside the door, Sergeant Mendoza smiled and said, "Nice speech, Coach."

He swept his hair back. "Thank you."

For the first time, he noticed the flecks of brown in her emerald green eyes and the sleek silkiness of her smooth dark hair.

He thought, *I will have to get my taillights looked at sooner than I planned.*

Just then, Sergeant Mendoza's radio crackled. Someone had called dispatch regarding a suspicious man behind the Bright Star. She gave Thump and Grant Lee a wave as she hustled to the Charger. Thump and Jenny loaded into Blue with Grant Lee riding shotgun.

Once back at the fieldhouse, the two men hurried out to practice. At the field, a large man introduced himself as Hector Rejas, the father of Valentino Rejas, the kid from Corpus Christi. Hector informed Thump they had completed the school registration process and filled out the forms needed for Valentino to play ball. With everything in place for Valentino's first practice the next morning, Thump sealed the deal with a firm handshake and a pat on his new offensive lineman's broad shoulders.

Those are the shoulders that could cause a problem for Diane Tran, Thump thought.

Hector was in a hurry, so Thump walked them out to their truck and then headed over to the field to catch the end of the workout. Dirk had just called up the squad and was talking to the team as Thump reached the sideline. The boys all stood and put their fists together for the break.

"One Team."

"One Heart."

For the first time since the start of the preseason, Thump heard laughter and playful banter from the boys leaving the field. They had survived six grueling conditioning sessions in three days. In the eyes of the Texas high school football gods, they had cleared the first hurdle of their gauntlet. Even the coaches seemed to have a little pep in their step.

T'Darian dressed and stopped by the coaches' office. Wearing a huge smile, he knocked and asked for Thump.

Thump turned from a conversation at the whiteboard with the Herrera twins about what Thump called a money play versus a two-deep, zone coverage: 171-Hash.

"What's up, T'Darian?"

"Coach, I just wanted to tell you we are having an open house barbeque over at Camp Promise this Sunday. Pastor Mike said to tell you that we all want you to come."

"Even Derek?" Thump asked with a smile.

"Yes sir, even Derek."

"Okay, Jenny and I will be there. What time are y'all having it?"

"Pastor Mike said to be there right after church. The church is sponsoring it. He said to tell you that all the coaches can come, but they don't have to. It's only if they want to come."

"Okay. I'll be there. Oh, and T'Darian?"

"Sir?"

"Can I bring a date?"

The entire room laughed.

"Coach, you can bring whoever you want, your dog, a date, whoever."

"I'm there already," Thump said.

"Okay. See you tomorrow, Coach."

"See you, T'Darian, and be ready to throw about 300 balls tomorrow. It is officially football season!"

"Yes sir."

T'Darian left to join Pastor Mike and Derek in the parking lot. Thump felt a lump in his throat.

Addressing the staff, he said, "Men, when our time is done, I can promise you this town will build a monument to what we've accomplished. It will be that big, what we are about to do."

"Amen, Coach," Isaac said.

"You got that right," Harrison replied.

Thump's attention returned to the whiteboard and his explanation of the 171-Hash read progression versus cover-two zone and cover-two man-under. After the Herrera twins demonstrated that they had studied their playbooks and understood the passing tree and the fundamental reads of the core passing plays, Thump dismissed the staff. It was around 1:00, a little later than their usual knock-off time, but tomorrow morning would be a difference-maker.

Thursday morning's practice would highlight how things had changed at Port Verona under Thump. The practice plan called for high-intensity instruction of the alignments, assignments, and execution of the techniques specified during the installation day activities the prior Saturday. Thump had directed the coaches never to have over three players standing in a line waiting for their turn during any individual segment. Just like the conditioning practices, five-minute periods divided the day into segments: individual, group, team, specialty, and conditioning. Thump scheduled the kicking periods randomly throughout the practice so that the boys mastered the psychological challenge of transitioning from offense to defense, or vice-versa. Practice was an intricately choreographed production. If it wasn't, then the wins would be only accidental.

Six consecutive practices in helmets, shoulder pads, and padded shorts with volleyball knee pads followed. Unlike the coaches back in his days as a player, Thump allowed the boys to remove their helmets when they weren't active in a drill. Because of the quick reps, the boys had no time during individual drills to remove their headgear. Knowing this would be a problem, Thump mandated that the assistants allow the kids to air out during the transitions and other sections of practice.

But even with his precautions, several boys tapped out with nausea and dizziness. Above the endzone, the seagulls circled for their morning endzone buffet. Thump couldn't help thinking that the sight provided a new meaning of the phrase, "early bird special."

On Thursday, the mid-morning temperature hovered near the three-digit mark as the tortuous Texas Gulf Coast sauna made breathing difficult. Because the ice machine ran empty before noon, Grant Lee used his connection with the manager at Sonic to get their regional distributor to double their daily ice order.

Every morning before sunup, Jason Maldonado met the delivery truck at Sonic, loaded his Tahoe full of ice and stored the bags in the junior high's cafeteria. During the intermission between practices, he carted them to the exhausted ice machine which, reduced to a large ice-container, was empty of all but a handful of cubes.

Late Thursday afternoon, back in his bungalow, Thump received a text from Dr. Tran. "SEE ME, MONDAY."

Monday it is, Thump thought.

Thump was well-versed in the rules of this game. Unlike an entrepreneur who addresses concerns quickly to maintain an

atmosphere of efficiency, power-tripping school administrators have
no real stake in their subordinate's performance. Egotistical, but
equally insecure, they regularly shake the cage so that the animals know
who's the boss. An enigmatic Thursday directive to report to her office
on Monday was a transparent attempt to rattle Thump's cage. She had
telegraphed her next move.

His fingers twiddled with the long black waves on Jenny's velvety
ear as he sipped a Dr. Pepper and rocked in front of his box fan.
Thump loved rubbing Jenny's ear. Soon, the two of them drifted off.

On this night, Thump fought no battles. No lance pierced his
armor. He slept confident in his knowledge of how to check Tran.

CHAPTER THIRTEEN

Thump awoke in his rocking chair, his neck torqued toward his shoulder and his mouth open. Sleeping in the chair had locked tight every joint in his body. He groaned. His throat felt as if he had gargled with sand. He checked his watch; it was 4:00 in the morning.

Jenny could use a day off.

As he jogged toward downtown, Thump upped his pace. He hadn't seen one moving vehicle and the sky was as black as a roofer's tar-stained boot sole. The booms of the massive, corporate shrimp boats, indistinguishable in the darkness, wore a devil's cloak.

Halfway through town, he noticed a familiar blue and red sparkle off to his right. Unfamiliar with the Port Verona streets, he stopped to get his bearing. From where he stood, the Port Verona Charger sat engaged in a traffic stop in the residential part of town, five to six blocks north of his location.

Fascinated by the courage and mental toughness of police officers, Thump was a lifelong cop fan. As a kid, he'd read Wambaugh's *Choirboys* and watched every episode of *Police Story* and *Adam-12*. Now, in the predawn darkness, he squinted toward the light show that cast a strobe effect on the adjacent homes. He couldn't make out any movement around the car.

Rose, what do you think? You think she needs help?

No, Thomas. Move on.

Rose, don't you think we should check it out?

No, Thomas. To approach an officer on a traffic stop is unwise.

Thump took a few steps toward the lights. *Yeah, but.*

Tell you what, Thomas. Let's walk a little farther, but please keep your hands in view. You know how police get nervous on a traffic stop.

Thump walked down the middle of the side street toward the light show. He couldn't hear a thing. No insects. No sounds. He listened for a conversation but heard none.

Rose, I'm no cop, but this doesn't feel right. Still, everything must be okay, or backups would come, wouldn't they?

Thump broke into a brisk pace. He could feel his pulse in his throat. Once he reached the police cruiser, he saw the open driver's side door. The pulsating blue and red compounded the reflections coming at him from all angles, but he noticed that this police Charger exhibited sheriff's department decals, and whoever the deputy had stopped, had disappeared. Also missing was the deputy. Thump peeked inside the Charger.

This car belongs to the county sheriff's department.

So, where's the deputy, Thomas?

No idea, Rose. We better get help. This looks bad.

The raised butterfly nets of the docked shrimp boats waffled the dawn's breaking light as Thump noticed a second police unit closing from the south. Its red and blue lights advertised its urgency. No siren, but he heard the police interceptor's characteristic snarl.

Thomas, watch it. Hold up your hands.

Thump moved to the middle of the street and held his hands high. From the opposite direction, he could see another set of lights throbbing. The lights closed fast.

The first cruiser screeched to a stop. Its spotlight's beam struck Thump in his face. Positioned approximately 50 feet from where Thump stood, the cruiser blocked the street in front of him as the second cop car approached from the north, taking a defensive position similar to the first one. The glare of their spotlights concealed the officers.

A voice from the first cruiser told Thump to keep his hands high and to turn around. Sweat poured down his face. He felt an intense need to sweep the hair from his forehead, but he knew better. The officer from behind the first cruiser directed him to walk backward. After he backpedaled a dozen or more steps, the officer told him to kneel and cross his feet behind him.

The pebbled pavement dug into Thump's knees as he knelt in the street and waited for the next command. He heard more voices coming from the abandoned Charger's radio. After a long pause, the officer ordered him to put his hands on his head and interlock his fingers. Suddenly, a handcuff pinched his wrist, and the officer jerked his arm backward. His face slammed into the pavement. Handcuffed and lying prone in the street, he heard what sounded like Sergeant Mendoza's voice.

"Wait! I know him!" Sergeant Mendoza approached Thump and lifted him to his feet. "He's okay, Gabriel. This isn't our guy," Mendoza said to the deputy.

Gabriel removed the cuffs from Thump's wrists and apologized.

"No problem, I understand," Thump said. He brushed the road grit off his face.

"Oh, my God, Coach! Are you okay? We got a call that a man attacked a deputy. Did you see anything?"

"No. When I jogged up, everything was just as you see now."

Speaking into the microphone attached to his uniform's epaulet, Gabriel radioed that the area was secure with a witness at the scene. Sergeant Mendoza told Thump to stay put while she and Gabriel searched the car for any immediate clues to the deputy's disappearance. During the search, Gabriel told her the missing deputy was the shift supervisor, Don Bunch.

The engine of Don's Charger remained running and his car radio functioned. His unit's dash camera continued to record. Approximately 10 feet from the cruiser, in the middle of the street, stood a small pool of blood.

Multiple police sirens oscillated in the distance while nearby residents congregated. Thump checked his watch and asked Sergeant

Mendoza if he could call Grant Lee to tell him to oversee practice later. She said he could, but he had to be sure and not say anything about the scene or what was happening.

Soon, units from the Tiburon County Sheriff's Office (TCSO) and the Texas Department of Public Safety (DPS) swarmed the area. The troopers secured all points of access to where Deputy Bunch's unit sat with its lightbar still flashing.

Mendoza directed Thump to the front seat of her car while she helped secure the scene for the sheriff's investigators. Isolated from the fracas, the cold air blasting from the dashboard vents helped Thump relax and compose his thoughts.

Grant Lee was en route to the fieldhouse when he received Thump's call. As ordered, Thump provided no details other than for Grant Lee to handle the two practices and to direct Jason to drive over to the By the Bay number 5 cottage to pick up Jenny. Thump told Grant Lee the bungalow was unlocked, and Jason should plan on babysitting her for the rest of the day. Being a coaching veteran, Grant Lee asked no questions. He assured Thump that he would "hold down the fort."

Thump knew he was in for a long day. After an hour of sitting in Mendoza's Charger and listening to her police radio, Thump saw a plainclothes officer arrive.

He wore faded jeans and a straw hat. Clipped to his belt were a badge and a silver revolver. His sun-etched face and unkempt mustache resembled that of a gaunt, weather-worn, West Texas rancher. He glanced toward Thump, then back to Sergeant Mendoza, and gestured in Thump's direction. She nodded and approached her unit.

Once inside her unit, Mendoza buckled her seatbelt and informed Thump that they were going to the Port Verona police station to wait for the Texas Rangers to arrive and interview them. She flashed a smile and reassured him that everything would be okay but that they should drive through Sonic first to get a breakfast toaster because, "it will be a minute before either of us has time to eat."

On the way to Sonic, she asked him about the team and if he had arranged for somebody to look after Jenny. Thump admired her coolness under pressure. Despite the intense circumstances, her tone remained warm and pleasant.

Upon arrival at the police station, Mendoza placed Thump in an interview room where he finished his sausage breakfast toaster and Dr. Pepper. Like those interrogation rooms he had seen on television, it looked dingy. Except for some suspicious brown stains, the faded green walls stood bare. Two metal-frame chairs with the plastic back supports sat across from a table that looked like it had seen action during the Korean War.

Sergeant Mendoza told Thump to wait until the Texas Rangers arrived to interview him. In the meantime, he would talk with the sheriff department's lead investigator. When the investigator entered the room about two hours later, Thump recognized him to be the West Texas rancher doppelganger from earlier. He spoke with a slow, gravelly voice.

"Mornin', Coach. I'm Deputy Jim Weir, Chief of Investigation for the Tiburon County Sheriff's Office. Coach Sutton, I hate to meet you under this kind of circumstance, but let's get right down to brass tacks. I have your statement here in a report from Sergeant Mendoza. Why don't you take a minute to look it over one more time to see if there is anything, I mean anything, no matter how minor, you left out?"

Thump read the report and verified its narrative.

Deputy Weir asked Thump to tell him more about his morning jog. Was jogging part of his routine? Was anything different about today?

Thump said one thing was different about this morning. He hadn't brought Jenny along.

"And Jenny, I understand, is your dog?" Deputy Weir asked.

"Yes sir, she runs with me, but today I thought I would just let her sleep in. I do that sometimes."

Weir pulled a wipe from his pocket and cleaned the lenses of his cheap reading glasses, the kind you buy at a discount store. He put the glasses back on and peered over the bridge at Thump.

"Have you guys found out anything about the missing deputy?" Thump asked.

Weir tapped the table. "No, Coach, we haven't. Is there anything you haven't mentioned to me? You didn't see anything on your jog? No unfamiliar faces in the area? Vehicles?"

"No, sir." Thump ran his fingers through his hair and leaned back. "I wish I had something to help you with."

"Yeah, me, too, Coach. Me, too." Deputy Weir sighed and looked up at Sergeant Mendoza. "I understand the two of you kind of know each other."

"Yes, sir. We have run across each other a few times on my morning patrol," Sergeant Mendoza said.

Deputy Weir removed his glasses and bit the end of the tooth-marked earpiece. "Yeah, I understand."

Turning back to Thump, he pulled a card from his front pocket and said, "Coach, that is about it for now. I want you to take this card and put my number on your phone. If you remember anything about those two boys or that car, call me. Day or night. And one more thing: Word will get out you were a witness even though you saw nothing. Just to be on the safe side, it might be best if you did your jogging at the high-school track from now on."

"You think? What's the big deal? I mean, like you said, I didn't see anything," Thump said.

"Coach, right now we don't know what we're dealing with, but come sundown, everybody in Tiburon County and beyond will know the head football coach at Port Verona was the first person at the scene of a deputy's disappearance. You forget you are a celebrity in this town."

Thump looked at Sergeant Mendoza. She nodded in agreement.

Perceiving the uneasiness in the room, Thump agreed without further discussion. "Okay, I'll do that."

Sliding his chair back from the table, Deputy Weir slapped his knees. He stood and offered his hand.

"Great. Coach, you go home and relax. Drink a beer or three. I imagine this was a traumatic experience for you. I know it is for the rest of us. Old Don and me, we grew up together in Reed City. We joined the Marine Corps on the same day. Over in the Nam, he saved a lot of lives. Came back home and never left. He retired from the Reed City Police Department after 40 years on the job, then signed right on as a road deputy with the Sheriff's Office. I tell you, that man loves the streets." Weir looked down. "Like a brother to me."

Deputy Weir advised Thump that he would take care of the Texas Rangers when they arrived. If the Rangers needed to talk to Thump, they would call his cell.

Weir told Sergeant Mendoza to go home and get some rest. It was around 11:30, and her shift should have ended at 11:00.

"Come on, Coach. I'll give you a ride home," Sergeant Mendoza said.

Neither Thump nor Sergeant Mendoza said a word on the short trip to Thump's place. Turning onto the shale drive, Mendoza radioed that she was, "10-6 at the location with the package."

After she parked the Charger beside Old Blue, she left the engine running. "You okay?" she asked.

"I don't know. I guess it's all starting to sink in."

Mendoza pulled a silver-barreled pen from her pocket along with a business card, then wrote something on the back before handing him the card.

"My private cell is on the back. I'll be up for some time. And I'm off on Saturday and Sunday." She smiled. "Weekends off are a privilege of seniority. If you need to talk to somebody, or even if you just want to visit, call me."

"Thanks, Sergeant."

"You're welcome, Coach Sutton." She touched his arm and repeated her suggestion, "You call me, okay?"

Her eyes.

Her eyes stopped time and motion. It was the second time her irises had paralyzed his thoughts.

"Coach, are you okay?"

Thump pulled the car's door handle. "Yeah, I'm fine. Okay, I might just do that."

As he approached his cottage porch, he heard the Charger's rear tires spit loose shale as the car left the driveway.

Rose, that girl has one heavy foot.

CHAPTER FOURTEEN

R epeated vibrations tickled Thump's hip.
Nine voice mails? Grant Lee, Jason, Isaac, Pastor Mike, five calls from Rod?

Thump returned Grant Lee's call and told him to get in touch with Dirk. The three would meet back at the fieldhouse at 5:00. Next, he called Jason to tell him to drop off Jenny at the number 5 cottage.

Isaac and Pastor Mike called about the kidnapping. They had learned of it while preparing for the open house at Camp Promise. No secrets in Port Verona.

After he briefed Isaac and Pastor Mike, Thump rolled up his pants and called Big Rod.

If Rod was anything like he was during their days together at Tallulah College, the stuff was about to get deep.

Rod's cell rang but once before he picked up.

"Thump! What in the name of John Henry have you been doing? I hear you attacked a deputy. Boy, you are stirring up the hornets, and you ain't even lost your first ball game yet."

"Now, hold on, Rod. Where are you getting your information? I was jogging on my usual route this morning, and I came upon that police car parked about two blocks from downtown with its lights flashing. I checked it out, and the next thing I realized, the law surrounded me. But that's all cleared up, now."

"Thump, my man. I need to get somebody to watch after you. I understand that deputy just disappeared. Gone without a trace, is that true?"

"Yeah, they told me not to talk about it, but he went missing before I got there."

"Man, oh man, Thump. And you already got the superintendent nipping at your tail. I heard about the Rotary Club fiasco."

"Fiasco? I thought it went great."

"No way, not as far as Dr. Tramp thinks."

"It's Tran, Rod. Her name is Dr. Tran."

"Tramp, Tran. Shrimp, prawn."

"Rod, cut the crap. What was it you wanted to tell me about the Rotary Club breakfast and Dr. Tran?"

"Well, the story I got from Matt over at the Farm Bureau is that she was boiling mad because you up and walked out after your little speech. I think the kids call it dropping the mic or something like that. You upstaged her, Thump. She had just made her big deal of announcement about the million-dollar federal grant she got, then you swept the rug right out from under her."

"Heck, Rod. I was just doing what a head coach does, get up there and get the fans excited. God only knows these fans around here have had nothing to be excited about for decades."

"I know, buddy. Listen: Have you already forgotten what I told you? You ain't supposed to get people excited. You ain't supposed to give them something to cheer about. She hired you to fall flat on your face!"

"Yeah, I got it. Hired to fail, you told me."

"That's right. You stepped on her toes; plus, you got yourself all over the social media and such with that thing with the missing deputy."

"Yeah, I hear you. But that isn't something I could help."

"Thump, you listen to me. What did I tell you? This is Port Verona, Texas. Truth ain't reality. Perception is reality."

"Okay, so what am I supposed to do about it?"

"Nothing you can do about it now except just have your I's dotted and your T's crossed come Monday. I already know you're meeting with her. You know what? It might be time for you to come strapped. She'll mess with your head. That's her expertise. She's smart, and I can promise you she knows every chink in your armor. I don't know anything else to tell you, Thump. Just be careful. Take a Xanax before you go in there with her. You need any? I got two prescriptions for my wife. I can bring you a handful."

Thump chuckled. "Big Rod, you got enough mustard to go with all that baloney? Things are going too good for anybody to stop this train from pulling out of the station. I feel it. Those kids believe in themselves. People around town expect something big to happen. Some petty jealousy won't derail our destiny. And she has got to understand she will get as much credit as I will when we turn the corner."

"Okay, Thump. I got your back. Maybe you're right. Maybe she'll realize the truth. Anyway, the old lady just hollered at me about the dogs barking. You call me if you need anything. And keep your head down. The entire county is buzzing about you and that missing cop. You know, Port Verona is home to a big drug dealing outfit down here, right? They call themselves *Del Mariachis*, or something like that. You may have stumbled onto something that is going down between them and the sheriff's department. My buddy Leon lives at the neck of Port Verona Bay, and he tells me that he hears airplanes, the kind that land on water, coming in all the time. It's a known secret that there is a major drug operation working in the area. Just keep your head on a swivel, okay?"

"I hear you. You know, you circulate more gossip than that interweb. Don't you understand that not one person has ever blindsided me? How do you think I got my name?"

"I know how you got your name! I'm the one who gave it to you in that interview with the *Fort Worth Star-Telegram*. It wasn't enough that you knocked out our tailback, but you had to coldcock our all-conference guard, too. Stomping on his throat like that, you looked just like Thump. You know, the rabbit from that Disney movie with the baby deer."

"That movie was *Bambi*, and your buddy tried to tear my left knee off! He clipped me three times. And you realize the rabbit's name is Thumper, not Thump? The *Star-Telegram* sports editor was a TCU grad. He ran your quote only as a goof on the quality of your Baylor education."

"Whatever, Thump. Monday, you just better prepare for a Category IV storm to hit the Cove. I got to go. Take it easy, buddy."

After hanging up, Thump saw an unpublished number pop up on his screen. He didn't pick up those types of calls, but he suspected it might be the Texas Rangers. And it was.

The Ranger reminded him to maintain as low a profile as possible and not to mention any details of the case to anyone. Thump said that he didn't know any details, so that wouldn't be a problem.

Car doors slammed outside the front door. Thump peeked out the window and saw Jason's Tahoe. When Thump opened the front door, Jenny attempted to leap into his arms.

"She never does that. Jason, what did you do, beat her?" Thump said with a laugh.

"No, sir. We had a good time. I took her to the Dairy Queen and got her a double cone."

Thump gave Jenny's chest a vigorous two-handed rub. "A double cone? Even Daddy doesn't get you a double cone!" Jenny collapsed in joy and rolled onto her back for a tummy rub.

"So, Jason, how did practice go?"

"The kids flew around, but everybody wondered where you were. Later we heard what happened. That had to be scary."

"Yeah, it was a crazy morning. Thanks for taking care of her. I can't tell you how much I appreciate your good work."

"Oh, no problem, Coach. Listen, the guy at Sonic said that they can't make an extra ice delivery tomorrow. How do you want to handle that?"

"Don't worry about it. You get to sleep in for another hour. Don't tell anybody, but I am considering cutting it down to just one practice tomorrow. We should be okay with the ice."

"Okay. Thanks. See you in the morning."

Thump headed over to the fieldhouse to do some cleaning. On the way over, his phone buzzed. It was Rory Brendle with the *Sentinel*.

"What's up, Rory?"

"Coach, I missed my time to talk to you at the Rotary breakfast."

"Sorry about that. I was in a rush to get to practice. Every minute counts."

"Yes, sir, I understand. I got with Grant Lee like you suggested, and he took care of everything I needed."

"That's great. Good to hear."

"Yes, sir. Anyway, I found out about this morning. Are you okay? I mean, this is off the record. I'm just calling to check on you."

"I'm okay, Rory. Thanks for the concern. It's been a long day, and it isn't even suppertime."

"I hear you, Coach. People say that this thing might be a drug-related retaliation type deal. I overheard something about the *El Marineras*, a gang in this area that originated in Corpus Christi. They have a huge presence right here in Port Verona."

"I don't know. They kind of kept me under lock and key the whole time I was with the sheriffs. They didn't tell me much other than to keep my eyes peeled and so forth. Truth is, I probably know less than you do."

"Really? Wow, that's some scary stuff. Well, thanks. Coach, you take care. I just wanted to reach out to you. All my best, and I look forward to stopping to see the team practice next week before the scrimmage. I need to take some head shots, maybe an action shot or two. My deadline is Wednesday, so I'll stop by."

"No problem, Rory. Thanks for checking on me. I appreciate you. I really do."

CHAPTER FIFTEEN

Despite Thump's arriving at the fieldhouse 45 minutes early for the staff meeting, Grant Lee and Dirk waited in the coaches' office. Grant Lee spoke first.

"Coach, we look good for tomorrow. We have no injuries to report, and the boys who suffered all the heat prostration issues are in the clear to take part. The trainer from Presbyterian Sports Medicine stopped by practice this morning. Our level of conditioning impressed her."

"What about the defense, Dirk? How are we looking?"

"The secondary is looking great. Derek flies to the ball like nobody I've seen. We have him at strong safety. The corners are solid, and T'Darian looks darn good at free safety."

"Yeah, okay. You can spot-play T'Darian in passing situations but find another full-time free safety in his place. T'Darian is our gunslinger. With those three soccer kids, we will have complementary firepower at the receiver positions. Listen, you need to consider Jose at the other safety. See if he can tackle. That kid can run all day; all three soccer boys can. Surely, one of them will lay a lick on somebody. What about the linebackers?"

"Yes, sir. We'll work Carlos and Luis at the corners. The linebackers? So far, we have Victor Lucio at the Sam backer along with the Vietnamese kid, Dan Ngo. They both show good feet and toughness. Looks like either could be your leader on the field," Dirk said.

"Then get both on the field. There is no tomorrow here. This is the future. The only way to turn around a program is to turn around the defense. No disrespect to Grant Lee, but the Barracuda defense has been toothless since 1964. We need something special out of you, Dirk. We must be great on defense. And I mean right out of the gate."

"Yes, sir, Coach."

"Now, what about the front?"

"Valentino appears to be the man at nose. He can play both A-gaps if we need him to. He's tough, doesn't say much, hardly talks at all, but he's agile for a big guy. We still have some question marks at the two tackle positions and the two outside linebackers," said Dirk.

Thump clapped his hands and pointed at Dirk.

"You darn right, Valentino's agile. If he were an inch taller, that kid would be on every recruiter's radar. Okay, so you know we need a guy with a motor at the weakside backer, right? Those tempo offenses will prevent us from flip-flopping the outside backers, so you need two guys with wheels. You and Grant Lee put your heads together and find them.

"Grant Lee, how's the offense looking? Are the kids picking up the system?"

"Coach, it seems everybody understands the alignment numbering system. They are getting the hang of the names of the plays and the snap count being married to the play. It took some work, but we're on track. The cards helped. Coach Dye and Coach Sewell have been working the offensive line in your absence, and they've done a good job with it."

"All right, that's two good men you can count on."

With everything ready to go for Saturday's practice, Thump dismissed the two assistants and secured the building after making sure he'd turned off every light. It was around 6:30, and if there was one thing he knew, it was that he deserved a watermelon Slushee. He would pass on dinner tonight; the day's events had disturbed his appetite.

Once back at cottage number 5, he settled into his grandma's rocking chair and took a pull off his half-empty Slushee. Jenny sat nearby, waiting for a treat that wasn't forthcoming.

"No, ma'am. Jason bought you a double dip earlier. It's dog food or nothing."

Jenny groaned and slinked toward her kitchen nest, where she circled the bedding three times and flopped. She let out a contemptuous sigh loud enough for Thump to hear from the living room.

Thump pulled Sara's card from his wallet, then flipped it between his fingers in the way a card shark might fidget with a poker chip. He wondered about Deputy Bunch: Did he have a family?

The familiar squeak of the old rocker soothed his angst as he prayed for a dream of solace.

CHAPTER SIXTEEN

To Thump, the Texas heat must have birthed Thursday's morning's practice from brimstone. Apart from six hopeful seagulls squawking in disappointment, the sun shone without mercy; the field withered without chatter. Thump wanted to jump their young tails, but he held back.

Ed Hattaway had taught him to see the big picture, to see past the now, but another part of Thump felt sorry for them. It tempted him to cut practice short. Then he remembered Ed saying, "Nobody wins by practicing soft."

Rule number eight: Go hard or go home.

They would go hard for two more days. At the end of Saturday's early practice, Grant Lee called up the team. Each coach thanked the boys for finishing their first week strong. Thump reminded them their first scrimmage was the following Friday. A chaotic cheer interrupted the praise session when Thump informed them that they would conduct no second practice; they could go home. With nothing of real value to add, other than a reminder to hydrate, he ended on that high note.

"One Team!"

"One Heart!"

Several boys sprinted the entire distance to the fieldhouse.

Later that evening, Thump checked his watch.

Time to make a phone call.

He held a super-sized soda cup once banned in New York City, and sucked on an ice cube soaked in Dr. Pepper.

She answered on the third ring.

"This is Sergeant Mendoza."

He spit the cube back into the cup.

"Hello, Sergeant Mendoza, this is Coach Thomas Sutton."

"You need to give that up," she replied.

A bit of chit-chat revealed they each had similar plans, kicking back and bathing in the sweet nothingness of the evening.

"Did they tell you anything?" Thump asked.

"No, they haven't found him. It looks bad, though. The speculation is he ran up on some bad guys after they had just made a big drug deal. A lot of weight moves between Corpus and Houston. The description of the car fits the method of operation for those kinds of dealings; Crown Vic, a big trunk, lots of room for false panels and so forth. I suspect the higher-ups have information they aren't releasing."

"Not even to you?"

"Especially not to me. This sounds big, probably cartel-related, and I'm just a small fish. The FBI is working on it with the Rangers. And the Sheriff's Office is shaking the trees of every local drug-dealing punk's backyard."

"Come on, it's not like you're Barney Fife."

"Barney who?"

He laughed. "Never mind, it's an old TV show I used to love and still do. I'll tell you about him when we get together."

"Oh, so you think we're getting together?"

"Yeah, I do. Tomorrow for church and then afterward at the big function over at Camp Promise."

"Really? Maybe I have plans."

"You do have plans. Your plans are to hang out with me tomorrow."

"You know, Coach, this isn't a football game, and I'm not some dumb teenage boy quarterback. You can't just bark out an order and expect me to follow it. Besides, I don't do the church scene."

"Don't you think, that after yesterday, maybe it would be a good idea to start?" asked Thump.

"The place might burst into flames if I walk in there."

"Well, I don't call audibles, so we're going with my original play. I'm picking you up at 10:30 tomorrow morning at your place. And after your baptism, we'll head over to Camp Promise for some frivolity."

"Frivolity? Where did you buy that word?"

"I spent half of my last paycheck on it. Impressed?" Thump asked.

"Okay, who am I to argue with the big, bad, head football coach of the Port Verona Barracudas?"

"Exactly. Text me your address and get to bed early tonight."

"You sure you want to do this? Tongues will wag all the way to Amarillo. Haven't you had enough excitement for one week?"

"Yes, ma'am, I'm definitely sure."

"Okay then, I'll send you the Google map for my place. It's out on the water by the western bay. It would be better if you pick me up at 10:15."

"Okay. 10:15, got it."

"See you tomorrow, Coach Thomas Sutton."

"See you tomorrow, Sergeant Sara Mendoza."

CHAPTER SEVENTEEN

After his most restful sleep in years, Thump showered and picked out his best polo and newest jeans. He broke out his new, bone-colored, linen sport coat and the pair of tan Oxfords he had ordered online the previous Tuesday. Because he would sooner slide naked down a giant razor's edge into a vat of rubbing alcohol than walk into a clothing store, he bought most of his clothes online. He smoothed the sides of his salted temples and examined his face for any anomalies. It would be his first date in three years.

"What do you think?"

Jenny tapped her tail twice and sneezed.

"Mixed review, eh? I'll be back after church to pick you up. Why don't you set out that autumn leaf print bandana I bought you? It highlights your eyes."

Twenty minutes later, he arrived at 116 Tiburon Bay Drive, a bright yellow, slatted cabin resting on a foundation of twenty pilings. The pilings elevated the dwelling above the threat of Category III and below storms. A neat vegetable garden flourished off to the south side of the driveway.

Under the house on a concrete slab sat a gleaming candy-apple red coupe, a 1971 Mercury Cougar XR-7 with a white ragtop, the kind seen back in the October homecoming parades of his youth. It was the car that always carried the homecoming court queen.

Sara's wooden screen door slapped open, but the height of the structure made a difficult angle for Thump to see her from the truck. As she descended the last of the wooden steps, she appeared as one of those stars from the old Hollywood musicals.

A beige sunflower print sundress with two thin straps left her brown shoulders nearly bare. Cinched at her narrow waistline and complemented with a deep pocket sewn into each hip, the skirt flowed to just below her knees. Her attire reminded him of the dresses his mother wore when she walked through her rose garden on Sunday, picking beetles from her babies' leaves.

"Babies," that's what his mother called her flowers.

Carrying a large canvas bag, Sara's approach to Blue's passenger door was more of a bounce than a walk. He had never seen her hair down like that, glistening in the morning light and cascading downward.

She jerked on Blue's heavy metal door. Its rusty door hinge whined in protest.

"Man, they don't make trucks like these anymore," she said.

"That's a good thing," Thump replied.

She scooted close and kissed him on the cheek. "You clean up nice."

"You look pretty sunning yourself," he said.

"Oh my. As in my sun dress? That might be the worst pun I've ever heard."

He backed Blue out onto the highway. Its rear mud-grip tires crunched the white shale like breakfast cereal.

"So, are you sure we should do this?" she asked.

"Look, it's nothing. Lots of people you know. Some you haven't seen in a while. It's a little solemn and somewhat happy at the same time. Just think of it as going to a funeral of an old friend from high school; it's just that God resurrected him is all."

"Wow, you never miss an opportunity for a bad joke, do you?"

The parked vehicles overflowed onto the church lawn. They packed the church that morning. Rule number one for small-town preachers: expect a large crowd the Sunday after a tragedy.

Even though Don Bunch was a lifelong Reed City resident and had spent little time in Port Verona, it didn't matter. Small towns backed the blue with a fervor not seen in the metro areas.

The moment that Sara said would wag tongues all the way to Amarillo didn't happen. With their minds focused on the curiosity of the kidnapping incident, the congregation paid little attention to her presence.

Sara's arm held on to Thump's elbow as they entered the sanctuary as just another couple there to worship and gain needed strength for dealing with the tragedy. As Sara was the face of the local police department, people expected her to show an interest in Deputy Bunch's disappearance. No one thought it noteworthy that she had just darkened the doorway of Second Baptist for the first time since she was a pre-teen.

Following the church greeting, the hymn-singing, the praise songs, and the day's offering, Reverend Ben approached the pulpit and opened his Bible, then pointed his finger upward and read, "Jeremiah 5:26 says, *Among my people are wicked men who lie in wait like men who snare birds and like those who set traps have deprived you of good.* Deacon Le Ky, will you please lead us in a word of prayer?"

Le Ky stood and said, "Please stand. Let us pray. Heavenly Father, we come here to worship Your awesomeness and to seek healing. We stand together as one family, seeking Your guidance and honoring Your loving presence during our times of plenty and our times of want. We ask that You bless those here in attendance today. In Jesus's name, we pray. Amen."

Reverend Wallace raised both arms. "And the church said?"

"Amen."

With the response, everyone settled in their pews. While last Sunday's sermon emphasized the temporary nature and fragility of the flock's time on Earth, on this Sunday, Reverend Wallace felt called to point out the permanence of perseverance.

"The fire which burns us also forges our mettle," he declared to be his central message.

Thump enjoyed the sermon. Reverend Ben Wallace reminded him of his high school football coach. His messages were sharp and insightful, just like Coach Brad Abraham's pregame speeches.

Before taking the Port Verona job, Thump hadn't attended much church. Usually, he stole a few precious last minutes of sleep before the Sunday preparatory marathon that so many head coaches loved. It was an expectation of most football coaches to work seven days a week, not because it took the full weekend to break down Friday's game film and analyze the next opponent; rather, it was to show the fans that your staff worked long hours.

Not every head coach bought into that expectation. A few of the rare, emotionally secure head coaches throughout the state would enact top secret stratagems to fool the hypercritical fans into thinking the coaching staff members were at the fieldhouse working all night. The most common of those ploys was a ruse that originated in Fort Hill in 1972 when Coach Squeaky Bill Jensen decided he would spend the weekend at his deer camp.

During World War II, Squeaky Bill commanded a Sherman tank under General George S. Patton. Squeaky knew that prior to being appointed to lead the Third Army, Patton acted as a decoy for the D-Day invasion while serving in command of the fictional First Army Group. The operation was part of a two-prong bluff to fool the Germans into thinking massive amounts of personnel, support systems, and military hardware were being staged for an invasion of the northern beaches. Instead, the tanks, planes, and transports were all inflatables and wooden props.

Squeaky Bill called his own diversionary scheme Patton's Parking Lot. On the weekends that he green-lighted Patton's Parking Lot, Squeaky Bill told his assistant coaches to park their vehicles at the fieldhouse and "vamoose" for the weekend. He told the staff that should any assistant return to town before dark on Sunday, that coach would look for a job before dawn on Monday.

After he bribed his Aunt Carolyn to stop by the fieldhouse to coordinate the lights with the time of day, Squeaky loaded his two Walker hounds, deer feed, and camping gear in the back of his truck then pulled out of town after midnight Friday. He loved emulating "the greatest general who ever lived," as he swilled warm beer and sang gospel songs during the entire four-hour trip to his deer camp.

Thump worked for one head coach who used Patton's Parking Lot a few weekends each season, and it was great. But at another one of his coaching stops, he worked for a sadistically tilted head coach who considered such gambits to be a disgrace to the Texas High School Coaches Association. Thought to be insane by many peers and several hundred career assistants who worked under him, Chester Bolton would keep his entire staff at the fieldhouse throughout the weekend, right up to an hour before school started. Only then would he dismiss the staff, admonishing them to shower and go teach their classes with "spit and vinegar in your veins."

While Thump pushed through those Mondays and saved his reputation as a classroom teacher, he couldn't save his second marriage. It was game five, and Chester Bolton's Calvert Coyotes were in the middle of a tight district race when, after having been at school since noon on Sunday, Thump arrived home late Monday night to find a note sitting on the kitchen table. Next to the note was an unopened can of Campbell's vegetable soup and a fork.

Written in his wife's hand, the note read, "Enjoy your dinner. When you get a real job, call me. Otherwise, don't bother."

Six months later, he signed the divorce papers.

The last note of the doxology sounded.

Thump heard, "Coach Sutton! Oh, Coach Sutton!" Three aisles south of his location, Dorothy Jean Butler pushed her walker toward him.

With Sara in tow, he waded through the exodus of the faithful to speak to her.

"Well, good day to you, Ms. Dorothy Jean! I'm so glad to see you."

"I'm glad I'm still here for you to see. And who is this you have with you today? Is this your precious daughter?"

"Ms. Dorothy Jean, this is my friend, Sara. I keep telling her how young she looks, but she doesn't listen."

Sara cut a look at Thump, then smiled and offered her hand to greet Dorothy Jean.

"Oh yes, I remember Sara dear. So pretty, and such warm hands. Coach, I want you and young Sara here to come by my house for supper on Thursday. I'm cooking up some fresh garden soup with a mess of okra, corn, potatoes, and tomatoes from my grandson's garden. We have things to discuss."

"Yes, ma'am, we'll be there."

Sara's grip on Thump's fingers tightened. His knuckles felt like lug nuts in the socket of a compressed air wrench.

Dorothy Jean said, "That's 702 West Third Street. Can you remember that? If not, I bet young Sara will. 702 West Third Street, Port Verona. We sit down to eat at 6:00 sharp. Don't be late."

Thump assured Dorothy Jean that he and Sara would sit down for supper at six. Navigating the crowded aisle, he noticed a hand holding a smart phone high above the crowd. Just like last week, a teenage girl recorded his movement.

Sara leaned in and whispered, "Such a celebrity, my father is."

Once in the pastor's receiving line, Thump scanned the church front lawn for any sign of Rod. He had been a Houston Texans superfan ever since they had filled the vacuum of the Oilers' absence, and today the Texans kicked off in the early game.

Reverend Wallace greeted them in his booming pastoral voice. "So happy to see you here today. How are you doing? I heard about Wednesday and I want you to know that we are all praying for you here at Second."

"Thank you, Preacher. This is Sara Mendoza."

"Ah yes. I know the lovely Sara, our community's guardian angel in blue; she has visited us once before, I believe."

His recollection surprised her. "Thanks, I enjoyed your sermon," Sara replied.

"Absolutely, my dear. We are all in prayer for you and yours. And please come back sooner next time."

Reverend Wallace's well-honed telekinetic power nudged Thump and Sara along so he could greet the next congregant.

"So happy to see you here today. How are you doing?"

"Man, he has that down to an exact science," Thump said.

"Yeah, he has to keep the sheeple happy."

Thump stopped walking.

"All right, we don't need any of that sardonic, embittered cop routine. That sermon was spot-on. Plus, the man remembered you from when you were in junior high. That has to count for something."

"Okay. You're right." She glanced toward Reverend Wallace's receiving line, then looked at Thump. "Let's go back to your place so I can change. I know you are not wearing that white sport coat to a barbeque."

"It's bone, not white. And no, I won't be sporting my Sunday go-to-meeting duds to the barbeque; I need to change into my black-tie outfit."

"You're a child, you know that?"

Jenny bounced when they arrived back at the bungalow. Thump ditched the jacket but kept the jeans, shoes, and polo. Sara changed into a pair of olive-green, tie-waist cropped pants coordinated with a neutral tank top. When she appeared from the bathroom, Thump bit his tongue. She looked like a page torn out of a fashion magazine.

Jenny's entire body wiggled as she waited at the door. Thump tied on her Barracuda red spirit bandana and pulled her Sunday leash from the wall.

They arrived at Camp Promise around 12:45. Piles of brisket sway-backed the serving tables. Nearby, the fixings sat coordinated to move the line along quicker.

Pecan trees squared off the perimeter and shaded the pale blue cottages that housed the residents and their house parents. A sizable crowd gathered as the boys scampered about the quad throwing the football.

Wearing a barbeque apron and a chef's hat, Pastor Mike waved from the pit where he stood tending to the meat.

"Coach! Over here!"

Fueled by mesquite, the four barbeque pits radiated heat in all directions. Sara felt as if she were working a grass fire with the volunteer fire department. Praising herself for wearing her oil-based makeup, she wiped away the watery tears and told Thump she had to excuse herself.

Pastor Mike, a spatula in one hand, slapped Thump on the back.

"Your presence is a joy, Coach. You all right? They find out anything on that deputy? We prayed for you all."

"No, they still know nothing. I'm good, Pastor Mike. I got my bodyguard with me."

Jenny sat down and leaned against Thump's leg.

"I see now you got more than just one bodyguard with you." Pastor Mike said. He turned to the grill to tend the meat.

Thump replied, "Yeah, she's a good one to have around; they both are."

"You got that right. I want y'all to have a good time today. Eat, drink, all you want. We got more than enough, and if we run out, the good Lord will provide."

Thump thanked him and ambled through the crowd to find Sara. Across the way, T'Darian hit a crossing route, the ball passing just over the defender's extended hands. After catching the football in stride, one of the younger boys juked the second defender and sprinted for the make-believe endzone.

From over by the line of people snaking their way through the serving line, Sara waved. Thump saw her and headed that way, then got behind her.

Four hours later, the music and laughter subsided as the crowd thinned. Thump lay back on the grass, his eyes closed. Sounds of laughter echoed over the grounds. Sara poked him with her elbow and tapped her left wrist. Understanding her signal, Thump, with his belly full and his hand sore from all the handshaking, got up and walked over to Pastor Mike to thank him again for the invitation.

Derek and T'Darian worked nearby, helping the pastor clean up.

Speaking to the two boys, Pastor Mike said, "Men of honor, come thank your coach for coming."

For the first time, Derek looked Thump in the eyes and smiled. "Thanks for coming, Coach," he said.

T'Darian broadcast his usual cheek-to-cheek grin and said, "Yeah, thanks for coming, Coach. Did you see me over there, earlier? I'll see you at practice tomorrow."

"Yeah, I watched you both. Thanks for having me, men."

"You welcome," they replied in unison and then returned to their work.

Pastor Mike whispered, "No head football coach at Port Verona High School has ever attended this barbeque in the 13 years we been having it." His hand on Thump's shoulder, he added, "The Lord sent you here, my friend. Not a man. Not a woman. The Lord sent you. You remember that."

"Yes sir, thank you."

"Officer, you protect this young man from harm. We need him. We all need him," Pastor Mike said.

"Yes, sir," Sara replied.

"All right, then. God bless y'all and thanks for coming. I got to get back to herding these young men. Coach, I'll see you on Friday at the scrimmage." Pastor Mike pointed to Thump, then turned and walked away.

Thump and Jenny rushed Sara home. She needed to get some sleep before her shift started at 11:00.

CHAPTER EIGHTEEN

By Monday morning, Thump had gone three days without his breakfast tacos. He pulled into the packed parking lot of the Taco Place.

"Look, Jenny. It's the Taco Place. Brand name recognition is one key to success. They taught me that at TCU before I switched majors. You wait here."

Maya's perkiness made it easy to see how she had earned two varsity cheerleader letters.

"Good morning, Coach. Haven't seen you in a few days. What can we get for you? Where's your sweet puppy?"

"I left her in the truck. Some places around here aren't comfortable with federal law and such. And I let her stay in the truck on cool weather days."

"You tell her Maya said hi. Okay?"

"Will do, Maya."

"How's the team looking?" she asked as she bagged his order.

"Not too bad. I think we have a chance to be pretty good this year."

"Oh, that's good. Like I don't want to be mean, but we kind of stink. It's hard to keep people excited when the team struggles. You know? I mean, we're great in basketball, but we always stink in football." She handed him the bag of tacos. "I'm glad you came."

Thump wasn't sure whether she meant she was glad he came to Port Verona to coach, or she was glad he came to buy tacos, or both. He returned to Old Blue and elbowed Jenny aside.

"You know Daddy wouldn't leave you for long. And, Maya said hi." Jenny pawed at the bag. "No, this is people food, not dog food. You already had breakfast."

Thump clutched the bag and raised the shifter into reverse. Down the highway, he saw the familiar Port Verona PD Charger approaching from the opposite direction. The siren yelped twice as it zoomed by.

"Well, Jenny, we've gone from a finger nod to a two-whoop salute. I'd say things are looking up."

That Monday morning, practice moved slowly. Lethargy was an expected consequence of a layoff. Thump never understood the reason behind it, but a lull always followed a break in intensity.

Ed Hattaway always said that you don't become a champion by lying on the couch. It was turning out to be a bad first day back, but Thump would let the assistants handle it. He had to maintain good karma for the upcoming meeting with Dr. Tran.

He smiled. Tran would be disappointed if she knew he had almost forgotten about it.

They wrapped up the day's second practice at 11:00. Thump let Grant Lee and Dirk handle the post-practice talk. If anybody could make something good out of a day like this, it was Grant Lee. He had turned out to be Thump's right-hand man. Watching him talk to the kids, Thump wondered why the lifelong Barracuda didn't get the job. Then he remembered: Doctor Tran wanted a flop.

The poor practice had fouled Grant Lee's typically great attitude, and his frustration boiled when he dismissed the squad.

"Your effort today eroded everything you accomplished last week," he told them.

In expressing his dissatisfaction through a negative slant, Grant Lee violated rule number nine: Coach the positive; overcome the negative.

Thump wanted his coaches to admonish positively, but he overlooked Grant Lee's transgression. He suspected that two-thirds of the team had no clue as to the definition of "eroded." Besides, he felt that Grant Lee would improve; nobody is perfect.

Relieved to get off the field, the boys dragged past him with their heads down. Thump checked his watch. He would hold a brief staff meeting on the field.

"Men, good job out there. It was rough, but we expected that. Things will pick up tomorrow. Thanks for pressing them. Stay after them and stay positive. We must stay positive. Grant Lee, Dirk, and Miguel, you need to meet and look at this week's practice schedule. We want a good scrimmage on Friday, but we don't want to waste time preparing for a scrimmage opponent. It's imperative we get our vertical game better and we must be able to run Green Bay and Packer out of the offset. On defense, I want to keep seven in the box and get after their run game. Keep it plain vanilla in the secondary. The boss has asked me to swim over to the Cove. If I need anything, I'll call you."

Thump grabbed a cup of ice water from the trainer and embarked on his march to meet the general. *I should have sent Grant Lee instead. At least he would have a chance at achieving half a victory.*

Dr. Tran's receptionist greeted him at her desk and notified the superintendent of his presence. Tran sat at her desk, her back to the door.

Without turning to face Thump, she said, "Good morning, Coach Sutton. Please take a seat."

Thump replied, "Good morning," and sat in the center chair of executioner's row.

At least a minute passed before Dr. Tran swiveled her executive chair around to face Thump. She let out a deep sigh and cupped her hands on her desk.

"Coach Sutton, you've been up to quite a lot this past week. I don't know where to begin, but I have before me some very disturbing allegations."

"Allegations?" Thump replied.

"Yes, it appears you took it upon yourself to decide that your football team is to utilize our championship soccer program's field. As athletic director, I assume you are cognizant of the facility usage policy and the role each of those components play in our overall athletic program?"

"Well, ma'am, I haven't seen a written facility usage policy, per se. I just thought that the football team should practice on the safest field. In fact, since we play our soccer games in the stadium, I thought the practice field served as the sole practice venue for football and soccer."

"Coach Sutton, I don't mean to be abrupt but in a formal meeting such as this, the proper protocol is to address a superior who holds a terminal degree as 'Doctor,' not 'ma'am'."

"Yes, Dr. Tran."

"It isn't necessary to say 'Dr. Tran' in your response, only in your address. It's just a little tip that will help you down the road when dealing with others who possess a terminal degree as recognized experts in their field. Perhaps when school starts, get with our award-winning speech and communications teacher, Ada Green. She can explain business etiquette to you and help you practice."

"Thank you, ma'am. I understand now."

"Well, let's get back to the purpose of our meeting. You said that you thought the soccer practice field was open for use by the football team. Is that correct?"

"Yes, ma'am, I did. The soccer field is the only manicured surface on the grounds. It's clear of gopher holes. It's wider and longer than the game field, a factor that allows us to spread the drills apart so no accidental collisions occur when we throw the deep routes to our receivers."

"But, isn't your kickerback practicing on the game field?"

"The place kicker? Yes, ma'am. He kicks on the game field because the practice field has no goal posts. Plus, practicing on the game field will provide him with a psychological advantage during our home games."

"I see. But no adult supervises this individual on the game field. Is that a correct perception?"

"I guess that could be the perception, but he isn't taking part in any strenuous activity. And we can see him from the practice field. Besides, he isn't alone, we teach the boys never to do anything without a battle buddy."

"Excuse me? You teach them never to do anything without a what?"

"We tell the kickers to practice with a battle buddy, a partner. Like, if they are lifting weights, it isn't safe to lift alone. And if they are doing some extra conditioning work, they need a partner. It's the same with our kickers and punters; they work together in case an unforeseen emergency occurs."

"And you call these partners, battle buddies?"

"Yes, ma'am. It's a fun little phrase we use. The boys seem to like it."

She paused and looked through some papers. "May I get you some tea, Coach Sutton?"

"No, ma'am. I'm fine. Thank you, though."

"Coach Sutton, you may not be aware that Port Verona lost one of its former students in Afghanistan not so many years ago. Are you aware of that?"

"Yes, ma'am. They were talking about his funeral yesterday at church."

"Church? What church?"

"Second Baptist."

"Yes, this community pains over the sacrifices of our men and women in uniform. You could almost say there is a patriotic fervor here that is unlike anywhere else in Texas."

"Yes, ma'am."

"Don't you think your appropriation of a military term is a little insensitive? These children are not soldiers, Coach Sutton. And I don't think their parents want them to mistake playing football with the sacrifice of serving their country overseas. I just think the use of the phrase 'battle buddies' is inappropriate in a school setting, and I want that practice to end today."

"Yes, ma'am. We will no longer use the phrase."

"Good to hear. Now, let's backtrack a bit. You appropriated the soccer practice field as your football team's training area. Is that correct?"

"Yes, ma'am. It seemed to be within my authority as athletic director to evaluate and make use of the facilities in a way that best serves our mission; that is, we will prepare athletes to compete in the safest and most productive manner within the range of the best resources. The best resource for practicing football is the soccer field."

"Yes. And an excellent mission statement it is. What I am wondering though, did you adequately assess the other practice field behind the fieldhouse? From what I gather, that location has served as the practice field for over 40 years. And it is much closer to the fieldhouse, should one of those unforeseen emergencies occur."

"Yes, ma'am. Grant Lee Davis informed me of the past usage of that area. Frankly, I wondered why the district used it as a practice field. It may have been necessary to use before you constructed the soccer field, but it's much too small. Mature pecan trees border each sideline. That's great for shade, but less beneficial for player safety. And the turf isn't Tiff Bermuda, which means goathorn stickers invade the fields each spring."

"Coach Sutton, a group of very concerned soccer parents contacted me. They question your judgment in encroaching on the venue of our state-ranked men and women's soccer program so that you may practice a football team who hasn't brought home a district championship in over 50 years."

"Yes, ma'am. However, as athletic director, I would like to think we provide equity for our athletes by allowing them to access our best resources. I'm also sure it violates the Texas High School Coaches' Association code of ethics to play favorites because of the won-loss record of a particular sport."

"Yes, I see your point. Coach Sutton, here at Port Verona it is a matter of boundaries, not favoritism. The short field adjacent to the fieldhouse has always been the football practice field, and it will remain so. Our field specialist from Texas A&M Kingsville tells us a quality soccer field needs a designated rest period. As you realize, a soccer ball is in constant contact with the turf, so it is imperative the district protects the soccer field from unnecessary wear. Whereas, a football rarely touches the turf, unless it is our football team's offense who is fumbling."

She leaned back in her chair and chuckled.

"Yes, ma'am. I understand, but the small field is not the best place to practice."

"No, Coach. I don't think you understand. That field is the best place for the football team to practice. And I would hope you, being a part of my administrative team, would appreciate the necessity of supporting the vision of this administration."

"Okay. I understand."

"On to our next matter. I heard of your involvement in an incident within the community this past Wednesday. And it caused you to miss two practices, am I correct?"

"Yes, ma'am. I suppose you learned of the details. The police detained me all morning. Prior to the first practice, I notified Grant Lee to take over. He is my first assistant and is very capable."

"Coach Sutton, you appreciate the fact that our athletic director's involvement in an incident of this nature brings with it a glaring spotlight upon our school district and its mission here?"

Thump's lip quivered.

"What I appreciate is that the incident was a tragedy which I experienced through happenstance on my morning run. I'm not sure how my presence affects the school district."

"It's disappointing that you can't see that. Coach Sutton, this is a small town, and one errant arrow can pierce the heart of our support. Now we hear rumors of a drug cartel being involved, and the media has linked our athletic director to the activities of a massive drug ring. You can't see how that would be a problem?"

"Yes, ma'am, but I'm not sure how I could have done anything different. I came upon the scene of a kidnapping. The police detained me so they could get information and locate the deputy. I mean, what was I supposed to do, run past the deputy's car and not care that something was wrong?"

"Possibly, Coach Sutton. I am just not sure you grasp how serious it is when an event of this nature involves my athletic director, albeit incidentally, with the death of a police officer. They plastered your name and face all over the major Houston networks."

"Yes, ma'am. What can I say? You hired me to come here and build a winner. And I plan to do that. I will do nothing to shame you or this district. I thought I was being a great role model by taking part in the investigation."

"Oh, you were, Coach. You were. I understand now that your involvement was just an unfortunate coincidence, and I will note that in your record."

"My record?"

"Yes, you are in the clear as far as the unfortunate incident with the police, but I will need to document your lack of practical oversight regarding the two boys kicking alone on the game field, in addition to your misappropriation of the soccer field."

Thump's head felt as if it would explode. Somewhere down that very long tunnel of unconscious realization, he could hear Rose's voice, but he couldn't quite make out what she was saying.

"Document?" replied Thump.

"Yes. I've already typed the report for you to sign. Just sign here on the bottom showing that you received a copy. Your signature doesn't mean you agree with what's written, it means only that you received a copy of the report. And I will need to add a supplement about the use of inappropriate language regarding the 'battle buddies' phrase, of course. Nothing to worry about now, unless there is a failure on your part to take immediate corrective action."

The corners of her bright red lips turned upward as she dramatically slid a pen across her desk. His hand exhibited a noticeable tremor. Somewhere far down that tunnel echoed Rose's voice. Thump signed the document.

"My secretary will place a copy in your box along with the supplement for you to sign."

Rising from his chair, he thanked her for her time.

"You're welcome, Coach Sutton. I am just so excited we start school next week. I can't wait to see all the kiddos. I trust that you are preparing some exciting hands-on activities for your history classes. I just love history. My dissertation at Georgetown was on the civilian experience during the Vietnam War. I suppose I may have cheated a bit, since I lived it."

"Yeah, they killed my brother over there. Regarding Vietnam, I suppose I deserve a doctorate of sadness," Thump replied.

Her eyes seemed to go black and her face steeled. "It was a tough time for a lot of families."

Thump turned to walk out.

Tran swiveled back to her computer and called out lyrically, "I hope we can socialize off-campus soon. I so enjoy our meetings."

CHAPTER NINETEEN

An hour east of downtown Houston, a small community attracts an annual throng of Alligator Festival celebrants. Like Port Verona, Anahuac traces its communal roots back to a time before the Europeans set foot upon what would become Southeast Texas. Like Port Verona, its rich bounty of wildlife sounds a siren to the area outdoorsmen.

The land's original overseers, the Anahuac tribe, hunted the thriving gator population and even used the gator's fat as a protective balm against the unrelenting marsh mosquitos. It was after midnight deep in the Anahuac wetlands when a torched vehicle caught the eye of Deputy Ina Ruth Sanders.

The smoldering heap of steel and plastic appeared to be an older domestic vehicle. Ina parked her unit and surveyed the area.

This particular road ended at Anahuac Bay, a dead end and a great place to dump a car. Nothing extraordinary, she thought. It was another dump job. Deputy Sanders radioed the East Chambers County Sheriff Office dispatcher to send a fire crew and a wrecker her way.

Most burned-out vehicle cases result from a person falling behind on a used-car loan. Only a few of the dumped vehicles that Ina Ruth worked during her long career ended up being anything more than that. Occasionally, she hooked a false insurance claim or the handiwork of some good old boys out on a drug-fueled rager. She had no reason to link the smoldering remnant to the murder of a sheriff's deputy 150 miles away.

Three hours southwest of Houston, in Tiburon County, the Texas Rangers and a four-county task force were rounding up the shot callers from *El Marineras* while undercover agents prodded the drug peddlers and prostitutes for information. In the Houston FBI office, a caucus of profilers worked nonstop at dissecting Don's life to find the one needle that could help sew the disconnected facts into cohesive clues. Not that the dash cam video didn't provide any.

It was on a need-to-know basis that Deputy Bunch's dashcam video captured three suspects at the scene, not just the two mentioned in the press release. Video enhancement also revealed the three suspects to be young athletic males under six feet and acting according to a rehearsed script.

Further analysis of the dash camera revealed that the suspects had baited Deputy Bunch into the traffic stop. His dash camera recorded the Crown Vic passing by his traffic checkpoint near the hardware store twice before he executed an investigatory stop on the vehicle. Detectives suspected the assailants used a police scanner to pinpoint Deputy Bunch and maximize their opportunity to interact with him. By doing so, the suspects picked the time and place to carry out their plan.

Two days would pass before the FBI database provided a hit on the burned-out car found outside of Anahuac. An East Chambers felony investigator had exercised due diligence and culled the vehicle identification number from the chassis. The number came back as a hit for a black 2002 Ford Crown Victoria stolen out of Houston. Taken from a grocery parking lot two days prior to the deputy's kidnapping, it belonged to Esther Rosenblatt of Bellaire, Texas, an urban enclave in Southwest Houston.

By that time, law enforcement had realized that the kidnappers had stolen the Crown Vic to facilitate Deputy Bunch's kidnapping. The question was, why Houston? The *El Marineras* had no presence in

Houston; their turf extended to a toehold on Galveston. North of Galveston County, they were nonexistent. The geographical disconnect puzzled the investigators. Worse, the discovery of the Crown Victoria in the dense darkness of a swampy wildlife refuge evaporated the last droplets of hope that law enforcement would locate Deputy Bunch alive.

The following day, the Texas Rangers declared the case to be a capital murder investigation.

CHAPTER TWENTY

By Thursday, the Barracudas were in sync. Coach Sewell and Coach Dye agreed in their approval of what had become of the squad and their effort. Isaac told Thump that he had never seen the defense 'display a motor' such as they have now. The coaches had established the depth chart, and the offensive unit had a full grasp of Thump's unique system. Thump had allowed the Herrera twins to install the empty backfield set but cautioned them not to use it during the scrimmage. Thump had vetoed the option series but had allowed Harrison to install the bootleg. The Herrera twins had installed four different screen passes: Cobra, Snake, Venom, and Galveston. Galveston was the screen that faked Harrison's play action bootleg. It looked good against a skeleton defense, but Thump didn't want to show it against Macedonia Catholic.

San Antonio's Macedonia Catholic, a private school powerhouse, would be a litmus test for the Barracuda defense. Jason's scouting report summary revealed they were a run-first, pass-never offense who would come out and hit you in the mouth on every play. Defensively, the Fighting Bishops appeared impenetrable.

"A program earns its salt on defense," Ed Hattaway used to say. Macedonia Catholic was salty.

It had been two days since the Tran inquisition and Rose had finally exorcised Dr. Tran's diatribe from Thump's forethought. If not for Rose and Jenny, Thump was sure that he would have lost his mind after that Monday. He didn't eat for two days. Rod's gossip appeared to be more truth than fiction. And now, the team practiced on a field that wasn't fit for a peewee football team. He tried not to think about the anvil suspended over him; but even though Rod had warned him, Tran had nested in his head.

His distress bled onto the practice field. The Herrera twins had to assume a larger role with the offense while Dirk and Grant Lee congealed the defense into a mobile mass-menace. Tran's treachery had rattled Thump; he wasn't himself. Neither Rose nor Sara could allay his consternation.

Sara's workload had intensified as the Bunch case overtaxed local resources. She had no time to call Thump to tell him that they had found the suspect car east of Houston. Like everyone else in the know, she wondered why *El Marineras* dumped the vehicle so far outside of their turf's boundaries. In one respect, it was a good move, but it seemed to be an unnecessary risk to drive a car wanted in a police officer's murder almost two hundred miles and through a metro area just to burn it. As expected, *El Marineras* wasn't cooperating in the investigation.

Certain that Deputy Bunch was dead, his body dumped somewhere between Port Verona and Anahuac, Sara had been hypervigilant during her early morning patrol. Law enforcement had tightened its squeeze on the *El Marineras* and no one knew when they might retaliate.

Thanks to Thump's expropriation of her Thursday evening, she would sample Dorothy Jean's okra soup at 6:00. After she locked the keys to the Charger in the wall storage unit at the PD, she texted Thump to remind him. His brain had turned to mush since the Tran confrontation, and she knew that he would not want to suffer the consequences of getting on Dorothy Jean's bad side.

Known throughout the county, Dorothy Jean was Port Verona's matriarch. A longtime widow whose husband once owned the entire footprint of the nuclear power plant just north of Reed City, Dorothy Jean was the biggest philanthropist south of Austin and was on a first-name basis with the state's lieutenant governor, the most powerful man in Texas. When Dorothy Jean spoke, Texas listened.

With the August sun peeling paint from the Tiburon Guaranty and Trust thermometer, Sara insisted they take her Cougar, whose AC still blew like it was 1971.

"Papi loved to say that he could drive a Mercury to heck and back," Sara said as she adjusted the vents, "because the air conditioning would forever blow cold."

"Except he didn't say 'heck,' did he?" Thump replied.

"Yes, he did. I never once heard Papi say a bad word. 'Heck' was it. He said to me, '*Mija*, if you talk filth, you become filth. I am facing angry people using foul language on my job daily. I write them a ticket, and they curse. You know what I do? I treat them with dignity, because no one has ever showed them how to behave under stress. You remember that.' And I did," Sara explained.

"I would have loved to meet your father," Thump said.

"He was the perfect husband and father. A real man, not like these machismo misogynists who think they own women."

After allowing Thump to drive from his place to Dorothy Jean's, all of four blocks, they arrived at 5:30 sharp.

At 702 West Third Street stood a pale green two-story Victorian with a burgundy steel roof manufactured to appear as an older wooden slate canopy. An olive-green trim extended to a wraparound porch highlighted by a large garnet swing that guarded the right corner of the veranda.

Upon entering the yard, the visitor encountered two vintage copper lanterns astride the red brick entryway. Flowers, their fragrance blending to form a sweet-scented medley, adorned the lawn. Twin live oaks commanded the front yard; their century-old limbs kissed over the bricked pathway.

"This old bird has quite a nest," Thump said as he pushed the circa 1940s doorbell.

Sara elbowed him in the ribs. Thinking it best to let him learn on his own, she hadn't briefed Thump as to Ms. Dorothy Jean's backstory.

Dorothy Jean's niece greeted them at the door.

"Mr. Sutton, Ms. Mendoza, welcome to my aunt Dorothy Jean's home. I'm Clara, her niece. I live in Reed City, but I'm over here a lot to check on things. Y'all come on in. Listen to me just a gabbing away while y'all stand here and starve half to death. How rude of me."

"Not at all," replied Sara, "thanks for having us."

"Y'all come on in here, Coach," Dorothy Jean yelled from her dining room.

Clara led them into the dining room.

"Well, hello, Ms. Dorothy Jean, thank you for having us," Thump said.

"My pleasure, Coach, my pleasure. And I see Ms. Mendoza accepted my invitation. You two make a beautiful couple. Now, come on in and y'all sit down. Lupe has already set the table. Lupe has been with me 46 years. She raised her three boys right here in this house. One is a major general in the army, one is a lawyer in San Antonio, and the other is a vice president in charge of exploration with Exxon. Lupe is like a daughter to me."

Lupe smiled and showed the guests to their chairs, then offered the blessing for the meal she had prepared. Upon his first taste, Thump concurred with the heralded reputation of Dorothy Jean's soup. With the small talk making its way around the table for several minutes, Dorothy Jean looked intently at Thump.

"Coach, I understand that there is someone giving you a problem up at the schoolhouse. Is there any truth to that?" Dorothy Jean said.

"No, ma'am. Things are going great. Everybody is very supportive."

Dorothy Jean pulled the embroidered napkin together into a bunch on the table, her index finger tapped the tablecloth.

"Now, Coach. You are in my home. Please. I may be old, but I am not feeble-minded. Please do not treat me as if I am. I know everything that goes on in this town."

Sara looked at Thump. Thump looked at Sara.

"Don't you look at that young person when I'm talking to you, Coach Sutton. I asked you a direct question, and I want an honest answer. Not much means more to me right now than our football team. Did I tell you that I was the head cheerleader when we won state? I'm sure that you know that year was 1964, and that same year was our last district championship." She rapped the table forcefully, emphasizing her words.

"Yes, ma'am."

"Now, let us start over. I have received information that there is someone up at that school administration building causing a problem for our boys. And is it not your job to see to it that they take care of your boys? What kind of coach would you be to let one individual interfere with the job you have in front of you? And I just don't think that you are the type to allow that."

"No, ma'am. I just—"

"Stop right there. Coach Sutton, I brought you here tonight for two reasons. First, I have a gift of seeing people for who they are, and you are special. Second, some people in this town think they can slide things by me without my knowing about it. And this faction is out to destroy what has made this town what it is.

"Hurricanes come and go. Coaches come and go. Kids graduate and move on. But it's the football team that we rally around. They haven't won much, and for the people in this town who love them, they don't have to win a lot. Not to say that I'm not sick and tired of these shiftless, back-of-the-bus, so-called coaches they have brought in here in years past; I am. Not to say that I'm not sick of going to church on Sunday and hearing about the beatings our boys took on Friday; I am.

"Do you know what used to be the nickname for our stadium? Blood Reef. Because if you played the Barracudas, we would spill your blood. Simply put, on Friday, our boys would murder the opposition."

"Yes, ma'am," Thump replied.

"So, what say you, Coach? Are you the coach who will change things or not?"

"Yes, ma'am."

Thump took a long breath.

"We have a problem at the administration building, but there is little that I can do about it. They have already written me up over some frivolous issue. And if the truth can be told here in this room, I have it on good authority that Dr. Tran didn't hire me to change the culture here. She hired me because my record—with me being an aged-out assistant coach—indicated that I would fail and provide the opportunity for the superintendent and board of trustees to disband the football program."

Dorothy Jean looked at Lupe and said, "Didn't I tell you, Lupe?"

"Yes, you did, Ms. Dorothy. Yes, you told me."

Clara stood and said, "Would anyone like some fresh lemon pie?"

Dorothy Jean smiled and said, "Absolutely, Clara. What a wonderful idea. Clara's husband grows his own lemons in the backyard. I promise you have tasted nothing like Clara's lemon meringue pie.

"Coach, I need to know exactly what needs to be in place for you to be successful. You have the scrimmage against those people from San Antonio, then you need to get ready for the South Cleburne scrimmage. After that, you kick off versus Fort Comanche at their place. What do we need to have in place to right this ship and make sure there is no more meddling in your business at hand, which is to return dignity and respect to this town?"

"Well, we need to practice on the soccer field. It's the only suitable surface outside of the game field," Thump replied.

"You stay off that game field until late November in the playoffs. I put $10,000 a year into that field to make it the class of the Texas Gulf Coast."

Clara returned with a silver platter with five dessert plates.

"Help yourself, everyone," Clara said with a smile.

Dorothy Jean said, "All right, we need you back on that soccer field come Tuesday at the latest. Now, what else?"

"I feel Dr. Tran saddled me with an extra history class to force me out of a junior-high athletic period and undermine our growth. We are understaffed as it is. If I try to maintain a presence at the junior high and teach the academic load handed me, the schedule will run me ragged before mid-season. The program will suffer."

"Are the other head football coaches on your schedule required to teach the same number of classes that you are assigned?"

"No, ma'am. Most head coaches teach maybe one academic class, sometimes none, especially during the season."

Dorothy Jean cut her eyes to Lupe, then looked over to Clara, and smiled.

"I also understand that you have some players who have moved in who are difference makers, those two boys at Camp Promise, the brothers from Dallas. Are you having any difficulties with their paperwork or eligibility coming from over there at that administration building?" Dorothy Jean asked.

"No, ma'am, not that I know of."

Dorothy Jean and Lupe laughed together. "Not that he knows of," Dorothy Jean said to Lupe.

"Well, Coach Sutton, would you believe me if I said you will have major difficulties with those two boys' eligibility, let's say, the week before your first district game?" Dorothy Jean raised her eyebrows.

"You're kidding."

"Coach, let's just say that the bandits are poised to ambush you at the pass."

"I'm speechless." Under the table, his right hand trembled.

Thump and Sara sat silent as Dorothy Jean detailed Dr. Tran's plan to sabotage the eligibility status of T'Darian and Derek. And to make matters decidedly worse, she would wait until the week before the first district game to execute her scheme. That kind of action would ruin their chances of winning. Tran had taken out an insurance policy guaranteeing Thump's failure.

"Yes, my dear. She is smart and cunning. Lupe and I took notice of her back when she was in high school. Lupe's oldest son studied with her right here at this table. Something was just not right about that girl. She detested the football players. You know, that's not normal for a teenage girl in Texas."

Thump laughed. "No, ma'am, it isn't."

"Speaking of high school girls, I remember this one from her days in the 'Cuda Cage. That's what we called the gym back in my day. Do you know she holds the record for assists?" Dorothy Jean nodded to Sara.

"No, ma'am, she never told me." Thump replied.

"Well, I'm sure she has a lot to tell you that you may not know. And that is why we must adjourn for the evening. And, Coach, do you pray?"

"On fourth and one, yes, ma'am."

Dorothy Jean turned to Sara and said, "Oh, he is splendid with the repartee, isn't he? You better keep your eye on this youngster.

"Well, Coach Sutton, if you study that old Bible that I see you fumbling through at church, you will find numerous references to God hearing the prayer of the faithful. Proverbs 15:29 tells us that *the Lord is far from the wicked, but He hears the prayer of the righteous.* Are you a righteous man, Coach Sutton?"

"I like to think so, yes, ma'am."

"You think so? Heavenly day, you either are or you aren't, my dear Coach. You don't coach your boys to think they just might be good, do you? I hope not. I hope you teach them to believe."

"Yes, ma'am."

"My lovely Coach, to believe is to win. You either believe or you don't. You either win or you won't. Now, you listen to this old lady. I assure you that if you earnestly pray, God will remove all your obstacles. Prayer solves everything. You go now and have fun at your scrimmage with those Catholics tomorrow. I will see you in church on Sunday, the both of you. Clara will see you both out. Goodnight, my lovely Coach, and to you also, Miss Mendoza."

Walking to the car, Sara said, "Bet you didn't know you would get a Bible lesson with your soup."

"No, but I should have expected it. I walked right into that last one, didn't I?"

"You did indeed, my lovely Coach," Sara chuckled.

Sara took the keys for the drive back to her place. Pulling in next to Blue, she said, "I suppose I'll see you soon. I'm off this weekend."

Despite the reminder that she was free for the weekend, Thump felt a curious vibe. She was hiding something, but he had no time for whatever it was. Tomorrow would serve as the first benchmark of the program's progress. He squeezed her hand and pushed open the passenger door.

"Thanks for coming. I always like it when you come around," he said.

"Same, here. See you."

CHAPTER TWENTY-ONE

Friday's scrimmage kicked off at 3:30 p.m. Thump had pulled off a coup by getting the home scrimmage moved from Blood Reef to the neutral site in Victoria. His Barracudas weren't ready for a home-field unveiling. Besides, this arrangement meant the turf would remain untouched until the first home game.

Few things can get a struggling head football coach fired faster than the game field. Superintendents often expected to see an Augusta fairway on a city-park budget. While the turf at Blood Reef had Dorothy Jean as a significant benefactor, she was unaware how small a dent her $10,000 donation made in the annual field maintenance costs, and he wasn't about to enlighten her.

Rule number 10: Make every booster feel as if their donation is all you will ever need.

Thy Al Huynh-Maldonado volunteered to babysit Jenny at her house. Thy Al had grown fond of her since the Friday she and Jason dog-sat while Thump was at the police station.

A caravan of two yellowhounds and Jason's Tahoe packed with equipment would leave the fieldhouse at 1:34 p.m. sharp. Isaac and Harrison would follow in Isaac's Barracuda. If a serious emergency were to occur during the scrimmage, Isaac and Harrison would follow the ambulance to the hospital, where they would stay until the injured player's guardian arrived.

As the buses pulled onto the highway, the Port Verona Police Department's Charger appeared behind Isaac's Barracuda. Wanting it to be a surprise, Sara didn't tell Thump that the chief of police had scheduled her to follow the team to Victoria.

Upon their arrival at Victoria-Chavez's Freedom Stadium, the team would take part in two group meetings starting at 2:41 p.m. One would be a defensive meeting led by Dirk Mason, the other for offense, with Miguel Herrera. The Barracudas would take the field at 3:00 p.m.

Thump had ordered the team to dress in their plain practice jerseys with no identifying numbers. He would allow no displays of individualism. The opposing coaches would identify T'Darian, Derek, and the soccer boys without the numbers on their jerseys soon enough.

The word was out that something was happening in Port Verona. For the first time in anyone's memory, a rival head coach and his staff sat in the stands to scout the scrimmage. In attendance was Coach J. P. Duhon, the most despised man in Texas Interscholastic League District 13-AAA.

People said Duhon was as crazy as he was mean. As a kid, he'd used his uncle's shotgun to shoot off his left index finger on a dare. Duhon earned a legacy as the most maniacal player ever to take the field in a Louisiana State University (LSU) uniform. Though never a defensive starter, he'd specialized as a wedge breaker during his days at LSU.

Once, after hurling his body airborne to split a middle wedge set by five Mississippi State Bulldogs, he seat-rolled to his feet and clotheslined the kickoff returner. Standing over the Southeastern Conference's leading kickoff returner's unconscious form, he raised his arms as a gladiator before the crowd of 80,000. He then sprinted to the painted tiger's eye at the center of the field and executed a backflip.

The following Monday, a geosciences professor at LSU determined that the crowd's roar following Duhon's clothesline had registered as an earthquake on the seismograph at the Howe-Russell Geoscience Complex. ESPN enshrined the clothesline tackle as one of the top-10 moments in LSU football history.

Disciplined many times by the Texas Interscholastic League for his boorish behavior toward game officials, the Nine-Finger Slinger would run the score up on his grandmother. Isaac said he had never seen Duhon scout a Barracuda team.

The first to go on offense, Thump's Barracudas would get 15 consecutive plays.

From near the offensive huddle, Miguel Herrera would call the plays from a script with allowances for consideration of the down-and-distance situation. Thump would stand behind the huddle with the rest of the staff while Grant Lee's wife videoed the scrimmage from the press box. Chelsea Davis had been a star volleyball player in college where she met Grant Lee. An experienced videographer, she had filmed Barracuda football for the last 10 years.

The game's umpire placed Port Verona's select ball, a Wilson 1001 engraved with the Barracuda logo, at their own 35-yard line. At 3:28 p.m., the white capped official blew the ball into play.

T'Darian stepped in front of the two-tiered huddle with the call, "East 7 Bear." The center sprinted to take a position over the ball as the two wide receivers, Jose and Carlos, ran to their spots left and right of the ball. T'Darian repeated the call, then broke the rest of the huddle. Luis, the fourth wide receiver, was the "7" designation. He aligned 1 yard outside of the left tackle, 1 yard deep in the spot known as the tight slot. From the pistol backfield set, Derek aligned two yards behind T'Darian who stood behind the center four yards deep in the backfield.

Once T'Darian checked both receivers and Derek's readiness, he barked the count, "Down! Hut! Hut!" and the center snapped the ball shotgun-style to T'Darian. Derek, his eyes on the outside hip of the tight end, burst forward while making a big pocket, his inside elbow high with the thumb of his left hand pointing into his chest.

T'Darian reversed-out to his right and placed the ball into the pocket, then rounded back to the left, faking the bootleg. The Barracuda line got a big push at the point of attack as Derek squared his shoulders to get north and south behind the surge. He was about to squirt into the secondary when a Macedonia Catholic strong safety slashed in to tackle him across his thighs. East 7 Bear was a five-yard gain. Against one of the strongest defenses of the Texas private-school league, the first play of the Sutton reign made a positive gain. Sticking to the script, Miguel mixed the outside zone with a bootleg and three quick passes.

After guiding the offense to a first-and-ten at the Fighting Bishops' 21-yard line, T'Darian called the team to the line. With the tight end split left, the Barracuda offense would operate from the five-wide receiver set. Derek set to the left of T'Darian.

Thump surveyed the secondary alignment. Macedonia-Catholic had tightened their coverage into a bump-and-run look with no free safety help. This alerted T'Darian to the possibility that the Fighting Bishops were sending pressure on the snap. Thump signaled T'Darian to read the wide side of the field.

T'Darian nodded and tapped his fists together. Out wide to the right, both Luis and Carlos read the audible to run double go-routes. To negate the Macedonia Catholic blitz and exploit their press coverage, T'Darian would grip-and-rip a deep pass to Carlos on the fade route.

Aimed at the back corner of the endzone, the ball arced downward into Carlos's outstretched hands for the season's first touchdown pass. T'Darian and Derek leaped in a celebratory hip bump. Jose and Luis ran to Carlos to congratulate him. Simultaneous to the celebration, Coach Harrison Dye heaped praise on his offensive linemen. Though wanting to burst into tears of joy, Thump displayed no emotion. The Barracuda offense still had four plays left in the series.

Thump directed the coaches to riverside the huddle and scolded the offense.

"This isn't the time to celebrate," he said. "Time to bear down and focus." With four plays in the sequence left, Miguel broke the script to go empty in the backfield.

Thump whispered to T'Darian. He should read the two-deep safety on the left side of the field. Thump knew Macedonia Catholic would expect the 'Cudas to run out the series on the ground. He had to teach his team to smell blood and go for the kill. For so many years, they had been the ones fed on.

To be satisfied is to lose, Ed Hattaway would say.

Miguel called L8 Slot 171 Hash.

As instructed, T'Darian read the two-deep safety weave outside the left hash to cover Jose's corner route. Adjusting his line of sight to target Derek racing wide open down the hash marks, T'Darian unleashed a bomb. Sixty yards downfield, Derek stretched for the ball and stumbled into a parallel layout. The official confirmed a fingertip catch at the Macedonia Catholic 13-yard line.

According to the scrimmage rules, the catch earned Port Verona a four-play possession at that spot, but the Barracudas wouldn't need them. Derek blasted through the shell-shocked Bishops' defense.

The offensive series ended. Because of the heat index and the high number of two-way players on both teams, a 20-minute intermission preceded the Barracudas' on defense.

Coach Mason and his boys were in for a bare-knuckled street fight. This was only a scrimmage; the scoreboard wasn't even lit. Port Verona's two scores were irrelevant to the Macedonia Catholic coaches. In its tight dead-T set, Macedonia Catholic's offensive formation spanned less than 7 yards in width. The Fighting Bishops' offensive line stood shoe to shoe.

With each snap, a green tsunami crashed into the Barracuda front. Thump marveled at the Macedonia coaches' patience and their players' mental toughness as they battered the Barracuda front seven with double-teams and triple-teams at the point of attack. Marching downfield in the manner of a Greek phalanx, the Bishops used all 15 of their plays, plus three more to cap off the drive with a quarterback sneak that plowed under the Barracuda interior front. It was smash-mouth football.

Grant Lee seethed. He had implored Thump to allow Dirk to stack the free safety behind Valentino Rejas, but Thump wouldn't budge. Thump wanted to stay in the base defense and let the boys fight it out on their own, but he doubted the Barracudas could match Macedonia Catholic in the physicality department. Few teams rivaled the Fighting Bishops between the tackles. They didn't average 10 wins a season by playing powder puff.

The scrimmage concluded after another two rounds of 12 plays for each cycle. The younger players and the Thursday night junior varsity players (JV Joes) wanted their chance for some playing time. Thump guaranteed they got it. One thing a head coach did not want after a scrimmage was an angry parent in his office the following morning. Nothing turns a football mom against a coach faster than her JV Joe not getting to play after she took off work early to make the game.

Rule number 11: Never hand them a stick with which to hit you over the head.

Both teams met at midfield for post-game fellowship. Watching the teams interact after the game, Thump remembered meeting some of his best friends in just such a setting. It was during the fellowship circle at midfield after the infamous nickname game when TCU's Tom Sutton first met Baylor's Rod Venson. One new friend, one mischievous sportswriter and 24 hours later, he was Thump Sutton.

After a few speeches to the team and a rousing cheer from the boys, Thump broke the squad and looked toward the stadium fence line to find Sara. Instead, he saw J. P. Duhon leaning on the chain-link fence, staring. Once Duhon saw Thump make eye contact, he turned his head and spit an amber stream of saliva. Most coaches would know better than to spit tobacco juice onto the sidewalk, but Duhon made a point of breaking the "no tobacco" regulation posted at every stadium he visited. It was his way of clotheslining the rules and sending a message.

Later, headed south through the coastal prairie, the yellowhound caravan of exhausted boys and sunbaked coaches lumbered toward the orange-tinted coastline. It had been a good first scrimmage, but Grant Lee Davis simmered over Thump's refusal to pack the box against the Macedonia Catholic's foot-to-foot rushing game.

Thump would let him stew. He understood Grant Lee. Once upon a time, he was Grant Lee. His pouting episodes were a side effect of the intensity he brought to the table; he would eventually get over it.

The inexperienced Dirk had his dauber down. Walloped all afternoon, the defense appeared impotent, but Thump knew better. The boys wrestled with one of the top small school rushing teams in the state. His defensive unit hadn't quit.

Thump's heart pitter-patted over the Barracudas' offensive production. After not showing Thump much during the preseason drills, Derek proved he was a Friday night player, the one whose talent burst forth on game night like a fireworks finale. Coupled with brother T'Darian's bazooka arm and the three soccer recruits, Derek would reinvent Port Verona football in a way no one could have predicted.

The team would have the weekend off for their parents to take advantage of the state's tax-free weekend to buy their school clothes. Thump suspected that the boys and coaches could use a rest.

Teacher in-service days started on Monday. Two full days of mindless faculty bonding exercises, multiple two-hour lectures on the ineffectiveness of a lecture, and monotonous, stale sermons on how high-interest student activities eliminate classroom boredom. On the field, the Barracudas would move into the final phase of the preseason, the afternoon practices. Although the schedule limited practices to just once a day from here on out, the afternoon temperature would be much hotter.

The buses' air brakes grabbed and hissed, bringing the caravan to a halt. A muddle of parents and fans cheered. Standing to address the varsity squad on bus number one, Thump heard his phone sound a familiar alert.

Checking his messages after dismissing the team, he read, "Please see me, 7:30 a.m., Monday."

Oh, great. What does she want now?

On Saturday evening, he and Sara would go on their third outing. Beforehand, he would spend a lazy afternoon with Jenny, then prep for what he called "Sara time."

"This time, maybe we can get through a date without delving into the Bible. Readings from Leviticus and Ecclesiastes don't exactly move the chains for me, Jenny."

Jenny tapped her tail in agreement. She was more than pleased that she would spend another evening with Jason and Thy. Just then, she woofed. She had heard Jason's Tahoe drive up.

While Jenny enjoyed her date, Thump and Sara would check out the new Tex-Mex restaurant in Reed City.

Maybe this time, she will let me drive the Cougar.

She didn't.

CHAPTER TWENTY-TWO

Because the Houston Texans had the week off, Rod attended church. He waved Thump over to sit next to him. Following the service, Thump stopped to visit with Dorothy Jean.

"I heard the boys put on a good show in Victoria, Coach. I expected that. I also expect you will get some improvement on the support down at the administration building. Now, you let me know if you don't."

"Yes, ma'am, I will."

"And where is your young friend, Miss Texas Basketball 1996?"

"The chief of police called her out on an emergency meeting with the Texas Rangers. She won't be back in town until late tonight."

"Well, you better take good care of that one. She's red-letter, you know."

"Yes, ma'am."

"I hear that big lummox, Rod Venson, calling you. You better go see him before he hurls a pickup truck at the both of us."

Thump laughed and said goodbye. He decided to skip Reverend Wallace's receiving line to catch up to Rod.

"What's up, Rod?"

"Bad stuff, my friend. Terrible stuff," Rod replied. "You need to be careful. One of my foremen told me that the *El Marineras* put out a contract on your girlfriend. They declared war on all Tiburon County law enforcement over the heat they've been getting from that deputy's kidnapping. Yeah, and I heard you were on the list. You and your girlfriend better keep an eye peeled."

"Okay, thanks." Thump pushed his hand through his hair. He wasn't sure what to make of Rod's information pipeline. At Tallulah College with no cable and limited radio reception in their room, Rod would ruminate aloud for hours on the Kennedy and moon-landing conspiracy theories. Back then, as a young coach, Thump loved his roommate and fellow aspiring coach, but he thought Rod had a few loose wires. It appeared that somewhere in his cerebellum those loose wires still dangled. Still, he also felt Rod's loyalty rivaled Jenny's.

"Hey, I hear that Macedonia bunch opened up a can of whiplash on your defense. I would have thought you had toughened up those boys by now. Don't let me down, Thumper. I vouched for you, remember?"

"I got it," Thump said, not bothering to correct Rod's malapropism.

"Well, you'd better. You have just one more week until showtime! You better get them to play some 'D' before that little Vietnamese superintendent makes a *banh mi* out of your buns!"

"Okay, Rod, I have to go run. I haven't run in three days."

Rod lit a cigar, waved, and floored the gas pedal. In less than a minute, the massive black Ford disappeared down the highway.

He is such a sensitive soul.

Jason and Thy returned Jenny sometime around 2:00 p.m., and Thump decided they both needed a nap.

Once the sun sank low, they took a long run together. Thump showered and grilled them both a steak; his cooked medium while Jenny preferred hers rare. After dinner, he sat down to read *Finding the Winning Edge* by the late Bill Walsh and others. The book was a classic within the coaching community.

At 9:37 p.m., Sara texted him: I'M OFF TOMORROW. WHY DON'T YOU COME OVER?

He replied that he and Jenny would be at her place in 20 minutes.

For the first time, they planned to enjoy a secluded romantic evening. Sara opened the windows and turned down the lights.

Cuddled on the couch, they spoke little. In the cottage's stillness, Thump nodded off.

After midnight arrived too soon. Jenny licked Thump's forearm and he awakened.

Sara's face pressed against his cheek. For the first time, his lips touched hers. It was a moment that seemed to just hang in time. Her kiss felt soft and warm like a peach fresh from a Hill Country roadside stand.

Thump felt an overpowering awareness that he had known those lips for a hundred lifetimes.

She pressed her nose to his nose.

"You better get going," she said as she pushed him off the couch.

"Okay, I'll text you during teacher in-service tomorrow."

On the drive home, he replayed Rod's warning in his head and hugged Jenny tight.

Earlier in the week, Thump had stopped by the Taco Place to ask Maya if she could babysit Jenny at his bungalow on Monday and Tuesday. He told her he would double her pay at the Taco Place. So that she could make a few more dollars before school started on Wednesday, Maya's dad okayed her absence. Thump felt relieved that Jenny would have a friend with whom to play.

The next morning, he left Maya her dog care instructions, then hurried over to the Cove for his 7:30 a.m. appointment with Dr. Tran.

Another long walk.

CHAPTER TWENTY-THREE

"Coach Sutton, I received some excellent feedback regarding your contest on Friday," Tran said. "Take a seat."

"Yes, ma'am."

"I've also consulted with my maintenance chief on your behalf and advocated for your usage of the soccer field. He consented on the condition you guarantee that your coaches will take care to do their individual drills outside the boundary we painted this weekend."

"Thank you."

"Also, I've spoken with Principal Saltzman about your teaching schedule. He feels he would prefer a full-time history teacher, one who is dual credit certified, to take that spot. We hired a local retiree to fill that vacancy until he finds a suitable candidate. Your only duty inside the building will be to monitor the lunches for the junior high and high school and help during the large recess over at East Bay Elementary. Vice Principal Thy Tran-Maldonado will get with you on the specifics regarding your assignment there."

"Yes, ma'am."

She held a compact mirror to her face and ran her finger along her pencil-thin eyebrows.

"I hope these new arrangements aren't too much trouble for you," she said.

"No, ma'am, they aren't. I'm a team player."

"Yes, it seems you are. Now, let us both get to the convocation. And don't forget I want you and I to go out together one weekend to get to know each other better. I hear there is a new Tex-Mex restaurant in Reed City. Have you been there?" she asked.

He smiled. "No, ma'am, I haven't."

"Well, good, let's schedule a dinner date this upcoming Saturday at 7:00 p.m. I will pick you up at your place. To be productive, we need to get to know each other from a personal perspective. We play for the same team."

"Okay, 7:00 p.m., it is."

"And Coach Sutton, don't forget: On Saturday, I'm Diane, not Dr. Tran."

"Yes, ma'am, see you then."

Having been a coordinator in the largest classification in Texas, Thump was familiar with the zero-class-load that most head football coaches enjoyed. Still, the "no classes" was a shock. One snap from the queen and his teaching schedule had gone from multiple preps in a heavy load to no academic classes.

Not believing that dual-credit hogwash Tran offered—but not upset at the outcome—he let the sleeping dog lie. He would miss being in the classroom to a degree; he loved history and wanted to maintain his finger on the pulse of the non-athletes and minor sport participants.

But the ugly truth of his job? His future employment depended on one thing: winning football games. Teaching history or running a fair athletic program wouldn't keep him employed. Despite Dr. Tran's subversive aim, the townsfolk expected him to change the culture and fill the seats at Blood Reef. Thump figured he should call Dorothy Jean and thank her before the next scrimmage. She had left her fingerprints at the crime scene. No one else could have overpowered Tran.

CHAPTER TWENTY-FOUR

Even though the teacher in-service days were little more than a summer break reunion for the old hands, Thump got a charge out of meeting the newest to the profession, the baby teachers. Their fresh mannerisms were almost enough to spark some old dogs to speak with excitement during the elbow partner sessions.

The phrase "elbow partner" tickled Thump. As a young coach, his ideal elbow partner was a tall, blonde cougar at the Houston Galleria's El Presidente Hotel bar.

Dorothy Jean had been right about prayer. After several fretful days of checking his mailbox, he'd found Jenny's official service-dog certificate and uniform kit from Austin. The state of Texas had accepted Jenny as a registered service dog with the right to enter any facility protected by the United States Constitution. It was a great day. Jenny would never have to leave his side, not even at an opponent's football stadium. For J. P. Duhon, Thump had prepared his own clothesline tackle.

By Wednesday's practice, the mercurial Grant Lee had put his pout to bed and was ready to help direct the scrimmage against the South Cleburne Bumble Bees. In front of the staff war room's whiteboard, Grant Lee and the rest listened as Jason Maldonado submitted his report on the Bees. While a scouting report on a scrimmage opponent was unusual, Thump felt the staff needed a dry run.

After distributing copies of the five-page packet around the room, the young scout began his presentation.

"Due to their declining enrollment and lack of support within the administration building, South Cleburne is a mediocre 4A program. Coached by Hound Dog Slusher, a former Nebraska fullback of the Tom Osborne era, the Bees reigned as 3A regional champions five years ago. They have talented skill personnel that fit well in the traditional I-formation attack and the Arkansas Monster. Hound Dog and his staff expect better things after three consecutive losing seasons."

Thump interrupted, "I wonder if South Cleburne thinks we should expect better things after 32 consecutive losing seasons?"

The staff enjoyed a good laugh. Jason continued.

"They have a small quarterback adept at running the belly option and the boot. Their favorite plays are the weakside isolation and the strongside power, followed by the toss sweep to both sides. The fullback hits the trap with speed and power; he is a big boy. They have a prospect at tight end and a tall, skinny basketball player out at the split end. They like to just throw him the ball high and let him out jump the defensive back. That could be a problem for Luis at the corner.

"Up front, they run the old Arkansas-50 with an inverted safety aligned to their defensive declaration. They may invert to the side of our tight end or they may invert to the side of our backfield strength. It's a crap shoot trying to guess where they will set their monster, but if we can decode their monster declaration, we will exploit their alignment."

"Jason, an excellent scouting report. You take good care of my dog, and you always come through on my crazy scavenger hunts for equipment. Plus, you're the ice-man. You deserve a raise."

"Thank you, Coach."

"We knew they would drag around today with it being the first day of school," Thump said to the group. "We need to get the pep back in their step tomorrow with a light team period and specialty run-through. Grant Lee, I'm counting on you to use your mojo and get them pumped. This is the final rehearsal before the curtain rises for the premier next week. Jason, make sure you pack everything. Last week, we needed three mouthpieces and a girdle. You know how absentminded those kids are."

"Got it, Coach."

Thump dismissed the staff early. Because Maya was at school, he left Jenny at the local groomer. It cost a small fortune, and he could see the arrangement perplexed Jenny, but at least she got a nice warm bath and a fluff. Tomorrow, with her identifying red and black harness, she would ride to work with Thump. The only doorway Jenny wouldn't darken was Nguyen's Bait Shop and Store.

It was a new world for the two of them. Jenny could hang out in his office with her toys and her bed. He could work in his oversized chair, listen to news radio, and break down video. Whatever the outcome, he would enjoy the season.

Thursday after the evening news, he was to meet Sara at Nguyen's. She recommended they meet there at 8:00 for a *banh mi*—the split bread sandwich which Rod had implied was to become of his buns, should he not keep his head on a swivel regarding Dr. Tran's long-range plan.

CHAPTER TWENTY-FIVE

Thump arrived early at Nguyen's and sat at one of the round two-seater tables near the cooler as the Charger skidded to a stop at the front of the bait shop.

Sara, in her police blue with the gold-trimmed silver badge, broadcast a sense of reverence. Confidence embraced her presence. Thump noticed every head turn at her approach. MacArthur had just landed in the Philippines. She pulled a chair out.

"Fancy meeting you here," she said.

"You come here often, Officer?"

"Only for the last 16 years. What about you?" she asked.

"I've been here twice. I'm new in town, remember?"

"Where's your other half? I hear you now have an official bodyguard."

"I'm not sure the matron of this establishment appreciates the rights guaranteed under the Americans with Disabilities Act," he said.

Raising her eyebrows, Sara replied, "Nice catch. You're right. Besides, I don't think a dog in the dining area would be great for business. In the kitchen, maybe."

Thump thrust his hands up in the manner of a school crossing guard.

"Whoa. I hope no one heard you say that. You could get 'canceled.' The kids at school would say that you aren't woke."

"That's how we cops are; we like to live on the edge. Besides, it's our job to be callous."

He stared at her with a stunned look.

She laughed. "Just kidding, silly. I'm just messing with you. You know I'm not like that. I've been eating here since before I was in high school. I love everyone except the criminals. So how are we looking for tomorrow night?"

"I'm more than ready for tomorrow night. It's Saturday night I'm not ready for," he said.

"What's happening Saturday night that doesn't involve me?"

Thump raised his finger and retrieved their order from the counter, then returned to the small two-chair table.

"You want a cold Dr. Pepper? It's God's nectar," he said.

"I thought you said it was the nectar of Texas."

"Where do you think God lives?"

He retrieved two sodas from the cooler and returned.

"Tell me, what is this thing on Saturday night you're not ready for?" she said.

"It's hard to say. It's hard to even get my arms around it."

"Okay, what is it?"

"Dr. Tran is taking me out to dinner."

She raised her napkin to her mouth and feigned a cough.

"Not *Las Amigas*? You and Cruella De Vil? Oh my gosh, she wants you! What are you going to do? I bet you a hundred dollars right now that she will want to take you back to her palace. Have you seen her house? It has white marble floors, a heated pool, a sauna, and a hot tub. Oh, my gosh! Tran wants you as her newest Dalmatian puppy!"

"Quiet down. No way," he replied.

"Oh, yeah. She did the same thing to the last coach. Charmed him and ruined his marriage. Then she fired him a year later. He was a weed before the scythe. And they say she seduced the previous high school principal and another coach from five years ago."

"You're kidding."

"Ask Isaac Sewell if you don't believe me. He knows. So does Harrison Dye."

"Okay, all of a sudden I'm not hungry."

"Now, who is the one who isn't woke? Although, she's an attractive, wealthy woman. Who knows, maybe she'll take care of you if you show you have what it takes. Just let me know if you go there. I don't do the triangle scene. You can appreciate that, right?"

"Shut up, you know I'm not going there."

Sara smirked and wrapped what remained of her sandwich in a napkin.

"I hope you're not. Anyway, I need to get back to work. Make sure you order the number three at *Las Amigas*. I hear it won't make you feel stuffed, just in case you do something physical afterward, such as bowl in Reed City or skinny dip in a rich lady's pool. Call me later if you aren't too tired. I'll see you tomorrow. I'm escorting the team."

She winked, then kissed her index finger and tapped him on the tip of his nose.

"Thanks," he said. "I like you being there."

"Me, too, Coach. Me, too."

After she stopped by each table to say goodbye to everyone in the store, she waved to Thump and hurried out to the Charger.

Thump retrieved another Dr. Pepper.

CHAPTER TWENTY-SIX

On Friday, Thump received the itinerary via email from the South Cleburne athletic secretary. The junior varsity would scrimmage first, but tonight belonged to the big boys.

Over at the junior high, the windows filled with faces that strained to catch a glimpse of the players.

Sara activated her lightbar, and the Charger's siren sounded its staccato whoop-whoop. At 4:01, she blocked off the north loop so that the team buses could exit the alley from behind the stadium and turn west. After Coach Sewell's Barracuda made the turn, she gunned the Charger.

The boys gazed at the cruiser as it roared to the caravan's point position. Never had they been ushered with such pomp, but now under Thump's leadership, they felt as if they were celebrities. Valentino Rejas commented that even when his old school in Corpus Christi played for the class 6A state championship in Dallas, they didn't have a police escort to the game.

Thump recognized the look of pride in their eyes. He owed the police department and Dorothy Jean a huge debt for this one. Dorothy Jean had arranged the escort and paid for Sara's regular duty replacement and the cost of using the Charger. She was one old cheerleader who put her money where her pom-poms used to be.

Thump's eyes watered. His breath felt shallow. He swept his hair back from his forehead and decided it was too early to think about the game. Jenny lay on the seat on top of his leather bag, so Thump nudged her aside and reached inside the bag to pull out an old *Mad Magazine*. On the long bus trips, he carried a pillow, a sandwich, a small bag of Lays, a chilled Dr. Pepper, a frozen Hershey bar, a large pack of Juicy Fruit, two *Mad* Special Editions, and a *Sergeant Rock* comic. He would need every bit of those supplies to calm himself.

Later that evening in the scrimmage versus South Cleburne, everything went as expected, right down to the near fisticuffs between Grant Lee and Hound Dog.

After the Bees completed a long pass near their sideline, the South Cleburne boys taunted Luis. Soon, their comments escalated into xenophobic insults, and Luis told Grant Lee about the taunts.

During the break, Grant Lee confronted Hound Dog.

Across the field, Thump filled a cup of water from the cooler as the South Cleburne sideline exploded into a mass of bodies pushing toward Grant Lee and Hound Dog. By the time Thump got to the altercation, Sara had pushed Grant Lee back toward the Port Verona sidelines.

Hound Dog followed Sara and wouldn't stop howling about Grant Lee being a hothead. Three years prior, a similar incident between the two foes sparked a near riot at the regional track meet when the South Cleburne anchor leg of the 1600-meter relay shoved Grant Lee's runner off the track. The incident allowed Hazelnut High to edge Port Verona at the tape and cost Grant Lee a regional championship. After Grant Lee accused Hound Dog of coaching his kid to jostle Grant Lee's runner, deputies separated the two.

Sara's patience for juvenile banter expired, she ordered both coaches back to the sidelines before she had to "get more involved." From that point, the scrimmage intensified.

Weeks earlier, Thump had installed the goal line package that he called the SWAT unit. The name was Thump's homage to the old police show starring Robert Urich and Texas native Steve Forrest. In police lingo, SWAT stands for Special Weapons and Tactics. Like the SWAT team, players were handpicked for a special role. In the Port Verona edition, Valentino Rejas's alignment provided the armor. From the halfback spot, Valentino served as a locomotive with a rocket engine. It was a devastating concept, and Thump wanted to see how the SWAT power play would look against a live opponent. The heightened intensity of the moment provided the perfect medium for a trial test of the SWAT unit.

It was Port Verona's final turn on offense from the South Cleburne 35-yard line when Thump ordered the SWAT unit assembled on the field. The coaches echoed the call.

A chant started along the sideline.

"Tino! Tino! Tino!"

Jason signaled to T'Darian, "Over, North 5, Packer."

T'Darian broke the SWAT huddle as the chant from the Barracuda sideline grew louder.

"Tino! Tino! Tino!" the crowd joined in the chant.

Four yards deep in the backfield, T'Darian barked the cadence.

In the way a cowboy crushes his beer can after it surrenders its last drop, the Barracuda line crushed the Bees. Valentino rumbled toward the defensive end. T'Darian reversed out and handed the ball to Derek as he slashed right toward his aiming point—the inside leg of tight end Reynaldo Gallegos.

Tino's hips sank as his upper body snapped; his feet churned through the contact. It was one of the most brutal blocks Thump had seen during his coaching career. The South Cleburne kid's arms opened out like a condor's wings. Valentino landed on top of him as the back of the defender's head bounced on the turf.

Derek hit the hole on a dead run and lowered his shoulder into the strong safety, then spun to the inside and ran headfirst into the last defender. Once Derek got rolling, it was as if he had transformed into a faster, lighter Valentino. He mowed down the free safety and broke free for the endzone.

Thump pumped his fist and smiled. Isaac and Harrison hugged each other while Grant Lee ran back and forth, jumping like a cheerleader. The rest of the boys rushed the field.

The Port Verona fans stood and chanted, "Tino! Tino! Tino!"

Hound Dog waved at Thump from across the field. No need to shake hands.

*Not a proble*m, Thump thought.

The boys had played a clean, hard-fought scrimmage. Thump knew that sometimes, it's better sportsmanship just to move on. He told Grant Lee to gather the team and motioned to Sara. The sun had set over an hour ago and Thump's weather app had alerted him to a storm moving north toward Port Verona.

The rhythm of the windshield wipers swishing back and forth in the light rain encouraged Thump to close his eyes and listen to the boys' laughter. The two-and-a-half-hour ride of joyful fulfillment would defy the dreariness of the approaching storm.

The sky rumbled. When he was a kid, Rose told him thunder was God and Gabriel bowling. The massive thunderheads instilled Thump with a childlike awe.

God sure loves to bowl on the Texas Gulf Coast, thought Thump.

The following afternoon, Thump's legs throbbed. His hips ached. The stress of the scrimmage, the long film study and game planning for the home opener had sapped him. If Sara told the truth, he would need to be sharp for his business date with Dr. Tran. He also needed to frame his strategy for the evening.

Underneath the fan alongside Jenny, he sent a text to Tran informing her that he would prefer to meet her at her place for a drink before going out to eat in Reed City.

She replied, "CAN'T WAIT!" with a wink emoji.

Sara had told the truth.

Jenny tapped her tail. Together, they drifted off.

CHAPTER TWENTY-SEVEN

Four miles north of Port Verona, an asphalt driveway snakes toward the white colonnade of a two-story white brick home, a contemporary colonial overlooking a retired rice field. Blue creaked halfway around its circle drive then wheezed to a halt.

Dr. Tran opened the front door and motioned for Thump to pull around to her garage in back, then she disappeared into the house.

He parked behind the third bay. By the time he had pushed open the rusty driver's door, she had reappeared and motioned for him to come in.

The kitchen resembled those from the home lifestyle shows that Ten-Months-In-San Antonio loved. Dr. Tran hovered near a white marble island and poured wine into two cabernet glasses.

"Tom, I'm so glad to see you. How was your game last night?"

"Thanks. It was just a scrimmage, but it went well."

"I'm thrilled to hear that. How about this weather we've been having? I enjoy the rain, don't you?"

"It's okay as long as I'm not standing on the sideline in a cotton shirt and Dockers. But, I like the smell of an oncoming storm."

"So do I. My, don't you look dapper. Here, drink a glass of wine. We have a few minutes before we need to leave. Let's sit on the couch. Do you like jazz?"

"I'm more of a Dr. Pepper man myself, but I can try a glass of wine."

An Ella Fitzgerald standard wafted through the residence. The ambience was just as Sara described. A white marble floor flowed throughout the main rooms. Large portraits of Vietnamese, recognizable by their conical leaf hats, hung on the wall along with photos of straw huts, beaches, and hillsides.

Thump pointed to the photo of the men in the field and said, "I've always wondered what you call those pointed straw hats."

"We call them *non la*. They not only protect us from tropical heat and rain, but women use them to carry vegetables or water. And they aren't just practical; they have a cultural significance. For example, young couples can hide their affections from prying eyes. Vietnamese are a modest people."

Thump nodded and smiled. For the first time since his arrival at her home, he made eye contact. He couldn't help but notice how attractive she appeared.

Maybe it's the wine, but this woman is gorgeous.

As if she knew what he was thinking, she smiled then asked, "Do you like my art?"

"You have some beautiful photos."

"I took those myself. I go back to Vietnam often. Did you know I was born there?"

"You said something like that at the Rotary breakfast."

"Funny, I give the same speech every year, but still I run across people who don't know. People don't listen so well, it seems."

"I suppose not."

"Tom, tell me, are you still running every morning? I admire a man who maintains his health and fitness. It shows a tremendous amount of self-discipline and commitment."

"I run almost every day because of my dog. She is part-Irish Setter. They love to run. The other part of her is Black Lab, so she also loves to swim." He walked around the room studying the photos. "You have a lot of talent, Diane."

"Why thank you, Tom. Very few people know that I'm into photography. I like to think my portraits capture a consciousness."

"They're fantastic. What about that one up near the balcony? That looks like an Army helicopter from the Vietnam War."

She laughed. "No, I didn't take that photo. I was just two years of age when someone photographed that helicopter over a village in South Vietnam. Since my doctoral focus was on that era of American history, I collected a few artifacts to display around the house. It's part of my heritage. Without the American soldier in Vietnam, I wouldn't be who I am today. That is part of what attracts me to you, what with you losing your brother over there. In that way, we have a unique bond, you and I."

She raised her glass to the helicopter photo.

"That is a Bell AH-1G Cobra, an attack helicopter introduced into the conflict in August, 1967."

"Wow, you know your history."

"See, we have a lot more in common than you thought."

"You think we should get going?" he asked.

"Yes! I'm famished. How about you?"

"I could eat a bite."

"Oh, Tom, you have such a dry sense of humor. I love that about you. Here, you take my keys. Vietnamese women validate their men. A Vietnamese woman would never drive when she is with a male companion of interest."

She stepped close to him and held the keys close to her cheek.

"You will learn much about me before the night is over."

After he opened the back door into the garage, Thump saw three vehicles: In the third bay, a gold Lexus; in the middle a black Suzuki GSXR 1000 motorcycle; and in the open stall nearest the door, a red Mercedes SL 550 convertible. Thump's face warmed, his pupils widened, and his skin tingled. She waited for him to open the passenger door. Closing her door, he ran his hand through his hair and walked around to get behind the wheel.

Once buckled in, he said, "Diane, is there anything I need to know?"

The driveway security lights created an aura about her face and hair as she spoke.

"We can put the top down after dinner. I want you to have some fun tonight. I've given you a hard time at work, but tonight we are two adults out to have a good time. Let's see what my baby can do. No worries, if you get a ticket, your little pretend girlfriend can just fix it for us."

Her comment backed Thump into a corner. He could say nothing.

As the red Mercedes sped north, the beat of a heart-thumping 1980s power ballad pumped through the surround system. The needle climbed to the 90-mph tic mark when Tran reached over and placed her hand on the top of his thigh. It was if his reckless speed turned her on. He could feel her long nails slide along the inside of his thigh as the lead singer moaned through the song's climax.

He prayed for a way out of the situation. He needed to construct a clandestine stopcock to stop Diane's amorous rush. Just south of Godsend, divine intervention arrived when he spotted the blinking light that warned drivers of the hairpin curve.

Rose had been right. This little town is a Godsend.

He let off the gas and slowed to a reasonable speed as the lead singer's pounding lyrics yielded to the bass guitarist's fade into the coda. Thump pressed the mute button.

"Enough of this noise, Diane. Let's talk more about your life. Once I sit down to eat, this hungry old ball coach may be an anchor on the conversation. We should start our dialogue now. I want to know more about you. For one, how do you look like you're 25 when I look 65? Do you realize that you look like a college coed visiting her sugar daddy for the weekend? Especially with me driving you around in a $100,000 sports car."

She pulled her hand back from his thigh and laughed. She flipped open her visor's illuminated vanity mirror, then used her fingers to smooth her hair.

In Texas, a good Tex-Mex menu fills the house. Just three weeks in business and the line at *Las Amigas* extended into the parking lot.

By the time Thump set the parking brake, Tran already had the manager on speaker phone. Not only was her table ready, the manager would meet them at the door.

As a *mariachi* band hovered about their serving area, Thump thought of Sara's advice. He decided she was right, even if for the wrong reason. He would order light.

Encouraging Thump to do the same, Tran ordered a frozen margarita with a double shot of *Dulce Vida* premium tequila for her appetizer. Using the excuse of being the designated driver, Thump audibled to a Dr. Pepper with an order of flour chips and white *queso*.

The drinks and Thump's appetizer were out in no time. After he took their requests from the dinner menu, the waiter signaled the *mariachi* band to the table. Tran had engineered the evening of every man's dream; the reception, the setting, the sports car, the perfect meal, and a beautiful partner with improper intent.

It was time to play defense. Once the band moved along, he set the front line in place.

"Diane, you are one of the most beautiful women I have ever seen in the school business. Why did you go that route? With your brains and looks, you could have done anything you wanted."

She sucked deeply from her straw.

"Tom, you're such a charmer. Why, nothing is more important than teaching. I came from nothing. When I came to this country, I felt sentenced to nihility. Sure, I had some relatives, but my family—my immediate family—were all dead. Before long, my memory of them faded to a point where I'm no longer positive what are real memories and what I contrive from my imagination. It's a terrible thing, not knowing. Thus, the act of gaining knowledge is my salve, my salvation. Learning has consumed my soul. I suppose there is nothing else I could ever do outside of teaching children the value of knowledge."

She took another deep draw from her margarita.

Thump felt his first down call went exactly as he had planned. Thirty years as a coach had taught him that when a play works, repeat the call.

"Is that what drives you to be the dynamic and focused woman that you are, losing your family?" he asked.

She clasped her hands; her eyes locked onto his.

"It's a loss I can't abrogate in my mind. I yearn to fill the void, but nothing can provide recompense for the anguish of being set adrift in life." She paused and looked away, then looked back to Thump and grinned. "But this margarita helps!"

Thump chuckled along with her laughter. She had knocked off at least half of the rita and was feeling the tequila.

The food arrived, and Thump motioned to the waiter.

"We'll have a second cold drink for me and another double for my lady, please."

She raised her glass and said, "To a coach who will go down in history!"

"Well, let's check out this food. It smells incredible."

By the time Thump was halfway through his stuffed jalapeno shrimp dish, she had knocked down the first drink and started on the second. Under the table, she removed one of her stiletto heels and had begun to caress his leg with her stocking foot.

Even though he knew he shouldn't, he enjoyed her playfulness. Her inebriation made her even more desirable. She had broken through the line and was running wild through his secondary. He needed a time out.

"Excuse me, Diane. I'll be right back."

"No problem, Tom." She grasped her straw and sucked down more of the icy lime-flavored drink.

In the men's room, he looked in the mirror and ran his hands through his hair.

She's tough. I need to get hold of myself.

He washed his hands, then pulled a towel from the dispenser.

The tequila is kicking her tail; I need to disguise my coverage and stick to the plan.

He looked at his watch; they had been at the restaurant a little over an hour. Returning to his seat, he noticed her margarita glass to be two-thirds empty. He sat to finish his third stuffed shrimp.

"Tell me about your rescue. I want to hear more about how you got to Port Verona and what happened then."

She put her hand on his.

"You are so tender and sweet. Okay, well, like I said, I was small. The enemy came to my village and killed everything. Every person, every animal. Some men from a nearby village found me in a scorched shelter. They said that they found me under my mother's body.

The men in our village had constructed A-frame bomb shelters. Two-thirds of the shelter was below ground. We were in one of those shelters."

"But you weren't being bombed by the Viet Cong. Why did the men build bomb shelters?"

"The Americans would sometimes mistake a village for a communist refuge of guerrilla warriors. It was common for the village men to build bomb shelters for the women and children who remained in the village. I don't believe the Viet Cong bombed my village, no. It was American artillery and bombs used to root out the VC from the villages."

She sucked on her straw and swallowed, then raised her finger as she spoke. "And the communists—the VC—would raid the villages if they suspected the villagers to be cooperating with the Americans."

"Wow. If I may ask, how did you come to be -"

She interrupted, "So financially independent? Thomas, when you come from nothing, you put a higher value on hard work and becoming something. I earned full scholarships for each of my three degrees. All the while, I worked and saved. In addition, I have a stake in a small shrimping fleet that also belongs to distant relatives of mine. And know this; shrimping is a tough way to live, but it is a lucrative venture when you keep worker costs low by using family and reinvesting your resources. Plus, I've been a high-level school administrator for over a decade. I travel overseas and all over the country to speak before large conferences, and I'm paid well.

Everything you saw tonight is mortgage free. I have no debt, only dividends. And," she tooted her hand as if it were a bugle, "don't tell anyone, but I am about to embark on my next journey in life."

"Retire? How? You're too young."

"I have 25 years in the system plus an immense portfolio. And you've already seen some of my assets."

"Yes, I see."

"Well, tonight I think that you need to see more," she said with raised eyebrows. Flashing the toothy smile that four premium tequila shots can ensure, she sucked down the last of her drink.

"How about dessert?" he asked.

"No, I have something for us at home."

She continued to slide her foot back and forth along the inside of his leg.

"How about this? I would love a *sopapilla*. Would you like one?" he asked.

"No, thank you. Too many carbs for me."

"Let's at least get one for the road. I'm sure you can handle another frozen rita." Thump waved to the waiter, then ordered a final round and a takeout box of *sopapillas* with honey.

It was third down. Maybe he could catch her napping with a blitz.

"Let's be real, Diane. You're a knockout. And I'm your basic shallow man who wants those same things other such men want. But the thing is, I've developed some feelings for you. I just don't want this to be one of those wild nights and nothing else."

"What are you saying, Tom? You're experiencing feelings for me?"

"Well, sort of, yeah. I mean, I am into powerful women, I suppose."

"Oh, like your little police cutie. I see now. I wondered what you saw in her. She's darling, but she isn't enough woman for you.

"Oh no, she isn't anything like you. But what worries me is I'm concerned a woman like you won't have much long-term use for a guy like me."

Diane sat motionless as she studied Thump's face. Her libido idled its motor for a moment.

From across the table, Thump saw her glassy eyes drift out of focus. Diane had downed one too many. She disposed of her straw and licked the glass's salted rim.

"I get it. You're alluding to those rumors."

"What rumors?" he asked.

"Don't you play coy with me, Thomas Udall Sutton," she said as she waved her finger. "I bet your little police cutie pie, Sara, told you all the lies. That I had an affair with your predecessor, and that other principal, and whoever else they imagined." She swirled the frozen slush with her finger. "Are you scared? Do you think I'm a big bad cougar out to eat you?"

"Okay. I heard some things, but I'm not a gossip. I believe nothing of what I hear and just half of what I see. Besides, you of all people know my past has more red flags than a bullfight. Why would I entertain anyone's judgment about another person's character?"

His words appeased her.

"Okay, after I kill this margarita, you can drive me home where I'll show you how we Vietnamese girls treat our men."

She downed the last four ounces of the margarita then waved and told the hostess to put the check on her tab.

Thump jingled the keys for the benefit of the hostess. "Don't worry, I'm the designated driver."

About a mile south of Godsend, Tran fell asleep with her head on Thump's shoulder. He eased the Mercedes into its garage bay and cut the motor as she nudged her face into his neck and mumbled. He understood her to say that the alarm disarmed through the car's security system.

Thump extricated his torso from her grasp, then exited the car and walked around to the passenger door. She clamped both of her arms around his neck. He couldn't help but notice that her physique resembled an athlete. Smooth, firm and lean.

She muttered something about her bedroom and pointed. Thump cradled her as he made his way to the bedroom. He planned to place her on the kingside bed and leave a note, but as he laid her on the bed, she pulled him on top of her and wrapped her legs around his hips.

With both her arms clutching his neck, she pulled his face close and kissed him.

Thump bench-pressed himself away from her body. It was fourth and short for his defense. He needed to make a goal line stand.

Then, in a peculiar tone of lucidity, she said, "Thomas, do you know the intoxicant that offers a type of mortal nirvana to the western male?"

His face was inches from her lips. She had locked her legs around his waist and used her taut arms to pull him downward to her face. He didn't answer. He just froze.

"Tom, you give up? You don't know?"

He felt as if he were going to black out. He was back in Mrs. Rachell's second grade class and she had ordered him to the chalkboard.

Tran laughed and released her grip. She fell backward into the plush bedding.

"Tom, you can't guess? Physical immortality for the western male is an Asian woman. In the Asian culture, we women possess the yin. It's our power, and it's endless. We nurture the yin by experiencing all of what the body offers. It's the only path to balance. You don't understand because you are Eurocentric in your views. Your women bind their yin with outdated Victorian mores and narrowmindedness. You know, you cannot achieve balance by ignoring the imbalance. Listen to your desire. Stay with me tonight, Thomas."

Thump's mind swirled in a vortex of wanton imagery. His willpower wavered.

You idiot, the Devil was the most beautiful, most eloquent angel in heaven.

Rose?

Who else? Get away from this monster, right now! This minute, run! If you stay here with her, she'll destroy us.

A minute passed in silence. Tran maintained her grip but had laid her head back on the pillows and closed her eyes.

As he freed his limbs from her pincer-like grasp, Thump said, "Diane, it's just not the right time. We'll have another. You sleep now.

I need some rest, too. Thank you for a beautiful evening. I had no idea that we could have so much fun together."

Her glassy and bloodshot eyes blinked. Her lips trembled as if she were about to cry. She rolled onto her side and sighed. It was the sigh Jenny made just before she fell asleep.

Thump turned back the far edge of the comforter and gathered his wits. From Dr. Tran's bedroom doorway, he looked back at her. Silent and still under the pastel duvet, she had fallen into a state of innocence.

He turned off the light and left her bedroom. Thump's defense had won the game with an epic goal line stand. Though he wouldn't be able assess the evening's damage for days, he felt good about the night. Driving home, he replayed the evening.

Underneath Dr. Tran's nastiness lies a lonely little girl who is still reliving the trauma of losing her family. Maybe after tonight, something special will happen.

He found Jenny pouting on the bed. *No problem,* Thump thought. If he had proven anything tonight, he proved that he knew how to handle a woman. Two of her favorite treats from the kitchen cupboard and she would grant him total forgiveness.

He was tired enough to go straight to bed, but he felt a little dirty after his bedroom wrestling match.

A high school friend of Thump's once had worked as a rodeo clown. He imagined that experience must have been something like his date with Diane. Running from the bull's horns all night had worn him to a frazzle. After taking a shower to wash away the psychological mud, he lay on his bed with a contented Jenny.

He searched his contacts for Sara and sent a text, "bow wow," with a puppy emoji.

She replied, "What are you doing home? You still have your spots?"

"Pick you up at 10:15, and this time I'm driving the Cougar."

She texted, "Just because you were with a cougar tonight doesn't mean you drive a Cougar tomorrow!"

A kiss emoji pinged onto his screen. He sent one back and closed his eyes.

Later that night, he dreamed he was a soldier in a South Vietnam village during the war. Friendly fire rained down on his position. He radioed the firebase to stop the bombardment, but he couldn't get through. Jenny yelped in the distance, and a small girl from a nearby burning hut cried. He tried to run to the girl, but he couldn't move. His feet felt as if they were being sucked into a pool of quicksand. Something warm streamed down his face. Then another blast knocked the radio from his hands.

Blood had begun to soak his uniform. He knew he had to get to his feet to save the little girl, but as he reached to pull his boots from the muck, he couldn't feel anything below his knees. Looking down, he saw a pool of blood and mangled tissue where his legs had been. He heard the screams of the little girl and Jenny's death shriek.

Jenny nudged him under the chin. Thump stroked her head and looked at his phone.

It was 8:11 a.m. His sweat had drenched the sheet. He kicked the covers off his body, rolled over, and pulled his grandmother's quilt over his head. Four minutes later, his phone's alarm sounded.

CHAPTER TWENTY-EIGHT

Reverend Wallace's sermon dragged, but that was okay with Thump. He liked the church scene. It zeroed his emotional pendulum. Dorothy Jean motioned Thump to meet her outside.

"So, I hear your youngsters had a nice scrimmage. But do you think we are ready for those Fort Comanche boys?"

"Thanks to your help, we're ready. At least we're a lot closer than we would have been without you," Thump replied.

"Why, Coach, what are you talking about? I am no more important nor influential than any other alumnus of Port Verona High School, and I cannot wait for Friday's game. Come kickoff, Clara, Lupe, and I will be right there on the 50-yard line."

"Thank you, Ms. Dorothy Jean. I hope we can live up to your expectations."

"My lovely Coach, it is not my expectations you need to worry about. There is a greater judge to whom you must answer. I will see you Friday night. Now, you two have a wonderful day of rest."

Dorothy Jean waved to another friend and then walked to her car where Lupe waited.

Sara brushed back her hair and whispered, "So, tell me, did you live up to expectations last night?"

He didn't know whether to frown or smile, but he knew he had better provide the right answer. "I believe I passed the test, if that is what you are asking, Officer."

"In what way? And whose test did you pass?"

Thump took her hands into his. He stopped to look her in the eyes, but she turned her face away.

"Whose test, Thomas?"

Thump kissed her on the forehead.

"Your test, I passed your test. It's the only test that I would take."

"I knew you wouldn't let me down."

"You did? Because I sensed a bit of doubt."

"Coach Sutton, a good police officer leaves no room for a reasonable doubt."

They would spend the day together, the three of them. Sara had prepared for a picnic at the park.

Even though she hadn't let him drive the Cougar that morning, it worked out to be a decent day. After nearly an hour of fetch, Jenny collapsed on Sara's blanket, the red squid between her paws. The late August sun sank beneath the edge of the bay.

Perched atop the picnic table, Sara leaned back and said, "Did you think you could love again?"

That's out of the blue, he thought.

Thump stalled for a chance to come up with the right answer. "What are you talking about?"

"Before, or after?" she asked.

Her riddle muddled his neurons. *This is going the wrong direction. What's she trying to ask? Rose, where are you?*

"Before or after what?" he asked.

"I think you know. Did you think you could love again before coming here? And did you think you could love again after your last divorce?" she said.

"You are way out of my zone of comprehension, Sergeant. So, tell me what's the deal with that Mercury? And since we are doing 20 questions, when do I get to drive it?"

"The Cougar?"

"Yeah, the Cougar."

"It's exclusive to this cougar," she said.

"Now, who has the bad puns? And besides, that's lame. You aren't old enough to be a cougar," he replied.

"Okay, well, what's the deal on that antique pickup truck you poke around town in?"

"It was my daddy's. My mama gave it to me when he passed away," he said.

"I like that you say it that way. That is so sweet."

"Say what which way?" he asked.

"I like that you still refer to your parents as your mama and daddy."

"Yeah, I'm a relic, that's why. What do you call your parents?"

"I called my mother 'Mother' and my father, 'Papi.' Mother died when I was still in elementary school. Papi passed away a few years ago from Alzheimer's."

"Wow, sorry to hear that."

"A drunk driver killed her and my baby brother just outside of Reed City. Their deaths devastated Papi. I don't think; no, I know he never recovered. He had a sadness about him right up to the day he died."

"No other brothers and sisters?" he asked.

"Nope. Just me. When I got older, he always used to tell me how I had her mannerisms. His eyes always lit up when he would say that. In junior high, I got into sports, basketball mainly. I wasn't too bad at it." She sighed. "Maybe, it was because I had a huge crush on my coach. I went to college and played basketball. That's where I met a guy. We were together through most of college. It was a kind of on-again, off-again relationship. After I graduated, he came down this way to live with me. A year after getting my degree, the regional law enforcement academy accepted me. He worked offshore and drank a lot. It ended up being not such a great time in my life."

"So, what happened to your boyfriend?"

"I don't know. He may be up around Huntsville now. I'm not sure."

"Why Huntsville?" he asked.

"He's doing 25-to-life for aggravated battery, plus another 10 for unauthorized use of an automobile," she said.

"Say what?"

"Yeah, one night when I was still in the academy, he came home drunk. I was asleep in bed, and he started ranting about something. The next thing I know, he was punching me. I ran out of the bedroom and got to the front door, but he caught me by my hair and dragged me back in the house. He grabbed a *Bois-D'arc* nightstick, the one Papi got as a retirement gift from his shift commander at the Department of Public Safety. Anyway, they say he beat me half to death with it. I don't remember any of it. Two weeks later, I woke up in a Houston hospital."

Thump looked at her in silence.

She continued, "Yeah, you see this smile you like so much? These four top teeth are porcelain crowns. Three of the bottom ones are implants. This hair through which you love to run your fingers? Check this out." Sara pulled back her hair and showed him a thin bare line that ran from her hairline to the back of her ear. She guided his finger along the scar. "A nine-hour brain surgery." She squeezed his hand. "I went back and graduated from the academy two years later."

For what seemed an hour, neither spoke.

Breaking the silence, she said, "So, the answer to the next question is?"

"What's the question? I don't get it."

"Before or after? Did I think I can love again?" she replied.

"Okay. I'll play. Tell me," he said.

"The answer is, I didn't think I could love again, before. And no, I don't know if I could ever love again, after."

"Before or after what? You're driving me crazy. I still don't get you," he said.

"You're a tad slow, aren't you, Coach? Did you guys at TCU not wear helmets when you played football?" Her eyes glistened with a mischievous look. "Race you!" She leaped to her feet and ran to the swing set, calling back to him, "I bet you can't run fast, either."

"You're right. You're too fast. You drive faster than I do, and you run faster, too."

He jogged to meet her as she plopped down on one of two chain swings suspended from a freshly painted support. She leaned back and kicked at the ground to push high.

In the next swing, Thump rocked back and forth in a nodding fashion.

"So, tell me the story on that rust-bucket truck of yours." Her voice danced in the rhythm of the creaking swing.

"I told you. My mother handed it down to me."

"Yeah, I get that. And?"

"Okay," he responded with a deep sigh. "And that rust-bucket truck is all I have left of my family. They killed my brother on his second tour in Vietnam. Mama always said he went back because he had a death wish, a darkness inside him. Daddy died in his sleep from a heart attack. Ten years later, Mama died of cancer. If you ask me, cigarettes killed them both. Not much else to say."

"How come you never mentioned your brother?"

"What's to mention? He came home after spending a year over there with the Marines. I was young, but I remember that Vietnam changed him. It was noticeable to everyone. In high school, he was a great athlete—a four-sport letterman. And he was a joker, the most popular guy in school. But after he came back, he just kept to himself. Before he went to Nam the first time, he used to throw me the football and we would play this game we called Punt Back."

"Punt Back—what's that?" she asked.

"It's a kind of football game in which you punt the ball back and forth, scoring points according to certain things, like if it went out of the endzone or if you caught the other player's punt on the fly—things like that. The object is to pin your opponent deep where he can't recover. He taught me to punt by playing that game. Now that I'm an old man, I think he might have been trying to teach me more than how to punt. Maybe, playing Punt Back was meant to teach me not to give up, no matter what life handed me. That lesson is why I'm still coaching.

But when he came back from that first tour, it was like something had broken him. He wanted nothing to do with me. He wanted nothing to do with anybody."

"Did you ever go see his name on The Wall?" she asked.

"The big one in Washington? No, but I visited the replica wall that travels around the country. It was a while back. I was coaching in Kerrville. They had it set up at the cemetery and I made a rubbing of his name, Brian Keith Sutton Jr."

"Brian, I like that," she said.

"You know, there was this mother at the cemetery that day. Her son, a helicopter pilot, died in action. She had a large-scale replica of the helicopter and everything together in a big display. I mean, this helicopter she had was maybe eight feet long. I think about her sometimes. Her face lit up when she talked about her son; yet, she seemed so sad at the same time. I don't know. That kind of stuff is why I'm not much into digging into my emotional closet, if you know what I mean."

She rolled her eyes.

"Oh, yeah, right. You're a big football coach, all tough and hard. Aren't you the one who treats his dog like an Irish princess? Not into sentimentality? Right."

She leaned back and pulled hard on the suspension chains. The swing peaked higher with each pendular period.

"Knock it off, Sarge."

He pulled his swing's two chains together and twisted them. He released the tension and spun like a top. He dragged his feet in the dirt to stop.

"Speaking of Jenny, I need to remind Jason and his wife not to feed her ice cream again."

Thump whistled to Jenny.

Sara replied, "Here with me, and you're thinking of your daughter. And that's why I don't enjoy dating single fathers; the best you can ever hope for is second chair."

CHAPTER TWENTY-NINE

Fort Comanche week dawned on the Barracudas.

The Warriors were on a long slide of seven straight losing seasons, and three head coaches in a row had lost their scalps trying to restore the winning tradition Fort Comanche once owned. The losing streak had begun after the Texas Department of Transportation built a loop just east of the Fort Comanche freeway exit. In no time, the enrollment dropped from a large 4A to a small 3A.

At Saturday's pregame meeting, Thump said, "I expect the Warriors to drop to 2A during the next reclassification, where they will probably return to the old days of dominance. Whoever is sitting in the head man's chair when that shoe drops will win, and likely win big."

Though that time hadn't yet arrived, the Warriors fielded a group of tough farm boys. "Not a lot of speed but good size" was the main point in the scouting report. In the staff meeting, Thump remarked that the Warriors were like a good breakfast taco without the green sauce. "Good, but just missing something."

Dr. Tran's last yin master had put them on the schedule for an easy win, but it hadn't worked as planned. Despite struggling with funding and low numbers, the Warriors had massacred the Barracudas the last two seasons. On Friday afternoon, the Warriors would step off their yellowhounds confident in their ability to stretch their current winning streak to three.

Jason's research on the latest Warrior chieftain, former NFL running back Orion Dixon, revealed him to be a conservative, defense-oriented guy content to allow his opponent to lose through their mistakes. Jason informed the staff that Fort Comanche would stuff the box in a 6-2 front and expand into a 4-4 look in passing situations.

Jason said, "They play a vanilla three-deep and never check out. Offensively, they operate from a power-I backfield with no tight end. Maximizing their full house running game is their ultimate objective. Their kicking game struggles in all aspects, but they're a threat to play the tricks."

By midweek, Thump had gained confidence in the boys' preparation and mindset. All week, he had emphasized to them that if you are a Barracuda, you are a member of the team everyone expects to beat.

In his Wednesday post-practice speech, Thump said, "Believing is the preamble to winning. Fort Comanche believes they will win this ball game. We need to strike hard and fast with no mercy to prove to them that their belief is unfounded. Then, and only then, we can go home to our moms, our dads, our families, and our friends different from when we left that morning. So, call before you get back to the house after the game on Friday because they might not recognize you. You won't be the same old football player; you won't be that loser from Port Verona. You'll be part of an undefeated Barracuda football squad. This Friday night you will return home a winner."

Thursday would be the first junior varsity game and the JV Joes played at the site opposite the varsity game venue. Isaac, Harrison, and the Herrera twins would accompany the junior varsity to Fort Comanche via yellowhound. Each Tuesday for the next eight weeks, Dirk and Grant Lee would assist Jason with the junior-high games.

Since their big date, Thump had neither seen nor heard from Dr. Tran. Not even an email. With it being the first home game, Thump thought the silence emanating from the administration office unusual.

CHAPTER THIRTY

W eeks had passed since the unknown perpetrators had kidnapped Deputy Bunch. Sara felt the community had already seemed to move past the incident. Even though law enforcement had located the suspect's vehicle, the investigation had fallen into a glacial chasm of federal indifference where it had iced over. So far, law enforcement knew someone had stolen the car out of Houston, but that was it. *El Marineras* wouldn't crack.

That Dr. Tran and *El Marineras* were out of the spotlight was fine by Thump, he had a game to win. For every program in Texas, the first game is the biggest game of the season, at least until the second. In his weekly Tuesday interview with the *Sentinel's* Rory Brendle, Thump tried to downplay its importance without dampening the community's excitement.

Game night finally had arrived at Blood Reef. High expectations filled the stands. During the pregame, Thump reconnoitered the stadium. As she had promised, Dorothy Jean sat at the 50-yard line between Lupe and Clara. Resplendent in Barracuda red, the Port Verona cheerleader-for-life wore a large, floppy, black straw hat banded with a broad white ribbon. In their Barracuda spirit t-shirts, Clara and Lupe held red and white pom-poms in their laps.

Scouring the sideline, Thump located Sara standing next to the Tiburon County Volunteer Fire Rescue unit. He remembered she had told him that the young part-time EMT had a crush on her.

No wonder. She looks as if she enjoys his attention.

But now wasn't the time for distractions. During his entire career, Thump had preached to the boys on the art of focusing on the task at hand. A high-school boy couldn't knock the snot out of the other high-school boy across from him if he spent the afternoon obsessing over his girlfriend standing a little too close to her science lab partner. And a head coach couldn't make the winning calls if a love interest's indiscretion preoccupied his thoughts.

After the national anthem, Victor Lucio and Carlos Castaneda stood at midfield as game captains. Once the coin landed on the thick Bermuda turf, the white-capped referee signaled Fort Comanche had won the toss and elected to take the ball. It was an old school decision in the current era of the second-half preference, but Thump understood the motivation.

By electing to take the ball, Coach Dixon chose the traditional route to send a message. Thump swiped his hand through his hair. A Fort Comanche opening score could siphon off the fragile confidence that Thump had instilled in his boys. In high school football, the team who scores first becomes the heavy favorite to win the game, especially if the opening score results from a time-consuming drive.

By the time Jose placed the ball on the round soccer-style tee, the packed house stood as one. Energy flowed through the stadium. It was the moment for which Tom Sutton had waited his entire life. Holding Jenny's leash tight, he watched the football explode from the tee and flip end-over-end to the waiting Warrior return man. Thump's time had arrived.

It wasn't long after Jose's kickoff that Thump's earlier concern proved valid. The home stands grew quieter with each snap as Fort Comanche marched downfield at the pace of a university alumni band.

After the Warriors' third consecutive advance of the chains, it was as if the sky had rained wet towels upon the home sidelines. The

Warriors burned a full five minutes off the clock before they topped off their drive with a successful two-point conversion. Directed toward Thump, a spattering of boos and jeers spilled from the stands.

The home fans cheered an impressive kickoff return by Carlos, then T'Darian and the offense jogged in from the sideline with the call. In Thump's opinion, an eight-point deficit was no time to be fancy. He suggested that Miguel keep the ball in Derek's hands.

From the tight end spread, T'Darian handed off to Derek on the zone play. Pressing the hole, Derek found little room behind Reynaldo, and instead of ducking under and pushing for a minor gain as he had practiced all preseason, he planted his inside foot and bounced to the edge.

Derek had tried to make something out of nothing, and the something which happens in that circumstance is usually bad. As Derek lowered his shoulder into the strong safety, the Warrior cornerback closed from the outside and punched the ball from his grasp. Derek reached in desperation for the tumbling ball, but the Fort Comanche free safety had filled the alley like a pro. Scooping the ball on the run, he sprinted unhindered for the score.

Back near midfield, Thump stood stunned, almost ill. Now up by 14, the small contingent of Comanche fans roared. No longer the 300 devotees from a dying Texas whistle-stop, they had morphed into the thousands of maroon-clad fans at Texas A&M's Kyle Field.

Meanwhile, the Barracuda fans sat back on their hands, looking as if the scoreboard had sentenced them to Huntsville's death row. Alone in her small pressbox suite and unnoticed by anyone, Dr. Diane Tran cupped her hands to her face and smiled.

After the fumble, Derek was inconsolable; he refused to go back in the game even on defense. Then later, just before halftime, Fort Comanche tacked on another score. As the teams went into the intermission, Thump pulled Isaac aside and asked him to fetch Pastor Mike.

Before going in the locker room to address the team, Thump attempted to soothe the staff's anxiety by telling them that they should expect trials when navigating an uncharted course. He reminded them that the bodies of lesser coaches littered the bottom of Port Verona Bay, and he reminded them that they were a stronger blend of sailors than those who had stood on the Barracuda sidelines before them.

They had a 6' 4" cannon on their deck. Down 20–0, the goal for the second half was to use T'Darian's gifts to push the game into overtime.

Just then, Coach Sewell returned with Pastor Mike. Thump asked the two of them to pull Derek aside. Thump told them to inform Derek of his intention to get the game to overtime, and that once they got there, he would put the game in Derek's hands.

Pastor Mike counseled Derek and admonished him for leaving the lineup. He implored Derek to strap on his spiritual armor and go back in the game when Thump called his number. Tears flowed as Derek nodded in agreement. Pastor Mike and Isaac hugged him tight and reassured him of their confidence in his ability. With halftime counting down to three minutes, the team filed out of the locker room with their arms interlocked.

From the front of the herd, Thump led them in their mantra, "One Team, One Heart, One Team, One Heart."

For Thump's Barracudas, Coach Dixon's exercise of his first-half option to receive was now a fortuitous decision. Port Verona would need the extra possession if they were to recover from the three-score deficit.

Back on the home sideline and ready for the kickoff, Thump looked up to confirm the press box crew were ready. Thump noticed Dorothy Jean and her cohort in their respective seats, but over half of the home crowd had dissipated.

The empty bleachers disappointed but didn't surprise Thump. Those beloved twin sisters, Faith and Hope, had left Port Verona years ago. Expectation relocated soon afterward.

Just before the team left the locker room, Thump had informed Derek of his disappointment regarding Derek's refusal to retake the field following the turnover. He told Derek that he would have to earn his return to the backfield through his effort on defense. What Derek didn't know was Thump had no immediate need for him on offense because they would run from the empty set for the remainder of the game. Derek wouldn't return to the backfield, at least until they had overcome the deficit and tied the score.

Senior backup Javier Castrejon replaced Derek. A middle-distance man on the track team, Javier was the district champion in the 800-meter run. He specialized on offense at the "slot" and "trips" position, the backfield alignment just outside the tackle. From that spot, he would release into the pass pattern to reduce the likelihood of defensive pressure.

Thump would turn T'Darian and the soccer boys loose. And Reynaldo's size out wide would make him the easy target for T'Darian to move the chains.

The strategy played out as Thump planned. Inspired by T'Darian's quick strike on a post corner to Carlos to notch their first score, Dirk's defense swarmed. Just as Thump predicted at the half, Fort Comanche deflated the ball, and stuck to their ground attack to run the clock.

Grant Lee adjusted his secondary by tightening their alignment to help corral the Comanche run game inside the tackles. Inside the box, Valentino demonstrated his prowess as a lateral force along the line of scrimmage.

With the clock wound down to the middle of the fourth quarter, the Warriors continued in their quest to grind out the clock, but T'Darian's arm and the five-wide passing game had reduced their lead to just six points. Another Port Verona touchdown plus the point-after would complete the dream comeback.

Just 35 yards away from the tying score, T'Darian hit Reynaldo for a 4-yard gain. But two downs and two deflected passes later, the Barracuda offense faced a fourth-and-six with less than four minutes to play. If Thump went for it, they would have time for a new series to shoot for the tying touchdown, even if the fourth-down conversion failed.

Then, from the headset, Roberto Herrera advised Thump that the ball placement at the middle of the field provided Jose with an excellent opportunity to make the field goal.

Thump thought, *Field goal? Not a chance. We're putting this one to bed.*

Ignoring the young coach, Thump decided they would go win the game, and after some extended contemplation of which play to call, Thump instructed Miquel to direct T'Darian to run the bootleg.

Miguel signaled, "9, Galveston," and the wide receivers hurried to get set.

T'Darian clapped his hands, and the Port Verona marching band fell silent.

Just before the snap, Grant Lee ran toward the field judge yelling, "Time out, time out."

The official stopped the action.

Thump's neck tightened; his face reddened. Before the game, he had warned the staff never to call a time out. Only he could call a time out. Grant Lee had overstepped his boundary at a critical moment. They had the element of surprise by going for the first down, but now the time out killed the opportunity.

Thump ran toward Grant Lee with his hands in the air.

"Coach Davis! What are you doing?"

Tugging at Thump's belt, Miguel said, "But coach, time was running out! We had only two seconds!"

The blood rushed from Thump's head. Miguel had been right. The system paired the bootleg with a "third hut" snap count. They wouldn't have gotten the ball snapped before the play clock would have expired. Thump bent at the waist to regain his senses as Grant Lee motioned the offense to the sideline to discuss the impending call.

Again, Roberto called over the headset.

"Coach Sutton, this is a chip shot for Jose."

With Grant Lee's save of the expiring play clock, Thump had dodged a bullet. He also realized he had violated his vow to always listen to his assistant coaches. Telling Harrison Dye to issue the special teams alert, Thump called for the field goal tee and tossed it to Jose who then placed the tee at an angle 7 yards behind the ball.

Just as Roberto had predicted, Jose's kick hooked through the middle of the uprights, but Dixon's boys still held the lead, 20–17. Dirk's defense needed to stop the Warriors in three.

After a mediocre kick return and two runs into the middle of the Barracuda front, Fort Comanche faced a critical possession down. If they could convert on the third-and-five, they would secure the win. Fans on both sides got on their feet.

Those in red chanted, "De-fense, de-fense, de-fense."

Those in maroon stood in silent prayer. This was Texas high-school football.

Dirk wanted to blitz the strong safety, but Grant Lee advised against it.

"In this situation, Coach Dixon will try to hit the back in the flat. Stay in the base. If you send the strong safety, the running back could slip open in the flat," Grant Lee said.

Dirk heeded his best friend's advice and called the base front: "30 Wide, Cover 3."

Grant Lee's experience paid a dividend when the Fort Comanche quarterback sprinted to his right to dump the ball into the flat. The Warriors had executed a precisely layered flood route to the wide side, but Dan Ngo read the quarterback rollout and raced to deflect the pass. With less than two minutes left to play, the Warriors would punt from their 35-yard line.

Carlos's fair catch put T'Darian and the offense to work in the two-minute drill. By the time the Barracuda offense advanced the ball into field-goal range, the clock had ticked down to 8 seconds remaining. Using his final timeout, Thump called for another field-goal attempt.

The snap and hold went perfectly. So did Jose's kick. The Barracudas and Warriors would face off in overtime.

After a brief intermission, the referee flipped the coin for the second time, and as with the first coin flip, the Warriors won the toss; but this time, Coach Dixon elected to go on offense last.

In an overtime period, the advantage is in possessing the ball last. By going on offense last, the coach knows how many points he needs to win or send the game into another overtime period. If the

Barracudas kicked a field goal on their first possession, the Warriors had to match only the field goal to extend the game to a second overtime period, but if the Barracudas scored a touchdown, the Warriors would have to match the touchdown. Going on offense last was a significant tactical advantage.

The boys in the Barracuda red jerseys huddled at the Warrior 35-yard line. Just as Thump had promised, he called for Derek to return to the backfield. It was a dicey move for the first-year head coach, but he knew that Derek had something to prove, and if this team would be successful this season, Derek had to step up to the challenge.

Thump told Miguel to keep it on the ground. No passes.

Derek's return to the game rattled Fort Comanche. Winning the toss gave them a slight emotional lift, but it didn't take. They had lost the mojo.

Expecting Port Verona to stick with the empty set, the Warriors came out to defend the pass. Running between Valentino and Victor, Derek tore through their front line like a Category-5 hurricane, scoring in just two plays with an 18-yard run and another 17-yard carry. Jose added the extra point to make it a seven-point Barracuda lead over the shell-shocked Warriors.

The Port Verona loyalists chanted and screamed while the Barracuda Wave of Sound blared what Thump thought might be the theme song from the original *Jaws* movie or something like it.

The visiting team would not manage another first down. Their last gasp came on a Hail Mary pass attempt into triple coverage. Orion Dixon's Comanches surrendered.

Having won their first home opener in 13 years, the Barracudas met at midfield to shake hands and wish the Warriors well in their season. After meeting briefly with their coaches, the 'Cudas broke the midfield huddle with their mantra and jogged to join the band for the school fight song.

Inside her booth, Tran's clenched hand yanked the 22-karat Barracuda spirit necklace from her neck and threw it to the floor. Given to her by the previous head coach, the pendant disappeared into a space beneath her chair as she stood to walk away.

Four hours of celebration passed before Thump could lock the fieldhouse. He texted Sara but received no response. No matter; he had no time to celebrate.

The staff would have to meet at the fieldhouse to analyze the online video of the next week's opponent and post the Friday night's game statistics for the kids. In addition, the coaches would attend Jason's scouting report session and write out the practice plans for the following week.

The coaching staff wouldn't finish until after 4:00 Saturday. A punch-drunk Thump dragged Jenny home, where they ate an early dinner and collapsed under the bedroom's ceiling fan.

Early Sunday morning, a cool front preceded by thunder, lightning, and heavy rain moved in from the north. Jenny darted to and from the bedroom and woke Thump around 3:30 a.m.

He knew what to do. Moving her doggie bed to the bedroom closet where she preferred to hide during storms, he closed the door after she nested. Once the storm passed, she would bark and alert Thump to let her out.

After the mental and emotional demands of the past 24 hours, he chose to clear his alarm setting. He would skip church to sleep in. In fact, considering how he felt at that moment, he wasn't sure he could attend the Sunday morning service again this season.

By Sunday afternoon, his voice-mail box had filled. Three of the messages were from Sara, the last one tagged as urgent. One was from Investigator Jim Weir of the Tiburon County Sheriff's Office, a curiously timed welfare check. Another message was from Lupe on behalf of Dorothy Jean, two messages from Rod, two more were from Rory Brendle, one was from Dr. Tran, and another from Pastor Mike.

Staring at the list of missed calls, he fought the temptation to press DELETE ALL."

Thump would drop off the grid for the time being. It was his day of rest. He would reach out to Deputy Weir and Pastor Mike, but the rest of the crew could take a long walk, especially Sara. Images of her flirting with the younger locals saturated his mind.

CHAPTER THIRTY-ONE

Alone in his robe and socks at breakfast early Saturday morning, Deputy Jim Weir scanned the scores from Friday night. On seeing the Port Verona score, his jaw dropped. Thinking it must be a misprint, but hoping it wasn't, he located Thump's contact information and called him.

Jim Weir liked Thump. Something about Port Verona's new football coach seemed familiar, but he couldn't put his finger on it.

If Thump had visited Pastor Mike's congregation, he would have heard a sermon that might have touched him. Inspired by Thump's management of Derek's frustration, Pastor Mike opened the service with a reading from Psalm 10:14-18, a series of Old Testament verses which related to one's being a good father to the fatherless. Pastor Mike then preached on God's love and patience for the good of humanity and God's desire for the exposure of wrongdoers.

Thump returned Weir's call, and they made plans to have breakfast together at the Godsend Hotel.

In the week following the win over Fort Comanche, the *Sentinel's* front-page color photo was an action shot of Dan Ngo's pass deflection, the key play in the defensive stand which forced the Comanches' final punt. The banner headline read, "DAN SAYS NO!"

Two weeks passed before Thump saw Sara out of uniform. Once, out on patrol, she had given him the old familiar finger nod, but he didn't ponder on how things had soured between them. Thump told himself that the broken relationship didn't matter.

One morning when he saw the Charger, he said, "Don't bother with her, Jenny. We didn't move all the way to the boondocks to find love. We came here to win some ball games."

From here on out he would maintain a lasered fixation on his team.

CHAPTER THIRTY-TWO

The Barracudas devoured their next two opponents and climbed to No. 16 in the 3A state ranking. Every business honored the Barracudas with a spirit window—a cartoonish caricature of a barracuda in pursuit of an opposing mascot.

Even Dr. Tran jumped on the bandwagon. One edition of the *Sentinel* highlighted an interview with her about how she discovered Thump and convinced him to come to Port Verona. Next up for the 'Cudas was the rivalry game with Reed City.

Sara texted Thump to tell him that she would escort the team. He didn't reply.

Because of the mismatch, no one was sure why, the *Sentinel's* sister radio station in Reed City had broadcast the seasonal matchup for the last 48 years. During that time, all but three of them were Reed City wins. While it would seem logical that the media would relegate the coverage of such a one-sided affair to the confines of Saturday afternoon barbershops and Sunday morning Bible classes, this was the "County Fair Shootout," a perennial game where the football took a backseat to the pageantry.

No matter how mismatched the teams, the Tiburon County Fairground Memorial Stadium's capacity crowd would overflow along the chain-link fence line where hundreds of townsfolk, shrimpers, farmers, and former Friday night heroes leaned into their neighbor's ongoing commentary of the happenings on the field and in the community. Although each school received an equal share guaranteed payout, the ticket sales, parking fees, and concession receipts from this one high-school football game funded two-thirds of the fairground's annual operating costs.

Along with most people in the county who couldn't get a ticket, Jim Weir sat at home with his feet up, listening to the game. It was the first time since LBJ's presidency that both teams would meet undefeated. Even the Sunset Bay Nursing Home had piped in the broadcast through their intercom. Law enforcement activities flatlined as every citizen and criminal tuned in to the game.

Favored by two touchdowns and regularly loaded for bear, Reed City was a classification larger than Port Verona. Given his fondness for the Barracudas' head coach, Jim figured, *Why not pull for Port Verona this one time?*

Then, just before kickoff, the chief investigator's phone flashed. A prime confidential informant for the Sheriff's Office, one who had helped him break an armed robbery ring last spring, had texted.

Mondo Escamilla, an *El Marineras* high-ranking member who knew his way around Tiburon County, had no qualms providing tips to the police regarding rival gang members or unaffiliated criminals, but he didn't come cheap.

Normally, when asking Jim for a meet, Mondo texted a third callback number. It was his way of making sure that a double agent had not compromised him. But this time, there was no number, only a message that read, "ergent, no cantdo uswal... meet WPA rode e of houston river... info bout pkg."

Even with Mondo's spelling and grammar, it was clear that he had information regarding Deputy Bunch's murder. "Pkg" was their code for Deputy Bunch.

Why did Mondo want to meet out in the hinterland? Jim wondered.

Works Project Administration (WPA) Road is a deeply rutted, single-lane dirt path which traverses a ten-thousand-acre cotton farm.

Traveled by mammoth tractors and other farm implements, its construction was meant to create local jobs during FDR's New Deal era. But now, with the main artery from Mexico being IH-69, WPA Road's inconspicuous connection between IH-69 and the Gulf of Mexico made it a peripheral dirt-road artery for the interstate's more nefarious travelers.

Jim thought the location of the requested meet to be out of the ordinary. Mondo usually asked to meet close to the city, and Jim wondered why Mondo wasn't sticking to the protocol of texting a safe number. This was an unusual setup, at an unusual time, in an unusual place. Jim considered ignoring the text but concluded that if meeting Mondo out on WPA offered critical info on Don's murder, he needed to hear it without delay. They had uncovered no further clues since Chambers County had recovered the Crown Victoria.

He texted Mondo, "ETA 25."

Jim's instincts told him to pack some extra firepower to go with his Smith and Wesson Model 66. Jim preferred the revolver over the higher capacity semi-automatic pistols "those youngsters" carried.

It wouldn't jam, and Jim always said, "If I can't drop one with six, I might as well just carry a knife."

Adding two .357 caliber speed loaders to his cowboy belt, he loaded his Remington 870 Police Special with twelve .000 rounds and leaned the shotgun on the front passenger floorboard and seat of his K5 Blazer.

Chevy's wide-stance, off-road capable Blazer had been out of manufacture for years, but it was the only vehicle that gave him total access to the county's terrain. Murderers rarely buried bodies in manicured city parks. Rather, they placed them in shallow graves out in the middle of pastures. The Sheriff's Office had maintained Jim's modified, military-package K5 for years. With its high ground clearance, four-wheel drive, and oversized, mud-grip tires, the large utilitarian SUV could get Jim to any crime scene any time of the year.

Once behind the wheel, Jim radioed the dispatcher to notify her of his destination. And as the number three man in the department, he exercised his authority to alert the pilot of ICAP-4 to be ready for takeoff.

ICAP-4, the intercounty air program chopper, supported law enforcement over the four adjacent area counties. Calling ICAP-4 to alert status would cut critical minutes from its response time, should the situation turn sideways out on WPA Road. Besides, other than ICAP-4, nothing else was available for backup. The entire Sheriff's Office road division was on duty at the game.

ICAP-4 confirmed its alert status. Live on its pad, the chopper vibrated as its rotor blades gained speed.

Jim checked his watch. It was 7:57 p.m. He radioed TCSO dispatch to 10-33 the net and flipped on the K5 Blazer's eighteen front-mounted spotlights. He slowed the K5 to a crawl.

Dispatch radioed, "All TCSO units, hold all radio traffic. The net is 10-33."

Seeing the taillights of what appeared to be a full-size sedan, Jim stopped approximately 40 yards from the vehicle. It sat parked in the middle of WPA Road.

Mondo leaned on its trunk, arms folded, glancing periodically back and forth. Mondo usually appeared twitchy. He typically never stood still for even a nanosecond but at this moment centered in Jim's spotlights, he looked frozen. With his rigid posture, he could have been mistaken for a mannequin.

Squatting in the middle of the road like a heavyweight boxer waiting in his corner, the K5 idled in gear with Jim's foot on the brake. He pulled his revolver from its holster and placed it in his lap. Blinded by the Blazer's spotlights, Mondo waved innocuously.

Jim thought he saw a shadow move inside the car, but he couldn't hear much over his unit's idling engine. He pulled the loudspeaker microphone from its dash holder.

"Mondo, keep your hands in view and walk toward my vehicle."

Mondo waved again, but he made no move toward the K5.

Something's wrong, thought Jim.

"Sheriff's Office, roll ICAP-4 my location, WPA Road east of Houston River."

Dispatch radioed, "10-4, ICAP-4, 10-78 WPA Road, east of Houston River."

The pilot flipped on his searchlight as he lifted the chopper off the ground.

"ICAP-4, en route WPA Road, east of Houston River. ETA, three," the pilot responded.

Jim keyed the public address microphone again.

"Mondo, if you want to talk, keep your hands in view and walk toward my vehicle."

Mondo turned around as if he was trying to communicate to someone in the car. He turned back to face the K5.

Jim called out, "Mondo, if you want to—"

Mondo burst into a sprint toward the K5, and two subjects exited the vehicle. A third man pushed open the trunk lid, then jumped out of the trunk and fired a shotgun. One of the rounds struck Mondo in the back. He died before his face hit the dirt.

The two others fired semi-automatic rifles at the Blazer. Jim dropped the microphone, threw his unit into reverse, and floored the gas pedal. Leaning over the middle console, he attempted to stay low behind the dash and look out the rear window while steering left-handed.

Disoriented by the glass and bullets flying through the Blazer's interior, he struggled to keep the SUV's oversized tires inside the ruts. One overcorrection and the vehicle could flip.

Dust from the front of the retreating Blazer billowed to obscure the shooters' sight. Speeding backward, Jim could hear bullets popping through his windshield and blowing out the rear window.

In the din of the bullets slicing through the Blazer's sheet metal body, Jim's radio barked.

"ICAP-4. ETA, two," the pilot radioed.

Bits of glass and hot metal peppered his shoulders and neck. Feeling the K5 was about to tip, he eased off the gas pedal and yanked the wheel hard in the opposite direction. Fishtailing in reverse and bouncing through a shallow ditch, the K5 sat perpendicular to the shooters, giving them a perfect broadside opportunity.

The shooters continued to fire as they advanced. Hot metal pierced the passenger side of the K5. Jim felt a heaviness in his right arm.

Searing hot metal fragments entered his left hip. He floored the gas again and turned the wheel. The K5 roared backward through the cotton field. Driving in reverse through a virtual sea of mature cotton plants and nothing else, he didn't need to see where he was going. Jim ducked lower between the seats and continued to steer with his left hand.

His radio crackled. ICAP-4 transmitted through the static. "Unit Three, activate your lightbar. ETA one minute."

Jim tactically maneuvered in a sharp zig-zag pattern away from the incoming gunfire. He could see nothing in front or behind him. The dust cloud camouflaged his escape, and the bullets' frequency diminished.

Jim grabbed the radio mic's cord and pulled it toward him. He couldn't feel his fingers, and he couldn't activate the microphone. He pressed its red button against his chest.

Out of breath, his words almost inaudible, Jim transmitted, "Unit Three. Shots fired, deputy down. Two long rifles."

The dispatcher responded, "10-4. Deputy down at WPA Road, east of Houston River. All local units, deputy down at WPA Road, east of Houston River. Be advised, plainclothes deputy is at the scene. Repeat, plainclothes deputy is at the scene."

Its engine valves clattered as the K5 bored through the sea of cotton bolls. Jim no longer heard the shots or felt the glass bits flying into his face and hair. Warning lights lit up the dash, and the engine sputtered. The K5 coasted to a stop where the engine died.

Jim tried to grab his shotgun from the passenger seat, but he couldn't grasp the stock. He reached across his body with his left hand, secured the 12-gauge pump and lay it across his lap. Yanking the driver-side door handle, he kicked open the door, fell out on his shoulder, and crawled behind the vehicle. He then stumbled into the surrounding darkness.

The assassins had shot out most of the K5 Blazer's lights. Abandoned in the cotton field, it looked like a bullet-riddled ghost ship.

The K5's radio receiver squawked.

"TCSO Unit Three, ICAP-4 is 30 seconds out. Activate your lightbar and advise."

Lying in a row between the hills of cotton, Jim heard the radio traffic, but he had no portable, and he didn't dare expose his position. Even if he wanted to move, a searing pain kept his left leg immobile. Sweat soaked his shirt. He felt lightheaded and nauseous. A warmth trickled down his right arm, and he still couldn't move his fingers. He looked down for his pistol, but he couldn't focus. Jim tucked the shotgun under his left shoulder and disengaged the safety.

The chopper hovered above the battered Blazer's remaining spotlights, which illuminated the cotton field just in front of the vehicle. ICAP-4's searchlight swept over the scene.

"TCSO Unit Three, respond."

The pilot radioed again.

"TCSO Unit Three, respond."

Silence oozed from the radio. The cotton plants bowed in deference to the gust whipped up by the rotation of the chopper blades. Though the pilot's searchlight revealed every bullet hole in the K5, he could see no signs of life anywhere near the vehicle.

"TCSO Unit Three, respond."

The pilot waited for a response, but none came.

Getting no answer, the chopper pilot called dispatch.

"Sheriff's Office, ICAP-4 is at the scene. Multiple damage to the deputy's vehicle. No visible suspects at the scene. We need backup at WPA Road, two miles east of Houston River. Be advised, plainclothes deputy is not visible."

If Jim could have retained consciousness, he would have heard a DPS trooper's siren wailing down WPA Road from the north. Two neighboring county's units and a Nineveh City PD unit followed just behind the trooper.

Back at the fairgrounds, the TCSO units remained gridlocked at the ballgame. In the closing moments of the greatest upset in the history of the County Fair Shootout, Jim Weir's near-lifeless body lay between two rows of broken, blood-stained cotton plants.

The Barracudas' convincing 42–14 victory shocked the county, but Deputy Jim Weir's survival would shock the world. Three high velocity rounds had shattered the deputy's hip, shoulder, and forearm. By the time the first responders loaded Jim onto Presbyterian Life Flight Rescue, hemorrhagic shock threatened his survival. Most first responders at the scene didn't believe he would make it to the hospital.

Deputies scoured the area into the next morning and recovered Mondo's body from the road. An autopsy would reveal that a blast of buckshot had severed his spine.

The assassins escaped. Yet, even while in a gun battle for his life, the lead investigator of the Tiburon County Sheriff's Office had processed the modus operandi of his assailants. As large-caliber bullets riddled his vehicle and tore through his body, Jim Weir realized his assassination attempt was a near copy of Don Bunch's abduction.

Only a few law enforcement officials were privy to the Deputy Don Bunch dashcam video, and Jim Weir was one of them. The recording revealed that on his approach to the driver's side of the dark-colored Crown Victoria, Deputy Bunch could see two subjects in the front seat. What Bunch couldn't see was that a third suspect lay in wait—in the trunk.

CHAPTER THIRTY-THREE

It was 2:00 a.m. when Thump and Jenny returned to his cottage after the Bay City game. Parked in a space near his door, the Charger faced outward, toward the highway. As Old Blue angled into its spot, Thump identified the figure behind the Charger's wheel.

He and Jenny hopped out of the cab and approached her window. Sara looked at him and lowered the glass, but she said nothing.

"Did you watch the game?" Thump asked.

"You know I was there."

"Yeah, but I figured you might have been busy."

"Busy? Oh, that's right, you think that I was getting busy with Isaac."

"Isaac? Who is Isaac?"

"Isaac Avila. The EMT that I dumped you for. Isn't that what you told your buddies? And then you shut me out of your life like I am some switch to turn off. For what? So you can save your energy and focus on your precious football team? You take me to church, you take me into your life, you ask me my life story, then you throw me out like trash." Tears streamed down her cheeks. "And you ask me about my family and talk about how you would have loved to meet Papi?" She put her palms to her face. "You go with me to the park. Our picnic?

186

The swings?" She pounded the steering wheel with her palms. "Then, you throw me away! You, of all people!"

Her front paws on the Charger's door, Jenny attempted to nuzzle Sara's neck. Sara continued to hold her hands to her face and cry.

Thump sighed. He felt nauseous.

"Sara, come inside for a minute."

"No, Thomas! You go inside! I'm still on duty. They paid me to escort you to and from the game. Until you go inside, my job isn't done."

"Listen, I know Dorothy Jean pays for this detail, so you aren't really on duty. Come inside. Let's talk."

"Go to heck, Thomas. You go straight to heck. Or, maybe you'd rather go to Diane's?"

"Are you nuts?" he replied.

"Oh, I heard you had a great time there. It's all over town how you carried her to her bedroom and kissed her. Yeah, Thomas. Everybody knows about your evening with Cruella. And from what I heard; she got your spots."

"You listen to me! I did not do anything with that woman. I went out with her because I had no other option. If I hadn't gone out with her, things would have just gotten worse. At least now, she leaves me alone."

"And you love being alone, right? Just you and your dog."

"Well, I thought so, but now—"

She interrupted, "But now, what?"

"Please get out of the car and come in to talk to me," he said. "Please."

"Why? What do you want? You want to tell me all about how you got carried away? That you can't love again? Is that why you concocted the story that I dumped you for Isaac? So you could dump me for nobody? And get away with it?"

"Please get out of the car and come in. Please."

Jenny jumped down from the car door.

Sara keyed her body radio's mic, "PV3 is 10-7 that location."

Dispatcher Mildred Thompson radioed, "10-4, PV3. You have the package?"

"10-4."

"10-4 PV3. Stay safe."

After Sara secured her unit, she followed Thump into the cottage. He brought her to the bedroom with Jenny and turned on the ceiling fan. He had never imagined Sara could be so vulnerable. After he retrieved two cold Dr. Peppers from the kitchen. Jenny hopped onto the bed next to Sara, then nested.

Thump dragged his rocking chair into the room and sat in front of Sara.

"Okay, I messed up. Before the Fort Comanche game, I saw you with that EMT guy. You had mentioned once that he had a crush on you. It looked to me like you were flirting. I was upset, and I just decided to—"

"Dump me?" interjected Sara.

"No, it's not like that. To me, here I am, this loser, this old man whose only successful relationship with a female is a dog, and I am falling for this beautiful, strong young woman who I adored from practically first sight. This town is her home and there is no way that she will stay with me. And they might fire me in eight months because that's why they hired me. They hired me to fail. So, let's say that you love me back. What happens then?

"This is your home. You have a young man, probably many young men, desiring a life here with you, and I'll eventually leave town. I don't know, I already feel." He stammered and took her hands, "I feel that I wouldn't be able to take it if I lost you. And I know if I again hold your hand in church, fall asleep on your couch, drive your Cougar, share another picnic, or laugh with you, I'll be forever in love. So, what can I do?"

Her eyes glittered like liquid emeralds, the copper flecks floating freely about. She studied his face; it was a face scrubbed of pretension. This was no locker-room pitch, no chalk talk. She had heard real words from a real man, a flawed man who loved her so much, he wanted to lose her before he could no longer have her.

She sat for a while, silent, then asked, "Are you going to answer my question now?"

"What question?" he asked.

"The question that you ducked that day at the park. Before, or after?"

He looked down; Jenny tapped her tail.

"Well, answer me. Before, or after?" she asked.

"Before? No. After? Yes."

She pulled her hands to her face in tears.

"I love you, Sara Mendoza. I love you more than football. I love you more than my own life. How's that for an answer?"

"Thomas, you hurt me. It's hard. I love you so much, but these last three weeks, you shut me out. You must promise me, I mean really promise me, you won't just walk away like that again. Emotional abuse and physical abuse both hurt. If you want this, you can't shut me out. Never again. Can you promise that?"

"I promise. I will never, ever leave you. And I will try hard to not be that stupid again. So now what?"

"Well, I'm not that easy. Just don't think that you can throw the L-word out there and get the key to the palace."

She leaned forward and kissed him. He pulled her into the rocking chair, his cheek pressed against hers. After several minutes of quiet rocking with the only sound being Jenny's snore and the creak of wicker, she whispered, "I have to go, but you and Jenny can stay at my place tonight. You can sleep on the couch. Jenny can sleep on the floor."

"How about Plan B?" he asked.

"Plan B is for you to sleep on the floor and Jenny gets the couch."

"Those are two bad plans, Sergeant."

"Get your overnight bag and pack Jenny's squid. You need some rest," she replied.

"Do I have a choice?"

"Five minutes, you and your daughter be in my unit. I'll be outside."

CHAPTER THIRTY-FOUR

Sara's fridge and pantry provided Thump with all the ingredients for a five-star Tex-Mex brunch.

Mixing the eggs and tossing Jenny a chunk of chorizo, Thump said, "Jenny, there are definite advantages to having a Latina girlfriend, and one of them is a well-stocked kitchen."

District competition started next week; the preseason was officially over. It was a good time for a bye week; the coaches were exhausted, and the kids banged up. Against Reed City, both Derek and Luis had gone down with injuries, Derek with a thigh bruise and Luis with a hyperextended elbow. Nevertheless, for Thump, it was the eye of the hurricane, a weekend off for the coaching staff and three days of a normal life for the boys. On Tuesday, they would start back with some light work and focus on the academics. It was the last week of the grading period, and the Barracudas couldn't afford to lose a single player.

Principal Saltzman had warned him that the losses due to the no-pass, no-play regulation usually cost the program two to three starters each grading period, but this year would be different. In the previous seasons, kids would look for an easy way out. Failing a class was a convenient avenue to escape the frustration and embarrassment of losing.

It was the *Catch-22* of high school sports. One of the most important aspects of the successful high-school football programs is the willingness of the kids to risk losing. And Thump had learned the only way to convince them to lay it on the line and risk it all was to prove to them they were already winners. Consequently, the only way to win was to win.

Relieved, but also anxious over Sara, Thump found the morning nearly as unsettling as reassuring.

"Where do we go from here, Jenny?"

Jenny's tail tapped as Sara emerged from her bedroom.

Flipping the French toast, Thump said, "If I could have guessed that you looked like that in the morning, I would have spent the night here long before now."

"You're a real comedian, Thomas. 'Course, you've probably heard that before, right?"

He knew better than to return her serve, so he turned back to the French toast.

With his Cary Grant voice he replied, "It's so early, let's not quarrel, dear."

She pecked him on the cheek and pulled three plates from the cupboard. Thump thought few things were more enjoyable than kicking back on a Saturday and binging on college football, but today didn't seem to be turning out as that kind of Saturday.

After she set the table, Sara sat down and asked Thump to lead the blessing. Thinking that she was mocking him for taking her to church, he laughed and reached for a tortilla. A slapped wrist and a stern look later, he saw she was serious.

"I thought you said you weren't into the church scene," he said.

"I wasn't. But I have always believed," she replied, "*Papi* said Grace. Besides, you have yourself to blame. Now, go ahead."

After breakfast, the darkness of another storm encroached the Gulf horizon. Thump sat motionless on the couch while Sara detailed the events on WPA Road. Untimely turnovers, an ineligible starter, a muffed punt—those things he could handle, but entanglement in a net of kidnapping and assassination attempts was nothing of which any football coach could imagine being a part.

Not only was he but one degree removed from both crimes, the love of his life was even closer. He could sweat blood to meet the demands of being a head coach and reviving a program, but on this day, he wondered how he could stand up to these forces. First, the nearly irrecoverable state of an abandoned football program, then a subversive superintendent, and now, he and the woman he loved were likely targeted for death. Sara squeezed his waist and pressed her face against his back.

The trunks of the young palms guarding Sara's patio began to flex in the building wind.

The next morning, he and Sara returned to church. Miss Dorothy Jean had stayed home, nursing a head cold. Whether it was paranoia or perceptiveness, they both felt as if every pair of eyes in the chapel had followed them to their seats in the church pew.

This church, this town, had never experienced anything like the recent events. An undefeated football team and two gangland attacks on law enforcement wouldn't be an improbable coincidence in Greater Houston, but to the residents of a Texas shrimping hamlet, such events were a dramatic misalignment of the stars.

After the service closed, they escaped without much hindrance, but as Sara approached the Cougar, she noticed Lupe waving.

Thump and Sara met Lupe near her car. Her face was shrouded by her gray, shoulder length hair. Thump thought her to be an attractive woman for someone her age.

Speaking in Spanish, Lupe first asked Sara if she was all right, saying she and Dorothy Jean had heard Sara and Thump were no longer together, but now that she had seen them, she was curious if the rumor had been a lie all along.

"We went a few weeks without seeing much of each other," Sara explained, "but things are much better now."

Continuing in English as a courtesy to Thump, Lupe said, "Well, I'm happy to hear that.

She then tugged Sara's elbow. "*Mija,* do you know anything about the shooting of the county deputy, the one from Friday night?"

Sara glanced toward Thump and said, "*Si,* it's tragic. They aren't sure who was behind the attack."

"Well, what I learned late last night may help. One of my grandnieces sees a young man. He is a suspicious character. They say he is one of those *El Marineras* gang members from one of the towns in the south."

"Do you know his name?" asked Sara.

"No *mija,* listen to what I'm telling you. My grandniece say she and the boyfriend had a big fight. She said he was upset. He told her he had to leave town for a little bit because his crew was taking heat from the police over things they hadn't done, serious things. She told him that she don't want her baby's father to go to prison over some lies and she say to him, 'Go turn yourself in to Sara at the police station. She can help you.' Then, they fought and he left town. But before he left, he swore to her on his baby's life that the *El Marineras* weren't behind the attacks.

Be extra careful; those attacks were not what they appeared to be," said Lupe.

Lupe kissed Sara on the cheek, then patted Thump on the shoulder. Thump heard her mumble something in Spanish as she wiped her eyes.

After walking a few steps toward her car, she smiled and waved back at them.

"What was that she said there at the end?" asked Thump.

"Just some *preocupación de la abuela,*" she said.

"Okay. You know I don't speak Spanish."

"Exactly," she replied.

"Okay, I get it. Now, I'm going to speak '*Manish.* Like it or not, you're going to allow me to drive."

"*Manish?*' Really?" she said as she opened the driver's door.

"So, what do you think about that story?" he asked as he settled in his assigned Cougar seat.

"I don't know, but you can believe there's something to it. I never doubt the veracity of intel that originate from someone's *la familia*. If Lupe's information is solid, we're searching in the wrong direction for Deputy Weir's attackers and Don Bunch's killer. We need to talk to Jim Weir. He would be able to decipher the clues."

"I heard he's in an induced coma and might not make it," said Thump.

Sara sighed and put the Cougar in gear. "I know. I know."

CHAPTER THIRTY-FIVE

Open week deviated from the strict regimen of after-school practices, film study, and meetings. Because open week can drop an anchor on a team's momentum, the coach must move the team forward. Every deckhand must regroup and refocus.

For the Barracudas, one significant upside to the open week was the recuperation and rehabilitation of Derek's thigh bruise. Leading the conference with a rushing average of 143 yards per game, he was a lock for the district newcomer of the year. Derek's talent forced the opposing defense to stack the box. In the secondary, the opposition had no choice but to play one-on-one coverage versus T'Darian's arm and the soccer boys' speed.

The administration posted grades on Friday. At 4:00 p.m., Principal Saltzman called Thump and reported that for the first time in seven years, Port Verona didn't lose a player to academic ineligibility. A full-page article in the *Sentinel* included two lengthy quotes from Dr. Tran about her influence and how she ordered the district's new emphasis on academic success within the extracurricular programs.

Her quote read, "During earlier athletic administrations here at Port Verona Independent School District, our scholar-athletes have performed far below the board's expectations. While it's commendable the football team has experienced success, what is most important is the newfound focus on our mandate to produce college-ready graduates. The glow of a productive outcome on a scoreboard dims when that achievement is compared to the fundamental attainment of our teachers and administration in their pursuit of the aims of this district. Coach Sutton is a man who understands what is important to the taxpayers and parents."

When he read the quote, Thump spilled his morning cup of Dr. Pepper.

So, she's back, Rose. I wonder what she's been up to these last three weeks?

Monday afternoon, he found out. Just as Dorothy Jean had foretold, he received an early morning call from the Texas Interscholastic League Office. The Director of Interscholastic Competition stated that he had received a formal complaint about Derek's transfer papers. And since the legality of Derek's transfer was challenged, T'Darian's transfer would be de facto investigated.

Dr. Skeet Akin from the eligibility committee ordered Thump to attend a hearing in Austin. And because the hearing wasn't until the following week, the boys were ineligible to take part in the district opener. At the hearing, Thump could present any evidence that may exonerate Port Verona, but should the evidence not prove the eligibility of both Derek and T'Darian, Thump would face serious sanctions up to and including suspension from coaching and forfeiture of the season's victories. Akin advised Thump not to involve an attorney, as this was an inquiry within the oversight of the Texas Interscholastic Office and carried no civil or criminal penalties.

An overwhelmed Thump called Principal Saltzman to ask that a substitute cover Isaac and Harrison, then he texted the two assistant coaches and asked them to meet him in his office.

He looked at Jenny where she lay snoring. He had assumed Dorothy Jean had quashed Tran's scheme directed at Derek and T'Darian. But his ally couldn't block Tran's most vile machination yet, and Thump pondered how he could counter this move. To Thump, it was incomprehensible that an educator would conspire to destroy the lives of two boys cast adrift in the tempest of life. But Diane Tran was balefully twisted. It was as Dorothy Jean said that night at the dinner table: Something wasn't right with her.

Although Dr. Tran had been secretive in her connivance, Thump knew she needed a District 13-AAA insider to file the complaint. Port Verona ISD would receive sanctions if Derek's and T'Darian's transfers were invalid, so Tran couldn't be the face of a castigatory investigation against her own school district. The trustees might see through her sedition. Thump wondered which of Port Verona's opponents agreed to spearhead the paperwork. He thought maybe Isaac or Harrison might have an idea.

Dr. Tran's scheme shocked neither Isaac nor Harrison. They had experienced Tran's predisposition for power, and many of the fans recognized her blueprint for football's endgame. It was an open secret that she hated football's inclusion as a school-related activity. Both longtime coaches had learned of her plan to disband the program following the season, and it surprised neither of them that she finally launched an apocalyptic strike.

Everyone else in Port Verona appreciated T'Darian and Derek's impact on the program. If the state declared those two boys ineligible, the decision would destroy what Thump had built, and Dr. Tran could forge ahead on her one-year agendum to gain board approval for her proposal to drop football.

Isaac suggested Thump call Pastor Mike to help break the news to the boys. He further advised that Thump edit the day's practice plan and appoint Grant Lee to oversee an intense strength and conditioning workout with an extended segment for each of the special-team phases. In their discussion, Isaac reminded Thump of their opponents' struggles during the preseason. Their first district opponent, Thelma, was experiencing a rebuilding year and ranked last in the district against the run.

Harrison agreed with Isaac. They believed that even without T'Darian and Derek, the Barracudas could handle the Blueticks.

Thump loved their optimistic nature, but he didn't agree with the assessment. He retorted that while Thelma might be porous versus the run, they had their own version of a Derek paired with a mobile quarterback, and the duo had combined for 17 touchdowns in five games.

Thump knew it didn't matter what Thelma brought to the table. The coaches had to keep T'Darian and Derek afloat during their week of purgatory or their ship would sink in the coming weeks. He asked Harrison to retrieve T'Darian and Derek from their seventh-period class. From there, he was to escort them back to Thump's office. They had only an hour to apprise Pastor Mike of the problem, so Isaac stepped outside the office to call Pastor Mike while Harrison spoke with Thump.

Harrison said he had family and close friends throughout District 13-AAA. He proposed that Thump spur Pastor Mike to reach out to the boys' previous school in Dallas.

"Coach, Pastor Mike has friends everywhere. I promise you; his influence is the only way to beat her."

Isaac interrupted. He had good news. Pastor Mike would arrive at Thump's office within the next 10 minutes.

On receiving the decision, Derek remained stoic and T'Darian burst into silent tears.

T'Darian's tears plunged off his cheeks and splattered on the floor into an unrecognizable dampness. The pain flooded his eyes.

Thump expected to hear from Dr. Tran, but she hadn't contacted him yet. Not wanting her to accuse him of unprofessional conduct, he told the boys that a Texas Interscholastic League investigation into their eligibility was ongoing, but he felt the state would clear them in time for next week's game. In the meantime, the Texas Interscholastic League had directed him to hold them from the Thelma game. He told the boys to keep their faith.

Derek looked up from the floor and said, "Faith ain't needed where the truth lives."

"Derek, we have faith and we have the truth. We have the original Previous Athletic Participation Form for both of you, and Coach Davis verified your credits from the transcripts. T'Darian's coach and the designees from Dallas Douglass High School signed off on the eligibility forms. The forms all have the same signatures, plus the signature of your middle-school principal. Your legal guardianship is a trust of Camp Promise, and Pastor Mike is Camp Promise's representative of record. It's in your files.

"Men, you listen. This is just a rock someone has thrown at me, and only me. When a team is losing, nobody cares how many rules they break. When a team is winning and things are changing, the haters grab for anything they can to pull you down. You're familiar with crabs, aren't you, T'Darian?"

"I heard people eat them," T'Darian replied.

"If you put a bunch of crabs in a big metal tub, they will try to climb out. They understand that staying in that tub will not end well for them. So, they climb and slide, and they climb and slide. Eventually, one crab gets a hold on the rim and pulls himself up. Just as he is about to escape, what do you think happens?"

T'Darian dropped his head and shrugged.

"The other crabs grab him and pull him back into the tub. In that way, crabs are just like people. We humans, if we see another person get up on that high point first, if somebody accomplishes something we can't, we get envious. The human might pretend to cheer on his friend, but the envy comes out, and the human does his very best to drag the friend back to his level. Men, our football team is that crab who climbed up to the rim of the tub. And just as we were about to make it over the hump, some other human crabs out there grabbed onto whatever they could to pull this program down. And what do you think they grabbed? I'll tell you. The two biggest parts of our team they could grab. They grabbed onto the two of you."

For T'Darian, it was a moment of realization, but Derek remained sullen and unresponsive. Thump understood Derek. He processed things in a more introspective manner.

Thump patted T'Darian on the back and said, "Men, I assure you; this isn't about you. This is about your coach and your team. We're the crab on top at the rim. We're fixing to break free of the losing ways of the past. Remember, you are just the two parts they could grab onto."

"Amen," Pastor Mike said.

Thump said, "You two men check the board and get your gear. Nothing changes. You are still practicing. Here in a minute, I'll inform the squad. Speak nothing to anyone. If anyone asks you about it, the only thing that comes out of your mouth is 'no comment' or nothing at all. Especially, don't talk to any of those teachers in the building. Not a word. Let me do all the talking. Coach Sewell and Pastor Mike will update you as we go. Now, get ready for practice."

Once the boys left, Pastor Mike asked what he could do. Thump briefed him on the eligibility process and his need to attend the hearing. Speaking in confidence to Pastor Mike and Isaac, Thump detailed the labyrinth backstory, including Dorothy Jean's prior knowledge of Dr. Tran's ruse. Thump advised Pastor Mike to contact his Dallas connections for ground support. If they were to counter her ploy, they had to be proactive in their effort to build an impenetrable case against the ineligibility claim. They needed to go on the offensive against the opposing coach with whom she was conspiring.

After speaking to the team, Thump received the text that he had dreaded. "Tom, please see me ASAP."

Summoned to the administration office, Thump left Jenny at cheerleader practice with Maya.

Dr. Tran wasn't at her desk when he entered. She stood in front of the panoramic family photo, the one of the family's first shrimp boat. Thump took a seat in the wooden chair.

She moved the second chair near and coiled close, then touched his arm and said, "Tom, I am so glad to see you. I have missed you. We've both been so busy. We should spend more time together."

"It's a busy time for both of us," he said, his arms folded.

"Yes, and you have been doing such a wonderful job. Everyone here is so grateful for what you've done with the football team. You've achieved a remarkable distinction. I never wavered in my belief that you were the right man for the job. I never doubted your tenacity and your ability."

"Thanks. Why did you call me?"

"Yes. I received information that the Texas Interscholastic League contacted you this afternoon. Is that correct?"

"They contacted me around 1:00 p.m."

"How do you propose we handle this predicament, Tom? I'm sure you have more experience in this department than I."

"I haven't received word of the specific violations alleged. Eligibility violations vary, but the boys' transfers are legitimate and documented."

"While this affair must result from a miscommunication, we will need to make sure that we have the evidence proving that the claims are unfounded. What do you have as your proof?"

"I have the original PAPF for each of the boys, and Coach Davis verified their enrollment status and the number of credits attained. Their birth certificates show the proper seals."

"Excellent, Tom. As soon as I receive documentation from the T. I. L., I'll forward it to you."

"Thank you."

"I'll travel to Austin with you on Sunday. I've booked two rooms at the Solis Regency downtown. Maybe we can mix in a bit of pleasure with our business trip," she said.

He pushed back the hair from his forehead.

"I'm not sure how much fun I would be. Even though I feel good about our chances of a favorable ruling, my future here hinges on this case."

"Well, let's not worry about that. You tell me later if you want to come along with me, Sunday afternoon. I think I can help distract you from the encumbrance forced upon you. You think about it. If you want to drive to Austin yourself and try to battle this thing alone, I'll respect your decision."

"Thanks, I'll do that," he said.

"Okay then. Thank you for stopping by. Let's not look too far down this road. Do we still have a chance on Friday against Thelma? I understand they aren't having the best of seasons, but I assume the loss of Derek Donaldson and T'Darian Law will make a win difficult."

"Yes, it will. But the boys are resilient and have learned what it takes to win. Whatever the outcome, they will play their best, and I'll be proud."

"Absolutely. I hope you come with me on Sunday so you can be fresh for the hearing on Monday. It will be a long week. I suppose I will let you get back to whatever you do. Until this development, your program has produced just as I predicted."

"Thanks, I appreciate that."

That evening, Thump lay in bed with Jenny watching late night television when Harrison texted him the identity of the District 13-AAA school that had challenged the boys' eligibility. In the least surprising circumstance of Thump's short tenure, Harrison identified J. P. Duhon as Tran's proxy.

Santa Gertrudis ISD had charged Thump and Isaac Sewell with paying Pastor Mike to steer the boys' cases into a placement at Camp Promise. If Pastor Mike had used his influence to place the boys at Camp Promise, a serious infraction had occurred. Duhon's complaint further alleged someone had forged the PAPF signatures from the Dallas schools. Santa Gertrudis claimed to have reliable information proving Dallas Douglass High School had denied T'Darian's credits based on excessive absences, and the evidence showed someone at Port Verona had altered the transcript or misrepresented T'Darian's earned academic credits on the state eligibility report. The evidence of a conspiracy outnumbered the dirty dishes in Thump's sink.

Dr. Tran had pushed her chips all in to force Thump to walk away from the table. He admired her tenacity. She refused to lose. And now, with Dr. Tran's stake at the table stacked in front of him, Thump pondered why Duhon and Santa Gertrudis had bothered to get involved.

Did the Santa Gertrudis ISD superintendent and Dr. Tran share a connection? It wasn't The Nine-Finger Slinger's nature to fear lining up toe-to-toe. No, this ineligibility claim was Tran's all the way.

It was imperative that Thump compartmentalize the week's preparation. It was Thump's time to part the Red Sea. If he failed, the

Barracudas would remain in bondage to their history of failure, and this football season would be the last one for Port Verona.

While Derek was a stellar young running back and defensive player, his skill set overshadowed the talent of a fine supporting cast. Carlos was faster than Derek, as was Luis. And Jose was a gifted scatback who owned the ability to break a tackler's ankles with his precise cuts. Tuesday's practice started an intensive prescriptive plan to offset Derek's absence and counter the loss of T'Darian at quarterback. Thump's offensive plan was to walk the aisle in full faith.

Pastor Mike and Coach Sewell's mentoring provided Derek and T'Darian with the strength to face the emotional challenge and use the setback as an opportunity to model their faith, but Thump understood that the events of Friday night would be a high hurdle. The suspension banned the boys from the sideline on game night. To help them cope, he arranged for them to sit in the press box and listen to the headset communication between the coaches.

Friday's edition of the *Sentinel* refrained from printing the specifics. Readers found a vague declaration that stated two Port Verona starters would be absent from the Barracuda lineup against Thelma. Neither Rory nor his editor wanted any part of publicizing what they suspected was a deliberate attempt by someone unknown to smear Thump and ruin the Barracudas' chance for a Cinderella season.

The townsfolk's usual kettle of small-town gossip boiled: Were the allegations true? Had the new coach made a fatal error in his recruiting? If not, who had initiated the charges against Derek and T'Darian?

Thump encouraged Rory to focus on who was playing in the game, instead of who wasn't. He felt spotlighting Derek and T'Darian further diminished the team's ability to overcome their absence.

"The game," Thump told Rory, "hinges not on the height of the hurdle placed in their path, but on those who clear the hurdle."

After the trauma of Monday, Thump looked to his players for the answer to his dilemma. This was a game that required special weapons and tactics. He would shuffle the skill personnel. The Barracudas would run from the SWAT offensive grouping for the entire Thelma game. Friday night against the Blueticks, the spread was dead.

Thump installed just two pass plays. One pattern called for Valentino to slip out from his power spot, and the other provided a quick strike alternative with Javier Castrejon as the lone wide receiver.

Carlos Castanada, a natural-born leader, would slide to the quarterback position while Luis Gonzalez and Jose Vasquez would alternate at tailback. Thump assigned Valentino an eligible number to wear at the power back position.

Coach Dye told the offensive line that they would "pound the power play down Thelma's throat and stomp it out the other end."

Given the suspensions of Derek and T'Darian, the Thelma Blueticks sniffed the possibility of a 1–0 district record. They saw this first district game as an opportunity to reinvent their season with a win. The message painted on the window of Herb's Bluetick Stop at the corner of the blinking light and Blue Pride Lane informed the passersby, "Last one to Port Verona is a Bluetick's Butt!"

The only advantage for the 'Cudas this week was that it was a return to the lights of Blood Reef and its restored tradition. By Wednesday, its 2,500-seat capacity had sold out at $6.00 a seat. In a surprise announcement, Dr. Tran had approved ticket sales for standing room along the fence line for $4.00.

Thump smiled at the irony of the superintendent's desire to destroy his team.

Isaac said, "That egghead still has no appreciation for the money our boys' winning streak has brought to the district. Just the windfall from this one crowd will be enough to fund a new college prep course."

Thursday after practice, Thump gathered the team in the south endzone where Coach Roberto Herrera held an unblemished game ball, its leather a fresh tannish brown with the Barracuda logo still shiny, its raised laces bleach-white, and its oblong form hardened from 8.7 pounds of air. Next to Roberto, Grant Lee held a deflated, scuffed dark leather football with the Barracuda logo unrecognizable, its dirty laces unraveling. Just out of view behind the huddle of players, Coach Dye held a long-handled spade.

Roberto held the newer ball high for everyone to see as Thump recited the team's passing statistics and reminded everyone of their come-from-behind win against Fort Comanche. And for those players who didn't know, Thump explained how he selects the fresh game balls and scuffs them with a fine grit sandpaper. As Roberto passed the newer ball around among the players, Thump described how the sanded grip of a new ball had enhanced T'Darian's grip.

Thump then asked Grant Lee to pass around the older, deflated practice ball. After each ball had made its round for everyone to touch, Thump placed them at his feet.

Under the left upright, Coach Dye had dug a hole. Thump asked the team which ball they should use for the game on Friday. A few of the boys mumbled, "the new one." The rest looked at each other with puzzled expressions.

Thump replied, "You would be correct to say we would use the new one, but tomorrow night is special. Most of you realize we have not thrown a bunch of passes this week in practice. And you are all aware of our plan and the fact we won't have T'Darian or Derek. But how committed are you to the plan? Do you believe? Or did you just write off this game?

"Men, it's important that you commit to your faith. In every culture, in every faith, a display of a physical commitment to the spiritual walk is a prerequisite, a beginning, to taking that walk." He tossed the newer game ball into the hole and said, "If you're prepared to accept our plan in full faith and you believe in yourself and this team's destiny, I want you to stand in line and grasp a handful of this sacred Friday night soil to help, for this week only, bury our passing game. Come tomorrow night, we won't throw the ball. We'll believe in our plan and we'll execute the SWAT offense. Valentino will bury those defensive ends, and we will win a game that no one believes we can win. Join with me in completing our commitment to each other."

Thump tossed the new ball into the hole and scooped a handful of dirt onto the pigskin. Each coach and each player followed, tossing a handful of dirt into the hole. Valentino took the spade and filled in the grave with the remaining dirt. The boys assembled close together near the grave.

It was a silly little motivational ploy that played out as Thump planned. Their eyes screamed with the intensity of the moment. Some had tears.

"One Team."

"One Heart."

As the boys filed off the practice field, Harrison Dye said, "Do you think they can do it?"

Thump replied, "They can't do it. But we can."

The next evening, during the pregame warmup, Dorothy Jean, Lupe, and Clara squeezed into their usual positions along the 50-yard line. T'Darian and Derek sat in the press box just to the left of Coach Roberto Herrera.

To maintain secrecy of the SWAT attack, Thump limited the pregame warmup on the field to individual defensive rotations and kicking game specialty sessions. Prior to going out on the field, he directed Miguel to run through the SWAT play sheet inside the gym. Rod Venson guarded the gym during the offensive warmup.

Should the Barracudas win the toss, Valentino and Carlos were to choose defense. Thump believed his defense would decide the game, and their first defensive series would decide if the outcome would be favorable or not.

In the choreography that was the pregame warmup, he exposed what Sara mocked as his "shaky manliness" and peered toward the ambulances. She nodded and flashed an insightful smile in his direction.

Ten minutes later, with the ball marked in play from their own 37-yard line, Thelma broke the huddle and aligned in the expected, double-wing, flexbone formation. Thelma's head coach was a midline veer guru who copied the offensive package used by Navy. It featured a motioning slotback behind a power fullback and a footloose quarterback.

Come high water or worse, Thelma would keep the ball on the ground. Though the Blueticks had lost all their earlier games, their fullback and quarterback had pillaged the opposing defenses.

The Saturday film study had showed that Thelma's predistrict opponents played the option from inside-out, so Grant Lee helped Dirk build a defensive game plan constructed around a hot, outside-in, read-blitz off the edge.

The plan dictated conditional blitzing. If the slot motioned toward the outside linebacker, he would blitz to the toes of the fullback. If the slot motioned away, he would soften the edge and rotate to the middle of the formation. Along with the outside linebacker tweak, the Barracuda free safety rotated toward the motion.

From the first possession, Dirk and Grant Lee's plan worked. Valentino Rejas, Victor Lucio, Reynaldo Gallegos, and Dan Ngo plugged the middle as the Port Verona outside backers splattered the mosquito that was the Thelma quarterback.

Early in the second quarter, Dan Ngo forced a bad pitch, and the Barracudas schooled at midfield for the recovery. From that point, Carlos engineered a seven-play touchdown drive.

Just before the half, Jose tacked on another three points. The home team led 10–0, and the Barracudas left the field before a capacity crowd of 3,000 ecstatic fans and one sullen superintendent.

Jenny nibbled on her halftime treat as Thump addressed the team.

"Your coaches are proud of you, your city is proud of you, and your teammates are proud of you. Just remember, they will adjust. They will counter and come at us. We must keep our intensity and keep our poise. If you can do that, you will never forget tonight."

Thump feared the Thelma staff would tweak their blocking scheme to account for the intense outside-in heat on the quarterback-fullback mesh point, but the change in Thelma's strategy never materialized. By the end of the third quarter, the unrelenting barrage of outside linebacker missiles launched at the quarterback's chin had fractured his willpower. Thelma would play the rest of the game relying on their fullback.

The 'Cuda momentum overwhelmed the disintegrating Blueticks. Just as Dirk had drawn it up, Valentino split the midline's double team blocks at the point of attack while Dan Ngo and Victor Lucio scraped into the B-gap. After Bluetick fullback Jon Early Pickens left the game midway through the fourth period with a thigh bruise, the Barracuda sideline celebrated. The Barracuda SWAT unit pounded the Thelma defensive front as Carlos, Jose, and Luis protected the ball and picked the Bluetick defense to death.

The horn sounded on a tight 10–0 district win. In what Thump speculated to be a deliberate act of social disobedience, the Barracuda faithful disobeyed the Texas Interscholastic League policy prohibiting fans from storming the field after the game. As the band sounded the final notes to the school song, Thump looked up to Dr. Tran's box and flashed a thumbs-up.

Oblivious to the message of Thump's gesture, she inferred that he would accompany her on Sunday.

CHAPTER THIRTY-SIX

Early Saturday morning, hours after the Barracudas' win, Fakhar Amin had just finished the graveyard shift at his family's southside Houston gas station. The sun peeked over the Atakapa Oil tank farm just a half-mile from the Space City Bank of Freedom. More than an hour late for his rendezvous with the private security firm contracted to watch over his 5:00 a.m. money drop, he scanned the parking lot. His vigilance noted nothing more than a trio of grackles fighting over a fast-food burger wrapper, so he decided to overlook the safety rules and make the drop unescorted.

Under the drive-through express awning, he had unzipped the custom plastic bag and approached the bank's business drawer when a hooded youth appeared from behind the corner.

Two blinding flashes later, the young father of two preschoolers lay in a pool of bright red. After the assailant freed the bank bag from Fakhar's clutch, he jogged north toward a black motorcycle waiting behind a row of manicured shrubs.

Other than the bank's security video, three bloody footprints, and the random $20 bills on the ground beside Fakhar's unconscious form, Houston Police Department robbery and homicide detectives found slight evidence. A 10-second clip on the Saturday evening television news mentioned another robbery by an unknown perpetrator.

CHAPTER THIRTY-SEVEN

Sunday, after church, Thump received a text from Dr. Tran.

"What time should I expect you to arrive?" she asked.

"Sorry, my dog is sick. See you tomorrow morning in Austin," he texted.

That evening, he made sure people in town saw Jenny playing fetch the squid with Sara and him while they picnicked near the town park's pavilion.

At 6:00 a.m. Monday, a select group gathered at Camp Promise. Rod Venson had volunteered to chauffeur the group in his luxurious RV while the witnesses, drinking coffee and hot tea, enjoyed the amenities and reviewed the evidence. Sara held the binder of hard copy; Pastor Mike and Isaac Sewell would testify about the validity of the boys' transfer; Harrison Dye would present a printout of his phone log; and Principal Saltzman would verify the transcripts as authentic.

Wrapped in a red-and-black afghan in the front captain's chair was the surprise witness, Dorothy Jean. Both she and Lupe prepared to testify before the hearing officer about their prior knowledge of Dr. Tran's scheme and the facts surrounding Tran's intention to unveil a last-minute declaration of T'Darian's and Derek's ineligibility.

Because Thump had learned the boys would not be required to testify, they remained in Port Verona to attend their Monday classes.

With Rod's RV just 30 minutes south of Austin, Principal Saltzman's phone buzzed. After reading the text, he handed his phone to Thump.

Dr. Tran's message to Saltzman read, "I have an urgent personal emergency. Cannot attend the hearing. You will act as the district's designee."

Puzzled, but not shocked that she had dodged the hearing, Thump called for everyone's attention and read the text aloud. Everyone in the RV raised a cup and cheered. Their speculation on Dr. Tran's urgent personal emergency made for a stimulating conversation when the RV hit the mind-numbing zombie march known as Austin traffic.

Thump entertained the group with a story from when he coached in Austin during the 1990s and experienced a snippet of the quirky "Keep Austin Weird" counterculture. Close to his rent house in the exclusive Tarrytown enclave lived a young couple who in their rebellion against technology's intrusion into their lives used an ancient, rotary-dial telephone. Absent of a television, their 1930s era four-bedroom corner home's ventilation was its room-to-room wooden frame windows beneath a canopy of several hundred-year-old live oaks, in which once, upon Thump's return from a Saturday coaching meeting, he spied the neighbor's teenage daughter reading a book. Thump had always professed no brochure could better explain the Austin experience than the image of that girl reading while reclined on the highest limb of the property's tallest tree.

They arrived 20 minutes early. A lone central office administrator, appearing half-disinterested and half-harried, represented Santa Gertrudis ISD. Dr. Akin called the hearing to order at nine o'clock. He directed Santa Gertrudis ISD to offer supporting evidence to their allegation.

The Santa Gertrudis assistant superintendent for curriculum development apologized for the inconvenience, but said she had little knowledge and no evidence of the case. The superintendent had sent her to hear the verdict and best answer any questions she could.

Scheduled in a two-hour window, the hearing lasted 15 minutes. A miffed Dr. Akin closed the hearing and offered an apology to Principal Saltzman, Thump, and the Port Verona witnesses. Saltzman and the others expressed their stunned relief, but Thump knew better.

While a negative ruling would have been a death sentence for Port Verona football, the success of Dr. Tran's scheme never hinged on the verdict. Her game was creating mayhem.

Permanently removing Derek and T'Darian from the program would be *lagniappe*. The goal was the collateral chaos seeded by the investigation. She had hoped that the hearing would unravel the football team and destroy the Barracudas' focus. She had wanted to destroy their chance for an outright district championship.

For Thump, the only surprise was Dr. Tran's absence. Thump had speculated she would have wanted to be at the hearing to claim responsibility for the case's dismissal. Her absence proved her long-range design for football's dissolution had disintegrated.

Despite the festive mood of his fellow Port Verona-bound passengers, Thump felt ill at ease. If a woman's scorn was unnerving, an evil woman's scorn was terrifying.

After the eligibility hearing, Dr. Tran sightings around The Cove became as a midnight ghost ship apparition out on the bay. Someone may have seen her in the copy room, exit through the back door, or enter the restroom, but no one was ever sure. Never a fan of athletic events, her rare courtside appearances at the volleyball games became nonexistent.

The final game against Santa Gertrudis would decide who took home the district hardware. At stake for Santa Gertrudis was their eleventh consecutive district championship.

CHAPTER THIRTY-EIGHT

In Houston, at an undisclosed meet on Friday, a snitch who went by O. B. Rhymes informed HPD detectives that the robbery and shooting of Fakhar Amin connected peripherally to the attempt on Jim Weir's life back in October, and the motorcyclist masked robber was a member of a Houston area gang, The Lighter Shade of Pale, commonly known as The LSP. A shooter known as Nick had bragged about the hits that he carried out on the "two old cops down south." But, because Weir survived, Nick was forced to return half of the $5,000 bounty on the chief investigator's head. Since Nick and his accomplices had already spent the cash, he committed the cash-drop robbery to recoup the $2,500.

O. B. Rhymes said, "Nick had to 211 that fool from the Shell to get the cash. So, he watched the dude, then popped him at the bank."

After Houston police detectives asked Rhymes to get more information on the motorcycle used in the Amin robbery, O. B. returned a few days later saying the motorcycle was a down payment on another "job on a cop down south in a week." O. B. said Nick declared he would "ride solo on this next job," because he needed to move fast.

Nick had bragged to O. B. that no cop could catch him on the bike. In a second interview, O. B. told the HPD detectives the plan was for Nick to allow the officer to pull him over on a traffic stop, then put two in her face and be back in town before she hit the ground.

At that point in the interview, HPD Detective Terrance Siddall raised his eyebrows.

"Wait a minute, O. B. You sure Nick said 'her' and 'she'?"

"Yeah, dead sure. He said the cop he's supposed to kill is a female cop. He even showed me a picture of her. She looked kinda cute, too."

When detectives pressed for more information about the night Don Bunch disappeared, O. B. said that Nick and two other LSP gangsters had jumped Don Bunch. Not only did O. B. corroborate all the facts regarding the attack, he laid out for the detectives a lot of the unknown, an unknown far worse than what law enforcement suspected.

O. B. outlined the events of Deputy Bunch's murder and related how and where the kidnappers dumped his body. O. B. said he got chills when Nick laughed as he described chopping up the deputy's body and transporting the parts in the Crown Vic to Anahuac.

When the detectives asked why Nick risked taking the body all the way to Anahuac, O. B. said that Nick told him it was part of the deal. Nick had to "chop up his body" and dispose of the parts in the marsh and "feed him to the gators." In the rambling interview, O. B. said that he heard Nick would make the hit on the female cop within a week.

"He got another way-far mirk on a blue penny, and it was his last part of the deal," Nick said.

Detective Siddall knew "penny" to be street slang for an attractive woman. "Mirk" meant "hire for murder." O. B.'s statement proved Nick planned to travel a long distance, probably to Tiburon County, to carry out the hit on the woman cop. Siddall and his partner had enough to move on Nick's crew, but they needed to nail the wizard behind the curtain. The detectives surmised that Nick might not even know who hired him. The deal was likely brokered through a third party, possibly a captain in Nick's gang.

Siddall's unit soon identified the female cop target as Sara and advised her chief to arrange for her a leave of absence, at least until they unmasked the mastermind behind the assassination attempts. Until the lead matured enough to allow them identify the shot-caller, they would have to sit tight.

CHAPTER THIRTY-NINE

During a phone interview with the *Sentinel*, J. P. Duhon grumbled that he was sick and tired of seeing that black dog at Thump's side. "My stadium ain't no dog kennel. If he brings in that fake seeing-eye dog, I'll walk across the field with one of those dog catchpoles and drag its flea-ridden carcass out of my stadium. I tell you, Rory, if that one-hit-wonder, nobody coach so much as thinks about bringing that dog into the Bull Pen, he better first call that witling Mississippi State running back I knocked out that day in Death Valley, and ask him for some rehab advice. Because, he will get more of the same."

On the order of the Port Verona Chief of Police, Sara took Santa Gertrudis week off. Corroborative FBI intel from the Houston office, verified another assassination attempt on law enforcement was imminent.

The net was closing in on the triggermen, and because Sara believed Lupe's grandniece's story regarding the *El Marineras'* lack of involvement, she contacted Jim Weir, who was convalescing at home under police protection. With Lupe's name scrubbed from the report, the Sheriff's Office disseminated Sara's information to the Texas Rangers and the FBI.

Thump and Sara remained unaware that the Houston Police Department had identified the gang who carried out the hits on Deputy Bunch and Deputy Weir. Investigators worried that, if charged, the gang members would lawyer up and refuse to name who ordered the hits. They needed more information. All anyone knew was that the threat against Sara was immediate, and the state had assigned a DPS trooper to her residence.

CHAPTER FORTY

Within an hour of the clandestine meeting with O. B. Rhymes, the Gulf Coast Task Force issued a priority alert, and this time, they included Sara in the notice.

After the task force meeting concluded, she left with little discussion. The Charger was the first to leave the Reed City courthouse lot.

Sara had limited Thump's knowledge of the investigation. As a civilian, he didn't need to know about a gang's plan to ambush her. She told him that she had asked for time off so she could be with him during the playoffs.

The playoff opportunity was a momentous occasion for the town, and she planned to be visible for the department. Besides, she wanted to spend more time with him during the week of the big game. She had fallen for the man and his dog.

Barracuda red mania electrified Tiburon County. No one had seen Port Verona more festive. People appeared happier and more welcoming. Church attendance across town ballooned, and Reverend Wallace's sermons turned livelier. Barracuda red decorations adorned Camp Promise, and Pastor Mike scheduled a bus to carry the entire camp to the Santa Gertrudis game to cheer for T'Darian and Derek.

In Reed City, a grassroots Barracuda movement organized support throughout the entire county. Five billboards, each rented anonymously, portrayed a composite mural of the action from earlier Barracuda games under a gray watermark of a human heart.

Each billboard's banner read, "ONE TEAM, ONE HEART."

One of the big three network stations from Houston scheduled its live high-school scoreboard show to be broadcast from the Bull Pen. Meanwhile, a San Antonio radio station planned to broadcast the game live across the Texas Sports Radio Network.

Even though the life of an officer was at risk, Port Verona's police chief ordered the city's patrol units to fly red and black spirit flags from their whip antennae. They were not to write any minor traffic violations for the entire week.

Instead of traffic tickets, the officers handed out red and black buttons which said, "Drive Safe, Go 'Cudas!"

No less impressive was the tribute paid to Jenny on Tuesday when the old lady at Nguyen's Bait Shop and Store told Thump, "Don't be such a silly big coach, you bring dog next time. I give her a snack. And you better tell that J. P. 'Dulip' coach from Santa Gertrudis he better not come here to eat. I tell my grandson, take mean coach out on sideline for you. My grandson loves his big coach and black dog."

On Thursday, the JV Joes finished their season with four wins and six losses, an improvement over the winless slate from the prior year. Monday, everyone would join varsity practice for the playoff games.

A lot of things had changed since 1964 when only one team advanced into the playoffs, one being that the Texas high-school postseason spanned six weeks and ended in late December. Four teams from each district advanced, a formula that guaranteed Port Verona a district finish no lower than second place. If the fifth-ranked Barracudas made it to the big show in Arlington, Thump's boys would play the week before Christmas on the home field of the Dallas Cowboys in a game televised live nationwide.

CHAPTER FORTY-ONE

Friday evening, the 'Cuda contingent would bus 90 miles to the Bull Pen.

Boarding the bus, Harrison Dye glared at the boys and said, "I want it so I can hear a mouse fart up in here." Except for the rattling diesel engine, the bus already sat silent. Coach Dye didn't need to remind the boys of the significance of the bus ride.

As expected, the silence screamed onboard the two buses. Two DPS units illuminated the highway. Close behind the troopers followed the team buses, the band bus, the pep squad/cheerleader bus, the Camp Promise bus, and five additional buses loaded with the student body. At the rear of the caravan, Sara and the chief followed in the Port Verona PD Charger. Three marked Tiburon County Sheriff's Office units blocked the cross traffic as the trooper escorts approached. Once the Barracuda buses passed the lead county unit, the trailing deputy leapfrogged to secure the next open intersection.

Two hours later, the caravan squeezed down a narrow asphalt-patched street that led to the Bull Pen. Santa Gertrudis fans on each side of the street stopped to glare at the buses. Most of the people jeered and yelled epithets and flashed the bull horn hand gesture, the signature sign of the Santa Gertrudis faithful.

Thump admired the Santa Gertrudis program. After a decade of district championships, J. P. Duhon had built in his image a town, not just a team. Santa Gertrudis fans were mean, and the stadium record bore proof of their ability to intimidate the visiting team. In the 13 years of the Duhon era, the Bulls' record was 71 wins and four losses at home in the Bull Pen.

The buses squeaked to a stop.

Thump led the squad through the designated team entrance, but a tall, double wrought-iron gate blocked their passage. Thump pushed open the gate.

Two grossly overweight Santa Gertrudis County deputies stepped forward and blocked Thump's path. The elder of the two punched his hand into Thump's chest.

"You can't read, Coach? The sign says, NO PETS ALLOWED IN THE STADIUM."

Sara pushed the deputy's hand from Thump's chest and said, "Deputy, you're lucky we aren't in Port Verona or I would take your butt to jail, right now. Put your hands on him again and it won't matter where we stand."

The bearded younger deputy laughed and said, "Looky here, Dale. The old coach got him a young wildcat for a bodyguard. Listen, Senorita Sargento, no disrespect to the mighty metropolis of Port Verona, but your badge don't mean squat here in Santa Gertrudis. You and your grandpa coach need to take that mutt on out that gate or else."

"Or else what, deputy?" came a voice from behind Sara.

From over her shoulder, Sara noticed the regional captain of the DPS substation in Reed City.

Captain Daryl Zachary repeated his question.

"Or else what, deputy? That dog is a licensed support animal. We apologize for not providing a heads-up on the matter, but in case you haven't heard, we've been busy dealing with some serious threats against your fellow law enforcement officers down in Tiburon County. If you please, Coach Sutton needs to get on about his business tonight, and we need you all here to keep your eyes alive. This isn't a time to be arguing

over some silliness about what this blowhard of a football coach y'all got
up here allows. We got cop killers out there we need to catch."

Deputy Dale frowned and looked at his partner.

"Yes sir, Captain. We're just doing our job here. Everyone here is
safe at the Bull Pen. Our fans don't like red, but they back the blue.
I'll make Coach Duhon aware of the dog's registration and all. I'm sure
he didn't realize the special circumstances."

"Thank you, sir," replied Captain Zachary, "and it was good to
meet you boys. I appreciate that you do a real smart job up around this
area, and I thank you."

"Yes, sir, we try. Well, y'all have a safe night."

It was a night of which Texas schoolboys dream, playing for the
legacy of an undefeated season before an overflow crowd in the largest
3A stadium in the state. The thick artificial turf of the Bull Pen was
softer than most grass fields, and its high definition video scoreboard
broadcast player statistics and replayed every critical play on the field.
Everything about the stadium was bigger and better; four more
towering light panels than the typical stadium, a two-tier press box
serviced by an elevator, and reserved folding chair seating from 30-yard
line to 30-yard line.

During the coin toss, the Barracudas elected for the second-half
option.

The teams took the field as J. P. Duhon reached for the can he
kept in his rear pocket and snapped the container four times. After he
pinched a large mass of cut tobacco, he stuffed the dip between his
cheek and gum.

A precision Barracuda kickoff dropped in the corner near the 2-
yardline. The Bulls' return man tripped over a Port Verona tackler at
their 28-yard line. From there, the Bulls would put the ball in the
hands of their senior all-state tailback, Deacon Sunday. Five
consecutive carries by Deacon moved the Bulls to the Barracudas' 35-
yard line where the Nine-Finger Slinger lived up to his nickname.

Faking the tailback waggle, quarterback Colt Marshall hid the ball
in the small of his back and froze in the perfect play-action fake.
Eighteen strides downfield, his blue-chip brother, Maverick Marshall,

snapped off his post route and broke toward the corner flag as Colt delivered a rainbow 3-ball shot. Maverick gathered the ball in stride for the quick score.

The Bulls tacked on the point-after and led 7–0.

J. P. Duhon's reputation in the big game was to go for the throat, so it didn't shock Thump when he called for an onside kick toward his sideline. Maverick Marshall synchronized his leap with the ball reaching its highest point at the required 10-yard mark. The home crowd's tornadic roar followed the Bulls' sideline explosion when the Bull Board showed Maverick's toes touch inside the paint.

Three consecutive carries by Deacon and the Bulls knocked at the Barracudas front door. The reeling Barracudas needed a miracle.

Thump looked to Dirk and told him, "Go after them."

Dirk signaled a strong linebacker whip stunt with Valentino slanting through the strongside A-gap. Keying on the directional read of Deacon's first step, Lucio knifed through the weakside A-gap into the Bulls' backfield.

Deacon planted his outside foot six yards deep and squared his shoulders to the hole.

Over the headset, Harrison Dye said, "Oh no, that hole is as big as a bat cave."

Deacon cut upfield just as Victor sunk his hips and executed a form tackle that separated the ball from Deacon's grasp. The football, loose on the turf, popcorned toward the sideline where Port Verona outside linebacker Angel Suarez scooped the ball and sprinted down the sideline. Neither quarterback Colt Marshall nor anyone else had a chance of catching the Barracuda track team's anchor leg.

Jose's kick would tie the score, but Thump was Duhon's equal in surprise tactics. As Jose planted and swung through his kick, T'Darian imitated Peanuts' Lucy and snatched the ball from the tee. T'Darian spun right and rolled wide. Alone in a drag route from his upback position, senior reserve linebacker Eugene Graham sprinted toward the back pylon. T'Darian cocked to throw but tucked the ball and went airborne at the front pylon.

The turf jarred the football loose from his grip and the Bull Pen shook with the crowd's roar. After a long conference among the officiating crew, the referee raised his arms. The two-point conversion was successful.

Undeterred by not running an offensive play in the quarter, Port Verona led 8–7.

Deacon Sunday rushed the ball sixteen times in the first half, but the schooling Barracuda defense kept him out of the endzone. Nevertheless, the Bulls cool-mannered Colt Marshall connected with his brother twice more for touchdowns of 36 and 44 yards.

Not to be upstaged by the Marshall brothers, the Barracudas slashed downfield with equal efficiency.

Just before the end of the half, T'Darian connected with Carlos on a 63-yard bomb, then hit Reynaldo Gallegos on a bootleg drag route to tie the game. Jose's PAT just before the horn gave the boys from the City by the Sea a tenuous 22–21 lead.

A shaken Dirk vomited on the sideline, but Grant Lee offered counsel and infused him with the confidence to pull himself together. Thump told the team they would need to help themselves on defense by keeping the ball away from the Marshall brothers. In the second half, they would run the ball and slow the game's tempo.

"We need to hand the keys over to Derek," he told the squad at halftime just before the three-minute warning. "Derek will carry us home."

Pastor Mike, welcome in the halftime locker room since the season opener against Fort Comanche, asked Thump if he could offer a blessing over the boys.

Thump nodded and said, "Coaches, let's step outside so Pastor Mike can have a word with the team."

A team of stone-faced boys emerged from the visitor's cramped locker room. Elbows interlocked, they walked with a silent intensity. On the field, two walls of parents, brothers, sisters, schoolmates, and otherwise indistinguishable Port Verona fans formed a path from the goalposts to the sideline.

Thump trailed behind the players and coaches. Midway to the sideline, Sara stepped in front of Thump. From her tiptoes, she said something in his ear. He smiled and jogged to the sideline to retrieve his headset.

During the second half, what had been a first-half cliché barnburner turned into the stereotypical slugfest with Santa Gertrudis showcasing a combination of power sweeps, isolations, and counters. No less authoritative was Port Verona's prowess in the rushing game as Derek slashed inside behind Reynaldo's blocking from the slot and power alignments.

The Bulls bled the clock as they pounded the Barracuda defensive front between the tackles. By the midpoint of the fourth quarter, Santa Gertrudis led, 28–22, but the Barracuda defense forced the Bulls to punt. Port Verona would have an opportunity for the winning drive.

Then lightning struck. With Port Verona driving for the winning touchdown, the center's snap zoomed over T'Darian's head. A herd of Bulls recovered, and with just over two minutes left in regulation, the Barracudas' last hope would be to use their timeouts and prevent the Bulls from earning a first down.

Thump watched from one knee, his arm around Jenny. If Dirk and Grant Lee could stop Deacon, T'Darian and the soccer boys would have one final chance to save the day.

As Thump expected, J. P. Duhon called on the Deacon to close out the game.

Colt Marshall stepped into the huddle, and calmly said, "Twins Left 46 G-Lead."

It was the bread and butter play of the Bulls' offense. The guard would kick out the outside linebacker, and the fullback would lead the way through the hole. Deacon would attack the 6-hole with a convoy of blockers.

From under center, Colt reversed out and handed the ball deep to Deacon. A small crease opened off-tackle, but Angel Suarez cross-shouldered the guard's kick out block. From over the top, Dan Ngo scraped tight to demolish the Santa Gertrudis fullback two yards deep in the Bulls' backfield.

Deacon bounced outside to avoid the pile-up. He had to beat only Derek Donaldson to break free down the sideline and seal the district championship.

A veteran defensive back coach, Grant Lee drilled his boys never to allow a running back the opportunity to square his shoulders. Daily, Grant Lee barked out what he called his leverage rule, "Keep inside-out leverage to the sideline."

Derek played as Grant Lee coached him. As Deacon dug for the sideline, Derek closed the distance. With his eyes focused on Deacon's near hip, he executed a flawless tackle just short of the first-down marker.

With 1:32 left to play and one timeout remaining for the Barracudas, the Bulls faced a fourth-and-short decision. J. P. Duhon elected to punt and place the game in the hands of his defense.

The Barracudas had been trained to swim in these waters. Carlos fielded the punt and Thump called for the SWAT unit.

Thump told T'Darian to run two plays. If they didn't get a first down, he would call his final timeout.

From the press box, Roberto reported that the Bulls sent their prevent package onto the field.

Thump had achieved the element of surprise. Once the referee wound the play clock, Thump yelled for T'Darian to hurry and snap the ball. His timeouts burned, Duhon couldn't switch the personnel package. Derek knifed through the Bulls' for 13 yards.

The game clock stopped for the chain crew to reset the chains. A desperate Duhon signaled his boys to fall and fake an injury, but never having been in such a frantic game situation, the Bulls' defense couldn't grasp what their coach tried to communicate.

T'Darian repeated the power play. Again, Valentino crushed the pass-conscious defensive end. Again, Derek slashed into the Bulls' secondary, this time for 14 yards.

As a frenzied Duhon berated his defensive coordinator, the Bulls' secondary coach finally communicated the order for a flop. Though the Bulls could now adjust defensively, the scenario had played out as

Thump had hoped. The Barracudas gained an extra timeout while the Santa Gertrudis medical staff examined the Bulls' free safety.

The stadium shook. The press box windows vibrated. Thump ordered the empty set grouping to replace the SWAT. Miguel huddled the entire team around the nine-yard sideline mark and waited until the referee wound the game clock.

As the coaches slowly herded the team back to the sideline, the empty-set grouping burst from the herd of players and aligned in the spread formation.

T'Darian fired a quick out to Carlos, then hit Luis on a slant for the first down. Thump burned his final timeout.

Twenty-six seconds remained in the game. T'Darian had led the team to within 18 yards of the tying touchdown. Derek, reduced to the role of pass protection, signaled he wanted the ball, but Thump wanted T'Darian to take a shot at the end zone.

Miguel signaled two plays, "Head 8, Shoulder 3," and the boys checked their wristbands.

Carlos moved to the right slot. Luis and Jose aligned wide right. To T'Darian's left, Reynaldo split wide. T'Darian called for the snap, but Victor Lucio hitched his delivery, and the referee stopped play for the offensive penalty. Because of the time remaining, the Barracudas received a five-yard penalty plus a five-second runoff. Thump signaled T'Darian to stick with the "Head 8" call.

The referee wound the clock. This time, Victor executed a clean shotgun snap.

T'Darian settled his feet to throw, but the Bulls' cornerback sank instead of jumping Jose's in-route. On the opposite side of the formation, the Bulls had bracketed Carlos. Pressure forced T'Darian to scramble. By the time he threw the ball away, the clock had ticked down to 00:09.

Coach Sewell tugged at Thump's elbow.

"Coach, they have four in the box and their ends are wide."

Thump looked at Isaac and bit his lip. The play clock ticked down, and the Barracudas stood 23 yards from paydirt.

"You think he can get it, Isaac? It's 23 yards."

"He can get it, Coach. He can do it," said Isaac.

Thump said, "Miguel, call East 7 Bear."

Miguel searched his play sheet for the corresponding signal but couldn't find it.

"Miguel, call the play! East 7 Bear!"

"I can't find it, Coach. We don't have it!"

Thump ran out to the nine-yard mark and screamed, "East 7 Bear! East 7 Bear!"

The stadium thundered. Over six thousand football fanatics stood screaming as the play clock ran down to 7 seconds.

T'Darian clapped his hands twice, but no one along the line could hear him bark the cadence. The offensive linemen peeked inside to see the ball and Victor delivered a waist-high snap. T'Darian countered and placed the ball into Derek's pocket. Instead of darting outside to the waiting strong safety, Derek powered forward behind Valentino's pancake of the lone linebacker. At the nine-yard line, Derek squared the free safety for the two-way cut (the cut Grant Lee had coached him never to allow on defense), read the safety's outside lean in his tackling demeanor, and executed a jump cut to the inside.

The home side went silent. Behind the visitors' bench, Port Verona fans tumbled from the stands and fell to their knees in joy. A large contingent of Port Verona students barked as they barraged the field with Milkbone dog treats. Thump held up the index finger, and Jose's kick put the game into the annals for posterity. After thirty-two straight losing seasons, the Barracudas were the undefeated District 13-AAA champions.

Alone in her white brick castle and listening to the jazz stream from her elaborate sound system, a relaxed Diane Tran sipped cognac while rereading *The Count of Monte Cristo*. Friday night reading was her favorite activity next to drinking, and now that she had absolved her mind of that worrisome football situation, she felt more content than she had been in years. Her retirement would be effective in four weeks, and she could live out her dream of returning to Vietnam. Everything was in order. She had liquidated most of her local assets and transferred her investment portfolio to an overseas bank.

Bequeathing many of her possessions to the Catholic Diocese in recognition of their rescue and relocation of thousands of refugees, Tran would coast through her final month, then move on to direct an elite international school in Hanoi. To paraphrase her second favorite author, Port Verona had been the best of times and the worst of times.

Now, it was time to go home.

CHAPTER FORTY-TWO

In late November, the Class 3A polls painted their top slot Barracuda red.

For the first time in forever, a football team from Tiburon County practiced after Thanksgiving Day. T'Darian had established himself as the field general of Thump's dreams, and Derek ranked third in the state in rushing. The Barracudas continued to improve at practice, even though they only blocked the barrels and ran simulated tackling drills.

After the Houston media promoted Port Verona's' epic turn-a-round, the National Federation of High School Coaches nominated Thump as a finalist for Coach of the Year. Cinderella had morphed into the 50-Foot Woman. If they captured the regional championship Saturday in Waco, the Barracudas stood two games away from wearing the ring.

By December, Thump and Sara's rooted relationship had matured into centennial heartwood.

The threat against Sara had dissipated, and the urgency to unravel the tangle of clues faded when the Port of Houston Police found Nick Vu's corpse under the Ship Channel bridge. Two small-caliber gunshot wounds to the chest had terminated Nick's career as a hitman.

A few days later, a terrified O. B. Rhymes told Detective Siddall that he heard the LSP suspected a snitch inside their organization, one who was helping the Texas Rangers solve the cop killings. Rhymes believed the gang planned to eliminate everyone involved. An old associate of Rhymes who washed dishes off Bellaire Boulevard told him that the LSP had placed a bounty on his head.

Talking to detectives, Rhymes insisted Nick was just the first to die.

Since the latest intel showed the future threat to law enforcement to be negligible, the joint task force disbanded. Task force shot-callers believed the LSP would clean the laundry and burn their Irish pennants. Leads would shrivel and die.

Detective Siddall didn't agree with the task force's assessment. For Siddall, a 36-year HPD veteran, the entire affair just didn't pass the smell test. His experience told him that every crime has a motive, yet despite the weeks of investigation, they hadn't determined a motive in either the murder of Deputy Bunch or the attempted murder of Jim Weir.

The day the task force disbanded, he called his wife and told her not to wait up; he planned to work through the night. The Houston Police Department needed a final face-to-face with O. B. Rhymes.

CHAPTER FORTY-THREE

Saturday in Waco, Derek scored five touchdowns to help Port Verona claim its first regional championship since the 1964 team's state run. The following Monday, the board granted Thump the approval to hire a part-time athletic secretary to handle calls coming in from across the state.

Expenditures had ballooned, but Dorothy Jean was more than happy to subsidize team travel costs to the point of paying for four-star accommodations in Waco, Fort Worth, and Arlington, plus five charter buses and two TCSO escorts while compensating Port Verona PD for Sara's time and use of the Charger.

The rumor that Dr. Tran was on her way out the door left Thump with mixed emotions, though he wasn't sure why. He guessed it was because he had experienced her vulnerable side and felt somewhat responsible for her pain. Thump assumed that a woman like Diane hated to lose more than anything, and in that manner, she was his kindred spirit. She had risen from nothing to own the town.

In time, everyone would forget about her accomplishments and the multimillion-dollar grant she bragged about that morning at the Rotary Club breakfast. Thump noted the irony. Diane was leaving Port Verona just as she'd left Vietnam.

CHAPTER FORTY-FOUR

The Texas Interscholastic League had scheduled the 3A state semifinals in Fort Worth. Port Verona would attempt to wrangle the Steers from Socorro Bend.

The scouting data and film breakdown revealed the Steers to be an I-formation team that resembled J. P. Duhon's style of attack. Thump knew the Socorro Bend head coach had once played for Duhon and cloned the Santa Gertrudis offense. The clone's one genetic flaw? Socorro Bend didn't have tailback Deacon Sunday preaching in its backfield.

With a record of 12 wins against two losses, Socorro Bend was a West Texas power-five program, but they intimidated neither Thump nor the boys. Unlike Old Blue, the Barracudas were hitting on all cylinders.

Saturday afternoon in Fort Worth, the Barracudas followed Derek to a 24-point halftime lead over Socorro Bend. For the first time in the playoffs, the J. V. Joes got to put on what Thump called their big-boy pants and tangle with a varsity team. At the start of the fourth quarter, Thump handed Miguel the keys to the offense and watched the Joes have fun.

Afterward, the Barracudas raced south to Port Verona.

The following Friday, they would travel to Arlington and play on the field with the big blue star, one more game for all the marbles and a lifetime to remember. Their opponent would be an undefeated Cartridge, the defending state champion. For the second time this season, Thump and the Barracuda red would spar with an undefeated opponent.

Thump stuck with his commitment to Sunday being a day of rest. After the church service and attending to the crush of supporters, Sara prescribed an evening under the stars.

First, she would take a long Sunday afternoon nap, then prepare her choice picnic basket lunch with a thermos of hot chocolate. The six o'clock news heralded an artic front's arrival at midnight in what would be a cloudless, crisp evening, a rarity between the bays.

By 8:30 p.m., the solstice moon hung low as if God had painted a massive lantern near the horizon. Thump lay on a blanket and watched a flannel-bloused Sara and Jenny play. He pulled a blade of grass and shredded it between his teeth.

Rose, Christmas with her on the Texas Gulf Coast is a Jimmy Buffett song.

A vibration interrupted his thoughts. He ignored it but thought better. It could be a parent or something important.

Tran.

Her text said she was leaving tomorrow for Vietnam and wanted to say goodbye. She asked him to meet her at midnight on her family's shrimp boat, the one in the picture—the *Nho Lai*. She said she needed to give him something before she left.

Thump texted he wasn't up for such a late-night rendezvous. Tran replied that the meet would take 10 minutes, no more. She had to be on her way to the airport; her flight left Houston at 4:00 in the morning.

"I want to say my last goodbye to my favorite coach."

Sara would go on duty at 11 p.m. to cover for a sick officer, so Thump agreed to meet with her. Sara rolled her eyes and shook her head.

"Her last act in Port Verona is to cast one more time for the one who got away."

"Nah, she's way past all of that. It's nothing."

"Okay, but I don't like it. I've heard some crazy stuff about her lately, even crazier than usual. Be careful."

"Don't be silly, Sarge. Besides, she told me to be sure and bring Jenny. She has something for her, too."

"What? Bring Jenny? Now I know that you better be careful."

CHAPTER FORTY-FIVE

To catch the big cat, a fisherman baits his trotline with savory enticements. On this night, Houston Police Detective Terrance Siddall fished the westside underworld, casting cash and opportunities for deals. Just before midnight, he and his partner hooked O. B. Rhymes outside a rundown club in a Sharpstown strip mall.

"O. B., over here," said Siddall.

A spooked Rhymes bolted, but a quick double-take confirmed that it was Siddall who called out. He crept to the plain brown Ford coupe to meet the two HPD detectives.

"So, here's the deal, O. B. I got you a place. A permanent safehouse. In New Orleans, no less. Nobody can jump you here in Houston, because you can go to New Orleans and get your music going with your rhymes and such. A whole new life."

"Thank you, thank you, Jesus. I heard they want to kill me tonight. I got to saying, O. B., this is you last night. By tomorrow morning, you dead. I heard they shot Henry and Van and throwed them in the channel like Nick. It's over for me, too. I been wondering if y'all going to save me. Where you was? Man, I'm starving. Been on the run, no food, no water."

"Slow down, O. B. You tweaking?"

"Yeah, a little. Let people say they gonna cut you up and feed you to the channel cats, how would you feel? You'd need a bump, too. Man, I'm hungry. You got anything to eat?"

"Tell you what, let's get you some food, some clean clothes, some cash, and a bus ticket to New Orleans. My buddy with the Jefferson Parish Sheriff's Office is waiting for you."

"Okay, okay. That's good news," said O. B.

"But first, I need you do something for me."

"What you mean? I did my thing. I gave you Nick. And look where he ended up. And I gave you the other two. What you mean? Do something?"

"Well, you're a little light. The shootings involved four people, maybe five. Who banked the hits?" asked Siddall.

"I don't know. How would I know that?"

"You don't know? O. B., the game is over. Tonight, you got a choice. I set you up on a bus to New Orleans and burn your file. Or I take you over to the Blue Spider, and I honk my horn until Rich La comes out."

"What you mean until Rich La comes out? Man, he'll kill me and you if he sees us together."

"That's where you're mistaken, O. B. He'll kill you, but not me or my partner. See, he suspects you snitched on his people. Now, they're dead and you're alive. Rich believes you got something to do with that. You know who hired your three idiot friends to kill those cops. Rich tells me you've been yanking my chain. He said that you know exactly where the money came from. And finally, and probably the most important thing for you to hear, is that Rich suspects you got his boys killed somehow. Now, Rich is not a big fan of Rhymes's song. So, what is it? Bus ride to New Orleans or channel dive with Rich?"

"Okay, okay. If I give you the lowdown, you promise you gonna get me to Nawlins?"

"Give me what you got or I promise to dial up Rich, and we are on our way to meet him at the ship channel bridge."

"Man, you trippin. Nick handled the money. I was a backup in case something bad went down. I dunno. Me and Nick go back to middle school. He gave me the bike the night before they shot him."

"You got the motorcycle?" asked Siddall.

"Yeah, I got it at my little cousin's house. Her boyfriend wanted to sell it in Mexico."

"Okay, keep with the story."

"Aight, I got you. Nick told me the money came from a woman. An Asian woman, older, but Nick says she looked hot, and she always carried a piece. Like, she came strapped every time he met with her. Nick said she acted like she had done this stuff before. Like, she was connected, like a real O. G. godmother or something. She laid it all out and paid cash. She's the one who told Nick to feed both cops to the gators, but that other one lived."

"Okay, so who is this Asian woman? She part of somebody's crew or what?"

"No, no, you ain't listening. I done told you she acted connected. She's a rich lady. I'm telling you, Nick said that she's a real high-up. She don't play. She done all this stuff before. She hired Nick and them to do the jobs for her. She owned the bike. Brought Nick to her house one time and partied with him. Nick said she owned a mansion with a Lexus, plus a Mercedes, and all that. I mean, she's old, but she looks hot. He sneaked some pics of her and sent them to me."

"You can't give me a name? You still have the photos?" asked Siddall.

"No, I didn't hear the name. She lives down by the coast where Nick and them grabbed the first cop. Yeah, I got the pics."

"Did she ever tell Nick why she wanted to kill those two deputies?" asked Siddall.

"Nah, I don't think so. Wait, she might have said somebody owed her something."

"Okay, where's the black motorcycle?"

"I told you, at my little cousin's," said O. B.

"You need to take us there," replied Siddall.

"So, will this get me on that bus?"

"O. B., this might just get you on a jet to the Bahamas."

CHAPTER FORTY-SIX

What had started as a relaxing day with his girls had turned crazy with this midnight meeting, but Thump supposed he owed it to Dr. Tran to humor her. Their relationship had traveled a rock-strewn road downhill to this low point. As Thump approached the boat, he recognized its name, the *Nho Lai*. She stepped out from behind the netting.

"Tom, welcome. I'm so glad you came. I have missed our conversations."

"Sure, no problem."

"I bet you wonder why I asked you and your dog to meet me out here on my boat, tonight."

"Sort of."

"Oh, yes, my coach of few words. The town's salvation. I suppose your brother felt the same way when he was a Marine in Vietnam, right? Like when he was saving us?"

"I was young. He didn't talk much when he came back from the first tour."

"Yes. What so affected him over there?"

"I don't know. I never found out. He didn't come back. Is there something I'm missing, Diane? You called me out on a shrimp boat at midnight to quiz me about my brother?"

She drew close. Thump could see her face, now. With her normally stylish hair pulled into a ponytail, she looked strange. Except for her customary bright red lipstick, her face was pale. Her skin almost lighter than white. She had always appeared younger than her age, but tonight she resembled a young girl. Normally attired in a stunning business ensemble, she wore black denim slacks complemented by a dark polo under a navy wind jacket.

The temperature had plummeted as the artic front bulldozed a frigid path toward the coast. Her breaths exhaled a mist-like vapor in the cold.

"What do you mean, Tom? Don't you miss your brother? I miss my family. We both have missing parts."

"Are you okay, Diane? You sound different. You told me to meet you because you wanted to give me something."

"Yes. You're in a hurry to get back to your little girlfriend, the one you like to visit the playground with."

"Okay Diane, what's wrong? Why are we doing this? You're going on to a great life. You love Vietnam. I envy you. You get to live your dream."

Thump checked his phone. Sara might be around the corner. She would be on duty by now.

"Of course, you envy me. I have a future and you don't. Brian Keith Sutton, Junior."

"What? Yeah, that's my brother's name. What about him?"

"Brian Keith Sutton, Donald Aaron Bunch, James Adam Weir, Jackson Ray Washington, Byron Randall Jones, and Lieutenant John Peter Rache, United States Marine Corps."

"Diane, what's going on?"

"Your brother was at my village that day with those other Marines."

"What? Brian was at your village? What are you talking about?"

"Yes, he and the others. They all owed a debt—the entire First Marine Division owes a debt. But what's a girl supposed to do, drive all over the country to exact retribution on every gray-haired Marine who ever murdered an innocent? I was blessed that fate brought me here to Tiburon County, the home of two of them, but the topping on the cake was finding you and getting you here to answer for your name. Your destiny was truly mine.

"Wait, what are you saying?"

Jenny moaned and pulled at her leash.

"I'm saying that your brother was the most honorable of his kind. He returned to my country to pay for his sins. He provided blood recompense for the women and children he and his fellow Marines butchered in my village."

"Okay, Diane, you must be drunk or having a breakdown. You said the Viet Cong murdered your family. Do you remember saying that? Multiple times?"

Despite the near-freezing temperature, sweat soaked his undershirt.

"What I have always said was what my elders told me. To try and save me from the memory. But I overheard their whispers. Why do you suppose I studied history at Georgetown? Why did I work at the National Archives? To remember. To find out the truth. And the truth is your pig brother's fellow swine came into my village on June 11, 1971, to commit vile acts upon the women and children there, so vile that I will not so much as let the words come from my mouth. Then, after your brother's friends desecrated the remains of those whom they had already defiled, after they garnered their trophies, they left the remains to rot."

The school superintendent with her cool, professional demeanor had morphed into an irrational, dark entity. Rage oozed from her pores. She panted and moved about.

"Your brother and his Marine friends would have found and tortured me if my mother had not shielded me with her body."

Diane tilted her head and smirked.

Thump had experienced some bad breakups, but he had never experienced such a presence in a woman. She seemed to perform rather than talk. Her odd facial expression and sardonic affect escalated the tension.

She's not right.

"Hold on, Diane. Are you sure that my brother, or Bunch, or those other guys even visited your village that day? Weir never mentioned my brother to me. If they were in the same squad, he would have recognized our last name, don't you think? Diane, think about it. You're upset. Let me call you some help. You can't fly to Vietnam in your state."

Her body trembled. She rocked side to side as she wiped her nose with her sleeve.

"God, it is so cold out here on the water," she said.

"Yeah, that cold front is moving in pretty fast. How about we get out of here and get you some help?"

She sighed and turned away as if she agreed, then spun around. Her eyes suddenly widened. Her voice became shrill.

"Do you suppose you came here by accident, Thomas Sutton, brother of Lance Corporal Brian Keith Sutton, United States Marine Corps? Are you that thick? The only accident was my mistake in underestimating you. How could I have known you would be so talented at motivating children to succeed? Your professional failures riddle your résumé. But I see it now.

The *Acintita Sutta* warns that we cannot comprehend the outcome of karma. It's unimaginable that you were sent here to finish what your brother didn't, but you were. Your brother and his Marine friends overlooked the crying baby lying under the ravaged young woman, but his dark karma sent you to fulfill his mission. Somehow, I survived your murderous brother and his pals, but you, the sword of his resilient evil, came to destroy me."

She pulled a small, chrome-plated, semi-automatic handgun from her jacket. A lifetime of muted grief had transformed her. In the shadows on deck, Thump thought her to be unrecognizable.

"Diane, hold on. I'm not my brother. And I don't believe he felt like he was my brother anymore after that first tour. Something happened to him. Besides, you can't be sure that you're describing my brother. Put the gun down, Diane. Don't ruin your life."

Her red lips curled.

To Thump, the moment froze. He felt he had reached her. What seemed like hours passed before she spoke.

"Tom, to be such a gorgeous specimen of a man, you are so dumb. Think about it. I'm not ruining my life. I'm ruining yours. Besides, you're a terrible date."

She fired two point-blank shots into his chest.

He lunged toward her to knock the pistol from her grasp, but she fired two more shots. The third bullet struck him in the cheek, tracking through his mouth to exit just in front of his left ear. A nearly simultaneous fourth bullet ripped through his right hand and entered near his right eye.

Disoriented, Thump stumbled backward over the boat's railing.

Free from Thump's restraint, Jenny sank her canines deep into Diane's forearm. Diane screeched in pain and dropped the gun. She fought with her free arm to gain leverage and flip Jenny overboard.

The loud splash signified it was over. Diane fell to one knee and cradled her injured arm. Blood started to drip from her fingertips.

She rose to her feet and looked overboard. Not a single ripple marred the glassy dark surface. She saw no sign of Thump or his dog.

After the acclaimed school superintendent retrieved her weapon from the deck and threw it into the bay, she jogged to her Lexus. She checked her travel bag for her boarding pass, identification, and passport. In her Gucci wallet, she had sequestered $1,000 cash.

She held her injured arm close to the overhead light and examined the bites. A deep red bruise highlighted the two puncture wounds and blood dripped from a deep laceration just above her wrist. She would treat the bites later.

With its satellite radio tuned to the smooth jazz station, the Lexus tore out of the park and turned north toward Houston Bush International. The woman had a plane to catch.

CHAPTER FORTY-SEVEN

It was after midnight in the Bayou City when Detective Siddall and a Houston Police Department vehicle recovery specialist processed the black 2012 Suzuki GSXR 1000. Since the motor bike displayed no plate, they ran the vehicle identification number found on its steering neck.

HPD Dispatch reported the motorcycle as registered to Diane Tran of Port Verona, Texas. A comparison of her driver's license with the photos sent to O. B. from Nick's phone confirmed her identity. Diane Tran had engineered the murder of Deputy Bunch and the attempted murder of Deputy Weir. Detective Siddall suspected that she had orchestrated the murder of Nick Flores and his two consorts, as well.

Around the hour that Siddall identified Diane Tran as a person of interest in Deputy Bunch's murder, Sara's unit sat cloaked by the scale model lighthouse in front of Nguyen's Bait Shop and Store. The veteran police sergeant had just aimed her radar gun at the traffic heading out of Port Verona when the gun's alarm squealed. It had locked on a vehicle traveling 52 mph over the limit. When the sedan zipped by her cruiser, Sara recognized the familiar gold Lexus.

The Dodge 5.7-liter police interceptor Hemi roared as the Charger bucked onto the highway asphalt. Once her pursuit overtook the Lexus, Sara reached for her radio's mic. She was about to call in the stop and flip on the cruiser's lights when Mildred's voice came through the speaker.

"PV3, we have a report of fireworks at the dock."

Sara's stomach knotted. She knew Thump should have met Dr. Tran at the dock a half hour ago. And now, Tran's Lexus rocketed north.

She wheeled into a quick U-turn and gunned the Charger back toward town. It took her less than 90 seconds to arrive at the docks.

She radioed, "PV3 is at the scene."

The Charger's high-intensity spotlight illuminated nothing out of the ordinary. She told Mildred that she would be out of the unit.

The harbored shrimp boats rested high on the water like aquatic gargoyles on guard. A frozen stillness hovered just over the tips of their masts.

Sara's flashlight swept the area. She recognized the bark of a distressed dog in the distance. It was Jenny.

The barking grew louder as Sara neared the grassy shoreline of the dock's east side. Her flashlight's beam danced off the water as she called for Jenny.

A soaked Jenny, her black coat almost invisible in the darkness, appeared. Her leash, also wet, dragged behind her, but she refused to heel. Instead, the yelping Irish Setter-Lab mix darted about the wharf.

"Mildred, roll Rescue One. We have a situation here at the dock."

"10-4, PV3. Do you need backup?"

"Negative, but I need Rescue One, code 3."

"10-4, PV3."

Sara grabbed for the leash, but Jenny bolted. She continued to run back and forth in a frenzy. Sara bent to one knee.

"Where's Thomas, Jenny? Show me Thomas. Find Thomas, Jenny."

Continuing her strident racket, Jenny scurried toward the water's edge and Sara realized where to find Thump. She sprinted around the inlet and down the boat ramp.

"Mildred, we have a man down in the water at the dock. Send backup. I am on the main boat ramp searching the water."

"Thomas! Thomas! Answer me, Thomas!"

Sara skirted the water's edge.

"10-4, PV3. All available units, officer needs help. Man down. Port Verona dock. Rescue One, we need you to 39."

Sara could hear the siren's wail in the distance. Rescue One was en route.

As she neared the shrimp trawler that belonged to the Tran family, she radioed, "Mildred, advise ICAP-4 to 10-18 this location."

Onboard the boat, Sara twisted her flashlight's lens to its widest aperture and cast a bluish white aura over the deck. She stopped to listen but heard only the irregular groan of the wooden boat's tackle rigging. Her lungs exhaled a visible vapor.

After clearing the stern, she searched the side of the boat nearest the water. It was clean, no sign of Thump. At the starboard bow, she found four shell casings. A few feet from the casings, closer to the rail, droplets of blood stained the deck. On the rail, she found a blood smear.

The cold air burned her throat. She tried to swallow.

"Mildred, confirmed signal 56. The victim is in the water."

Tears welled. Her vision blurred. Her voice cracked as she called out again.

"Thomas! Thomas! Answer me!"

The whooping from Rescue One grew louder. She could tell by the sound of the siren that the ambulance was moments away. She scanned the water and listened, but other than the distant siren, all she could hear were the yawns of the rigging and Jenny's continuous barking.

Her radio squawked, "PV3, ICAP-4 is delayed. ETA 30."

Sara trembled. She bent forward at the waist and looked at her watch. Anxiety pressed her shoulders low. Her boots cemented her feet to the deck and her knees wobbled.

"Papi, I need you. Oh God, please help me." She fell to her knees. "God, help me find him."

The flashing red lights of Rescue One reflected off the mist. She could see the red hue approaching her location.

She pushed herself to her feet and keyed her mic.

"Mildred, issue a BOLO on Diane Tran. Last seen headed north at Reed City Highway and First Street approximately 10 minutes ago at a high rate of speed."

"10-4, The Diane Tran?"

"10-4. Mildred, I'm going into the water."

Sara shed her gear, boots, and radio then dived into the icy bay water. When she broke the surface, she heard the BOLO.

"All local and state units stand by for a BOLO. All units be on the lookout for a 2012 gold Lexus four-door, Texas plates CCC 900. Suspect is Diane Tran, Asian female, age 45, black hair, five-foot-three in height, 93 pounds, last seen headed north out of Port Verona at a high rate of speed. Suspect in a signal 56 is possibly armed and dangerous. Repeat, the vehicle is a 2012 gold Lexus four-door, Texas plates CCC 900."

Sara suspected that if Thump had survived the shooting, he would have only seconds left before he lost consciousness and slipped below the surface. Thinking he would have hidden under the wooden structure; she swam to search the space under the wharf. She couldn't allow herself to think otherwise. Bobbing in the water like a cork, she held her flashlight high as she one-arm crawled among the pilings.

The siren of Rescue One stopped its long wail. Doors slammed shut.

Sara could hear the EMTs approaching the boat. Her fingers and toes ached. She yelled out to the Rescue One crew. Even with her flashlight, she swam in a casket of icy darkness. She called out that she needed more light.

Three streams of light swept over the edge of the *Nho Lai*. From the north, more sirens approached. To her right, she noticed a shadow that seemed out of place. She directed the EMTs to aim their flashlight beams toward the shadow.

Thump's body appeared suspended just inches from a piling. With each small crest of a wave, his nose dipped into the murky bay. Under the dock, a reddish-brown pool diffused into the gray water.

Thump had looped an abandoned dock line around his right arm and neck. He gurgled blood from his swollen mouth. His right eye pushed outward against the blackened eyelids. Sara yelled for help.

Isaac Avila and another EMT jumped in with flotation devices. A drizzle of sleet began to blanket the area. Brilliant red and blue fireflies atop the emergency vehicles illuminated the dock as first responders flooded the landing.

Throughout the search, Jenny stalked the water's edge, pacing, whining, and barking. As the rescuers struggled to lift Thump from the water, she lay down in the grass and whimpered.

CHAPTER FORTY-EIGHT

On the Life Flight to Houston, Thump's left eye fluttered for a moment.

"Life One—B.P. 80 over 20, respiration shallow and unsteady. He's crashing."

Thump stumbled through the fog of Death's presence. Nearby, he saw a wisp of a figure moving, as if she was searching.

"Sara?" He received no response. "Sara?"

The figure turned to look over her shoulder at him as the fog about him melded into a frigid pool of water. He saw it was Sara, but she didn't recognize him.

Before, never. After, forever.

She faded from his sight. Thirty seconds before the chopper touched down, Thump's heart stopped.

CHAPTER FORTY-NINE

Five days after the shooting, Grant Lee led the out-manned Barracudas against the much deeper roster of the Cartridge Cardinals. Determined to keep the Barracudas' dream alive, Derek carried the ball as if the gods of football had molded his cleats.

Port Verona trailed by seven late in the fourth quarter. With less than a minute left in regulation, T'Darian hit Carlos in the back corner of the endzone to pull within one point. After Jose kicked the successful point-after, the boys in Barracuda red faced an overtime period.

Though the Cardinals scored on their opening overtime possession, Derek's power runs brought the Barracudas to within an extra-point of tying the score. Grant Lee called for the point-after kick. They would regroup for a second overtime.

But the boys delayed in assuming kick formation. They milled about as Grant Lee screamed out at them to line-up. As the boys moved reluctantly to take their positions, Derek broke protocol and called the Barracudas' only timeout of the overtime.

The team wanted to end it. They wanted to go for the win.

"For Coach Sutton, they said."

CHAPTER FIFTY

D r. Tran had abandoned her Lexus at Houston Intercontinental and boarded the 4:00 a.m. flight to Hanoi via Los Angeles. By the time the puzzle pieces fit, and law enforcement realized her exit strategy, first-class passenger Diane Tran nursed her tightly bandaged arm somewhere over the Pacific. Once in Hanoi, she went underground.

Multiple federal and state felony charges, including a capital murder indictment for the Bunch slaying, would lead to an international dragnet for the dishonored superintendent. After INTERPOL found her, the U.S. State Department appealed to the Vietnam government for her extradition back to Texas, but the Socialist Republic of Vietnam denied the extradition because of her status as a natural-born Vietnamese citizen.

The board of trustees promoted Principal Saltzman to the superintendent position after he guaranteed to support the continuation of all athletic programs offered at Port Verona Independent School District.

Dorothy Jean Butler deeded her home to Sara before she and Lupe embarked on a bucket list tour of the world and moved to a home in Belize. Prior to leaving Port Verona, Dorothy Jean commissioned a bronze statuary in the city park near the spot where Thump, Sara, and Jenny often picnicked during that championship season.

The monument depicts Thump on one knee, his left arm outstretched, his finger pointed toward the bay. Jenny leans against him with her head high. Thump's right arm is around her neck. Close behind Thump, four players in their football uniforms look toward the water in anxious expectation. Following the statue's placement, the townsfolk birthed an annual preseason tradition.

Every year during the week of the first football game, Port Verona holds a community pep rally at the memorial. A brief address by the superintendent and mayor, a prayer, and the athletes individually dedicate their season by laying a Barracuda red rose of commitment.

Afterward, with Sara and Jenny at his side, Thump kneels to lay the final rose.

Together, everyone raises their fist and grabs onto a Barracuda brother's or sister's arm. Linked together as one, those in attendance close the dedication with the traditional Barracuda callout.

"One Team."

"One Heart."

CITATION

Turse, Nick. *Kill Anything That Moves: The Real American War in Vietnam.*, 2014. Print.

Made in the USA
Las Vegas, NV
05 July 2021